Margaret Oliphant

The wizard's son. A Novel.

Band 3

Margaret Oliphant

The wizard's son. A Novel.
Band 3

ISBN/EAN: 9783743341005

Manufactured in Europe, USA, Canada, Australia, Japa

Cover: Foto ©Andreas Hilbeck / pixelio.de

Manufactured and distributed by brebook publishing software (www.brebook.com)

Margaret Oliphant

The wizard's son. A Novel.

A Novel

BY

MRS. OLIPHANT

AUTHOR OF "THE CURATE IN CHARGE," "YOUNG MUSGRAVE," ETC.

IN THREE VOLUMES

VOL. III.

London

MACMILLAN AND CO.

1884

THE WIZARD'S SON.

CHAPTER I.

WAS this then the conclusion of all things—that there was nothing so perfect that it was worth a man's while to struggle for it; that any officious interference with the recognised and existing was a mistake; that nothing was either the best or the worst, but all things mere degrees in a round of the comparative, in which a little more or a little less was of no importance, and the most strenuous efforts tended to failure as much as indifference? Walter, returning to the old house which was his field of battle, questioned himself thus, with a sense of despair not lessened by the deeper self-ridicule within him, which asked, was he then so anxious for the best, so ready to sacrifice his comfort for an ideal excellence? That he, of all men, should have this to do, and yet that, being done, it should be altogether ineffectual, was a sort of climax of clumsy mortal failure and hopelessness. The only

good thing he had done was the restoration of those
half-evicted cotters, and that was but a mingled and
uncertain good, it appeared. What was the use of any
struggle? If it was his own personal freedom alone
that he really wanted, why here it was within his
power to purchase it—or at least a moderate amount
of it—a comparative freedom, as everything was comparative. His mind by this time had ceased to be able
to think, or even to perceive with any distinctness the
phrase or *motif* inscribed upon one of those confused
and idly-turning wheels of mental machinery which
had stood in the place of thought to him. It was the
afternoon when he got back, and everything within
him had fallen into an afternoon dreariness. He
lingered when he landed on the waste bit of grass
that lay between the little landing-place and the door
of the old castle. He had no heart to go in and sit
down unoccupied in that room which had witnessed
so many strange meetings. He was no longer indeed
afraid of his visitor there, but rather looked forward
with a kind of relief to the tangible presence which
delivered him from meetings of the mind more subtle
and painful. But he had no expectation of any visitor;
nor was there anything for him to do except to sit
down and perhaps attempt to read, which meant solely
a delivering over of himself to his spiritual antagonists
—for how was it possible to give his mind to any fable
of literature in the midst of a parable so urgent and
all-occupying, of his own?

He stood therefore idly upon the neglected turf, watching the ripple of the water as it lapped against the rough stones on the edge. The breadth of the loch was entirely hidden from him by the projection of the old tower, which descended into the water at the right, and almost shut off this highest corner of Loch Houran into a little lakelet of its own. Walter heard the sound of oars and voices from the loch without seeing any one: but that was usual enough, and few people invaded his privacy: so that he was taken by surprise when, suddenly raising his eyes, he was aware of the polished and gilded galley from Birkenbraes, in which already Mr. Williamson, seated in the stern, had perceived and was hailing him. "Hallo, my Lord Erradeen! Here we've all come to see ye this fine afternoon. I told them we should find ye under your own vine and your own fig-tree." This speech was accompanied by a general laugh. The arrival of such a party, heralded by such laughter in a desolate house, with few servants and no readiness for any such emergency, to a young man in Walter's confused and distracted condition would not, it may be supposed, have been very welcome in any case, and at present in his exhaustion and dismay he stood and gazed at them with a sort of horror. There was not even a ready servitor like Hamish to assist in the disembarkation. Duncan had rowed cheerfully off upon some other errand after landing his master, and old Symington and old Macalister were singularly ill-adapted for the

service. Lord Erradeen did his best, with a somewhat
bad grace, to receive the boat at the landing-place.
The gravity of his countenance was a little chill upon
the merry party, but the Williamsons were not of a
kind that is easily discouraged.

"Oh, yes, here we all are," said the millionnaire.
"I would not let our English visitor, Mr. Braithwaite
here, leave without showing him the finest thing on
the loch. So I just told him I knew I might take the
liberty. Hoot! we know ye have not your household
here, and that it is just an old family ruin, and not
bound to produce tea and scones like the Forresters'
isle. Bless me! I hope we have a soul above tea and
scones," Mr. Williamson cried with his hearty laugh.

By this time the young, hardy, half-clad rowers had
scrambled out, and grouped themselves in various
attitudes, such as would suit a new and light-hearted
Michael Angelo—one kneeling on the stones holding
the bow of the boat, another with one foot on sea and
one on shore helping the ladies out. Walter in his
dark dress, and still darker preoccupied countenance,
among all those bronzed and cheerful youths looked
like a being from another sphere : but the contrast was
not much to his advantage either in bodily or mental
atmosphere. He looked so grave and so unlike the
joyous hospitality of a young housekeeper surprised by
a sudden arrival, that Katie, always more on her guard
than her father, looked at him with a countenance as
grave as his own.

"I am not the leader of this expedition, Lord Erradeen," she said; "you must not blame me for the invasion. My father took it into his head, and when that happens there is nothing to be done. I don't mean I was not glad to be brought here against my will," she added, as his face, by a strain of politeness which was far from easy to him, began to brighten a little. Katie was not apt to follow the leading of another face and adopt the woman's *rôle* of submission, but she felt herself so completely in the wrong, an intruder where she was very sure she and her party, exuberant in spirits and gaiety, were not wanted, that she was compelled to watch his expression and make her apologies with a deference quite unusual to her. "I hope it will not be a very great—interruption to you," she said after a momentary pause.

"That could never matter," Walter said, with some stateliness. "I could have wished to have notice and to have received my friends at Auchnasheen rather than here. But being here—you must excuse the primitive conditions of the place."

"Hoot! there is nothing to excuse—a fine old castle, older than the flood—just the very thing that is wanted for the picturesque, ye see, Braithwaite; for as ye were remarking, we are in general too modern for a Highland loch. But you'll not call this modern," said Mr. Williamson. "Will that old body not open the door to ye when he sees ye have friends? Lord! that just beats all! That is a step beyond Caleb Balderston."

"Papa!" cried Katie in keen reproof, "we have been quite importunate enough already. I vote we all go over to Auchnasheen—the view there is much finer, and we could send over for Oona——"

"Is it common in this country," said the member of Parliament, "to have two residences so very near? It must be like going next door for change of air when you leave one for the other, Lord Erradeen."

At this there was that slight stir among the party which takes place when an awkward suggestion is made; the young men and the girls began to talk hurriedly, raising up a sort of atmosphere of voices around the central group. This however was curiously and suddenly penetrated by the reply which—who?— was it Walter? made, almost as it seemed without a pause.

"Not common—but yet not unknown in a country which has known a great deal of fighting in its day. The old castle is our family resource in danger. We do our family business here, our quarrels: and afterwards retire to Auchnasheen, the house of peace (perhaps you don't know that names have meanings hereabouts?) to rest."

There was a pause as slight, as imperceptible to the ignorant, as evident to the instructed as had been the stir at the first sound of those clear tones. Walter himself to more than one observer had seemed as much startled as any of them. He turned quickly round towards the speaker with a sudden blanching of his face which had been pale enough before; but this was only momentary; afterwards all that was remarkable in him was a strange look of resolution and determined self-control. Perhaps the only one completely unmoved was the Englishman, who at once accepted the challenge, and stepped forward to the individual who it was evident to him was the only duly qualified cicerone in the party, with eager satisfaction.

"That is highly interesting. Of course the place must be full of traditions," he said.

"With your permission, Walter, I will take the part of cicerone," said the new voice. To some of the party it seemed only a voice. The ladies and the young men stumbled against each other in their eager curiosity about the stranger. "I will swear there was nobody near Erradeen when we landed," said young Tom Campbell in the nearest ear that presented itself; but of course it was the number of people about which caused this, and it could be no shadow with whom the M.P. went forth delighted, asking a hundred questions. "You are a member of the family?" Mr. Braithwaite said. He was not tall, and his companion was of a splendid presence. The Englishman had to look up as he spoke and to quicken his somewhat short steps as he walked to keep up with the other's large and digni-fied pace. Katie followed with Walter. There was a look of agitation and alarm in her face; her heart beat she could not tell why. She was breathless as if she had been running a race. She looked up into Lord

Erradeen's face tremulously, not like herself. "Is this gentleman—staying with you?" she said in a scarcely audible voice.

Walter was not agitated for his part, but he had little inclination to speak. He said "Yes" and no more.

"And we have been—sorry for you because you were alone? Is it a—relation? is it—? You have never," said Katie, forcing the words out with a difficulty which astonished her, and for which she could not account, "brought him to Birkenbraes."

Walter could not but smile. A sort of feeble amusement flew over his mind touching the surface into a kind of ripple. "Shall I ask him to come?" he said.

Katie was following in the very footsteps of this altogether new and unexpected figure. There was nothing like him, it seemed to her, in all the country-side. His voice dominated every other sound, not loud, but clear. It subdued her little being altogether. She would not lose a word, yet her breath was taken away by an inexplicable terror.

"He is—like somebody," she said, panting, "out of a book," and could say no more.

Old Macalister came towards them from the now open door, at which stood Symington in attendance. The servants had been disturbed by the unusual sounds of the arrival. Malcalister's old face was drawn and haggard.

"Where will ye be taking all thae folk?" he said, no doubt forgetting his manners in his bewilderment.

"Come back, ye'll get into mischief that road," he cried, putting out his hand to catch the arm of Braithwaite, who, guided by the stranger, was passing the ordinary entrance. He became quite nervous and angry when no heed was paid to him. "My lord, you're no so well acquaint yourself. Will you let that lad just wander and break his neck?" he cried, with a kind of passion.

"Never mind," said Walter, with a strange calm which was as unaccountable as all the rest. "Will you tell your wife to prepare for these ladies—when we come back."

Here Symington too came forth to explain somewhat loudly, addressing his master and Braithwaite alternately, that the roads were not safe about the old castle, that the walls were crumbling, that a person not acquaint might get a deadly fall, with unspeakable anxiety in his eyes. The party all followed, notwithstanding, led by the stranger, whom even the least of them now thought she could distinguish over Katie's head, but of whom the servants took no notice, addressing the others in front as if he had not been there.

"My lord, ye'll repent if ye'll no listen to us," Symington said, laying his hand in sudden desperation on Walter's arm.

"You fool!" cried the young man, "can't you see we have got a safe guide?"

Symington gave a look round him wildly of the utmost terror. His scared eyes seemed to retreat into

deep caverns of anguish and fear. He stood back out of
the way of the somewhat excited party, who laughed,
and yet scarcely could laugh with comfort, at him.
The youngsters had begun to chatter: they were not
afraid of anything—Still—: though it was certainly
amusing to see that old man's face.

Turning round to exchange a look with Macalister,
Symington came in contact with Mr. Williamson's solid
and cheerful bulk, who brought up the rear. "I'm
saying," said the millionnaire confidentially, "who's
this fine fellow your master's got with him? A grand
figure of a man! It's not often you see it, but I always
admire it. A relation, too; what relation? I would
say it must be on the mother's side, for I've never seen
or heard tell of him. Eh? who's staying with your
master, I'm asking ye? Are ye deaf or doited that ye
cannot answer a simple question?"

"Na, there is nothing the matter with me; but I
think the rest of the world has just taken leave of their
senses," Symington said.

CHAPTER II.

JULIA HERBERT had failed altogether in her object during that end of the season which her relations had afforded her. Walter had not even come to call. He had sent a hurried note excusing himself, and explaining that he was "obliged to leave town," an excuse by which nobody was deceived. It is not by any easy process that a girl, who begins with all a girl's natural pride and pretensions, is brought down to recognise the fact that a man is avoiding and fleeing from her, and yet to follow and seek him. Hard poverty, and the memories of a life spent in the tiny cottage with her mother, without any enlargement or wider atmosphere, and with but one way of escape in which there was hope or even possibility, had brought Julia to this pass. She had nothing in her life that was worth doing except to scheme how she could dress and present the best appearance, and how she could get hold of and secure that only stepping-stone by which she could mount out of it—a man who would marry her and open to her the doors of something better. In every other way it is worth the best exertions of either man or woman to get these doors opened, and to come to the possibility of better things; and a poor girl who has been trained to nothing more exalted, who sees no other way, notwithstanding that this poor way of hers revolts every finer spirit, is there not something pitiful and tragic in her struggles, her sad and degrading attempt after a new beginning? How much human force is wasted upon it, what heart-sickness, what self-contempt is undergone, what a debasement of all that is best and finest in her? She has no pity, no sympathy in her pursuit, but ridicule, contempt, the derision of one half of humanity, the indignation of the other. And yet her object after all may not be entirely despicable. She may feel with despair that there is no other way. She may intend to be all that is good and noble were but this one step made, this barrier crossed, the means of a larger life attained. It would be better for her no doubt to be a governess, or even a seamstress, or to put up with the chill meannesses of a poverty-stricken existence, and starve, modestly keeping up appearances with her last breath.

But all women are not born self-denying. When they are young, the blood runs as warmly in their veins as in that of men; they too want life, movement, sunshine and happiness. The mere daylight, the air, a new frock, however hardly obtained, a dance, a little admiration, suffice for them when they are very young; but when the next chapter comes, and the girl learns to calculate that, saving some great matrimonial chance, there is no prospect for her but the narrowest and most meagre and monotonous existence under heaven, the life of a poor, very poor single woman who cannot dig and to beg is ashamed—is it to be wondered at if she makes a desperate struggle anyhow (and alas! there is but one *how*) to escape. Perhaps she likes too, poor creature, the little excitement of flirtation, the only thing which replaces to her the manifold excitement which men of her kind indulge in—the tumultuous joys of the turf, the charms of play, the delights of the club, the moors, and sport in general, not to speak of all those developments of pleasure, so-called, which are impossible to a woman. She cannot dabble a little in vice as a man can do, and yet return again, and be no worse thought of than before. Both for amusement and profit she has this one way, which, to be sure, answers the purpose of all the others in being destructive of the best part in her, spoiling her character, and injuring her reputation —but for how much less a cause, and with how little recompense in the way of enjoyment! The husband-hunting girl is fair game to whosoever has a stone to throw, and very few are so charitable as to say, Poor soul! Julia Herbert had been as bright a creature at eighteen as one could wish to see. At twenty-four she was bright still, full of animation, full of good humour, clever in her way, very pretty, high-spirited, amusing— and still so young! But how profoundly had it been impressed upon her that she must not lose her time! and how well she knew all the opprobrious epithets that

arc directed against a young woman as she draws towards
thirty—the very flower and prime of her life. Was she
to blame if she was influenced by all that was said to
this effect, and determined to fight with a sort of mad
persistence, for the hope which seemed so well within
her reach ? Were she but once established as Lady
Erradeen, there was not one of her youthful sins that
would be remembered against her. A veil of light
would fall over her and all her peccadilloes as soon as
she had put on her bridal veil. Her friends, instead of
feeling her a burden and perplexity, would be proud of
Julia; they would put forth their cousinhood eagerly,
and claim her—even those who were most anxious now
to demonstrate the extreme distance of the connection
—as near and dear. And she liked Walter, and thought
she would have no difficulty in loving him, had she ever
a right to do so. He was not too good for her; she
would have something to forgive in him, if he too in her
might have something to forgive. She would make him
a good wife, a wife of whom he should have no occasion
to be ashamed. All these considerations made it excusable—more than excusable, almost laudable—to strain
a point for so great an end.

And in her cousin's wife she had, so far as this went,
a real friend. Lady Herbert not only felt that to get
Julia settled was most desirable, and that, as Lady
Erradeen, she would become a most creditable cousin,
and one who might return the favours showed to her,
but also, which is less general, felt within herself a

strong inclination to help and further Julia's object. She thought favourably of Lord Erradeen. She thought he would not be difficult to manage (which was a mistake as the reader knows). She thought he was not so strong as Julia, but once fully within the power of her fascinations, would fall an easy prey. She did not think less of him for running away. It was a sign of weakness, if also of wisdom; and if he could be met in a place from which he could not run away, it seemed to her that the victory would be easy. And Sir Thomas must have a moor somewhere to refresh him after the vast labours of a session in which he had recorded so many silent votes. By dint of having followed him to many a moor, Lady Herbert had a tolerable geographical knowledge of the Highlands, and it was not very difficult for her to find out that Mr. Campbell of Ellermore, with his large family, would be obliged this year to let his shootings. Everything was settled and prepared accordingly to further Julia's views, without any warning on the point having reached Walter. She had arrived indeed at the Lodge, which was some miles down the loch, beyond Birkenbraes, a few days after Walter's arrival, and thus once more, though he was so far from thinking of it, his old sins, or rather his old follies, were about to find him out.

Lady Herbert had already become known to various people on the loch-side. She had been at the Lodge since early in September, and had been called upon by friendly folk on all sides. There had been a thousand

chances that Walter might have found her at luncheon
with all the others on his first appearance at Birkenbraes, and Julia had already been introduced to that
hospitable house.   Katie did not recognise Lady Herbert
either by name or countenance.   But she recognised
Julia as soon as she saw her.

" I think you know Lord Erradeen ? " was almost her
first greeting, for Katie was a young person of very
straight-forward methods.

"Oh yes," Julia had answered with animation, " I
have known him all my life."

" I suppose you know that he lives here ? "

Upon this Julia turned to her chaperon, her relation
in whose hands all these external questions were.

" Did you know, dear Lady Herbert, that Lord
Erradeen lived here ? "

"Oh yes, he has a place close by.   Didn't I tell you ?
A pretty house, with that old castle near it, which I
pointed out to you on the lock," Lady Herbert
said.

" How small the world is ! " cried Julia ; " wherever
you go you are always knocking up against somebody.
Fancy Walter Methven living here ! "

Katie was not taken in by this little play.   She was
not even irritated as she had been at Burlington House.
If it might so happen that some youthful bond existed
between Lord Erradeen and this girl, Katie was not the
woman to use any unfair means against it.

" You will be sure to meet him," she said calmly.

"We hope he is not going to shut himself up as he did last year."

"Oh tell me!" Julia cried, with overflowing interest, "is there not some wonderful ghost story? something about his house being haunted; and he has to go and present himself and have an interview with the ghost? Captain Underwood, I remember, told us——"

"Did you know Captain Underwood?" said Katie, in that tone which says so much.

And then she turned to her other guests: for naturally the house was full of people, and as was habitual in Birkenbraes a large party from outside had come to lunch. The Williamsons were discussed with much freedom among the visitors from the Lodge when they went away. Sir Thomas declared that the old man was a monstrous fine old fellow, and his claret worth coming from Devonshire to drink.

"No expense spared in that establishment," he cried; "and there's a little girl, I should say, that would be worth a young fellow's while."

He despised Julia to the bottom of his heart, but he thought of his young friends on the other side without any such elevated sentiment, and decided it might not be a bad thing to have Algy Newton down, to whom it was indispensable that he should marry money. Sir Thomas, however, had not the energy to carry his intention out.

Next day it so happened that Lady Herbert had to return the visit of Mrs. Forrester, who—though she

always explained her regret at not being able to entertain her friends—was punctilious in making the proper
calls. The English ladies were "charmed" with the
isle. They said there had never been anything so
original, so delightful, so unconventional; ignoring
altogether, with a politeness which Mrs. Forrester
thought was "pretty," any idea that necessity might
be the motive of the mother and daughter in settling
there.

"I am sure it is very kind of you to say so; but it is
not just a matter of choice, you know. It is just an old
house that came to me from the Macnabs—my mother's
side. And it proved very convenient when all the boys
were away and nothing left but Oona and me. Women
want but little in comparison with gentlemen; and
though it is a little out of the way and inconvenient in
the winter season, it is wonderful how few days there
are that we can't get out. I am very well content
with the Walk when there is a glint of sunshine; but
Oona, she just never minds the weather. Oh, you will
not be going just yet! Tell Mysie, Oona, to bring ben
the tea. If it is a little early what matter? It always
helps to keep you warm on the loch, and my old cook is
rather noted for her scones. She just begins as soon as
she hears there's a boat, and she will be much disappointed if ye don't taste them. Our friends are all very
kind; we have somebody or other every day."

"It is you who are kind, I think," Lady Herbert
said.

" No, no; two ladies—it is nothing we have it in our power to do: but a cup of tea, it is just a charity to accept it; and as you go down to your boat I will let you see the view."

Julia, for her part, felt, or professed, a great interest in the girl living the life of a recluse on this little island.

" It must be delightful," she said with enthusiasm; "but don't you sometimes feel a little dull? It is the sweetest place I ever saw. But shouldn't you like to walk on to the land without always requiring a boat ?"

I don't think I have considered the subject," Oona said; " it is our home, and we do not think whether or not we should like it to be different."

" Oh what a delightful state of mind ! I don't think I could be so contented anywhere—so happy in myself. I think," said Julia with an ingratiating look, " that you must be very happy in yourself."

Oona laughed. " As much and as little as other people," she said.

" Oh not as little ! I should picture to myself a hundred things I wanted as soon as I found myself shut up here. I should want to be in town. I should want to go shopping. I should wish for—everything I had not got. Don't you immediately think of dozens of things you want as soon as you know you can't get them ? But you are so good ?"

" If that is being good ! No, I think I rather refrain

from wishing for what I should like when I see I am not likely to get it."

"I call that goodness itself—but perhaps it is Scotch. I have the greatest respect for the Scotch," said Julia. "They are so sensible." Then she laughed, as at some private joke of her own, and said under her breath, "Not all, however," and looked towards Kinloch Houran.

They were seated on the bench, upon the little platform, at the top of the ascent which looked down upon the castle. The sound of Mrs. Forrester's voice was quite audible behind in the house, pouring forth a gentle stream. The sun was setting in a sky full of gorgeous purple and golden clouds; the keen air of the hills blowing about them. But Julia was warmly dressed, and only shivered a little out of a sense of what was becoming: and Oona was wrapped in the famous fur cloak.

"It is so strange to come upon a place one has heard so much of," Julia resumed. "No doubt you know Lord Erradeen?"

The name startled Oona in spite of herself. She was not prepared for any allusion to him. She coloured involuntarily, and gave her companion a look of surprise.

"Do you know him?" she asked.

"Oh, so well! I have known him almost all my life. People said indeed——" said Julia, breaking off suddenly with a laugh. "But that was nonsense.

You know how people talk. Oh, yes, ιe have been like brother and sister—or if not quite that—at least—. Oh yes, I know Walter, and his mother, and everything about him. He has been a little strange since he came here; though indeed I have no reason to say so, for he is always very nice to me. When he came home last year I saw a great deal of him; but I don't think he was very communicative about—what do you call it?—Kinloch——"

"He was not here long," Oona said.

"No? He did not give himself time to find out how many nice people there are. He did not seem very happy about it when he came back. You see all his habits were formed—it was something so new for him. And though the people are extremely nice, and so hospitable and kind, they were different—from those he had been used to."

Oona smiled a little. She did not see her new acquaintance from the best side, and there came into her mind a slightly bitter and astonished reflection that Walter, perhaps, preferred people like *this* to other—people. It was an altogether incoherent thought.

"Does he know that you are here?" she said.

"Oh, I don't think he does—but he will soon find me out," said Julia, with an answering smile. "He always tells me everything. We are such old friends, and perhaps something—more. To be sure that is not a thing to talk of; but there is something in your face

which is so sweet, which invites confidence. With a
little encouragement I believe I should tell you everything I ever did."

She leant over Oona as if she would have kissed her :
but compliments so broad and easy disconcerted the
Highland girl. She withdrew a little from this close
contact.

"The wind is getting cold," she said. "Perhaps we
ought to go in. My mother always blames me for
keeping strangers, who are not used to it, in this chilly
air."

"Ah, you do not encourage me," Julia said. And
then after a pause added, with the look of one preoccupied by her subject—"Is he there now ?"

"I think Lord Erradeen is still at Kinloch Houran, if
that is what you mean. That is another house of his
among the trees."

"How curious ! two houses so close together. If you
see him," said Julia, rising to join her cousin who had
come out to the door of the cottage with Mrs. Forrester,
"if you see him, don't, please don't, tell him you have
met me. I prefer that he should find it out. He
is quite sure, oh, sooner than I want him, to find me
out."

And then the ladies were attended to the boat in the
usual hospitable way.

"You will get back before it is dark," said Mrs.
Forrester. "I am always glad of that, for the wind is
cold from the hills, especially to strangers that are not

used to our Highland climate. I take your visit very
kind, Lady Herbert. In these days I can do so little
for my friends : unless Sir Thomas would take his lunch
with me some day—and that is no compliment to a
gentleman that is out on the hills all his time—I have
just no opportunity of showing attention. But if you
are going further north, my son, the present Mr.
Forrester of Eaglescairn, would be delighted to be of
any service. He knows how little his mother can do for
her friends, perched up here in the middle of the water
and without a gentleman in the house. Hamish, have
ye got the cushions in, and are ye all ready ? You'll
be sure to take her ladyship to where the carriage
is waiting, and see that she has not a long way to
walk."

Thus talking, the kind lady saw her visitors off, and.
stood on the beach waving her hand to them. The fur
cloak had been transferred to her shoulders. It was the
one wrap in which everybody believed. Oona, who
moved so much more quickly, and had no need to pause
to take breath, did not now require such careful wrapping.
She too stood and waved her hand as the boat turned
the corner of the isle. But her farewells were not so
cordial as her mother's. Julia's talk had been very
strange to Oona ; it filled her with a vague fear. Something very different from the sensation with which she
had heard Katie's confessions on the subject of Lord
Erradeen moved her now. An impression of unworthi-
ness had stolen into her mind, she could not tell how. It

was the first time she had been sensible of any thought
of the kind. Walter had not been revealed to her in
any of the circumstances of his past life. She had
known him only during his visit at Kinloch Houran,
and when he was in profound difficulty and agitation, in
which her presence and succour had helped him she
could not tell how, and when his appeal to her, his
dependence on her, had seized hold of her mind and
imagination with a force which it had taken her all this
time to throw off, and which, alas! his first appearance
and renewed appeal to her to stand by him had brought
back again in spite of her resistance and against her
will. She had been angry with herself and indignant
at this involuntary subjugation—which he had not
desired so far as she knew, nor she dreamt of, until she
had fallen under it—and had recognised, with a sort of
despair and angry sense of impotence, the renewal
of the influence, which she seemed incapable of
resisting.

But Julia's words roused in her a different sentiment.
Julia's laugh, the light insinuations of her tone, her
claim of intimacy and previous knowledge, brought a
revulsion of feeling so strong and powerful that she
felt for the moment as if she had been delivered from
her bonds. Delivered—but not with any pleasure in
being free : for the deliverance meant the lowering of
the image of him in whom she had suddenly found
that union of something above her with something
below, which is the man's chief charm to the woman,

as probably it is the woman's chief charm to the man.
He had been below her, he had needed her help, she
had brought to him some principle of completeness,
some moral support which was indispensable, without
which he could not have stood fast. But now another
kind of inferiority was suggested to her, which was
not that in which a visionary and absolute youthful
mind could find any charm, which it was difficult even
to tolerate, which was an offence to her and to the
pure and overmastering sentiment which had drawn
her to him. If he was so near to Miss Herbert, so
entirely on her level, making her his confidant, he
could be nothing to Oona. She seemed to herself to
burst her bonds and stand free—but not happily. Her
heart was not the lighter for it. She would have liked
to escape, yet to be able to bear him the same stainless
regard, the same sympathy as ever; to help him
still, to honour him in his resistance to all that was
evil.

All this happened on the afternoon of the day which
Walter had begun with a despairing conviction that
Oona's help must fail him *when she knew.* She had
begun to know without any agency of his: and if it
moved her so to become aware of a frivolous and foolish
connection in which there was levity and vanity, and
a fictitious counterfeit of higher sentiments but no
harm, what would her feelings be when all the truth
was unfolded to her? But neither did she know of
the darker depths that lay below, nor was he aware of

the revelation which had begun. Oona returned to the house with her mother's soft-voiced monologue in her ears, hearing vaguely a great many particulars of Lady Herbert's family and connections and of her being "really an acquisition, and Sir Thomas just an honest English sort of man, and Miss Herbert very pretty, and a nice companion for you, Oona," without reply, or with much consciousness of what it was. "It is time you were indoors, mamma, for the wind is very cold," she said.

"Oh yes, Oona, it is very well for you to speak about me : but you must take your own advice and come in too. For you have nothing about your shoulders, and I have got the fur cloak."

"I am coming, mother," Oona said, and with these words turned from the door and going to the rocky parapet that bordered the little platform, cast an indignant glance towards the ruined walls so far beneath her on the water's edge, dark and cold, out of the reach of all those autumn glories that were fading in the sky. There was no light or sign of life about Kinloch Houran. She had looked out angrily, as one defrauded of much honest feeling had, she felt, a right to do ; but something softened her as she looked and gazed— the darkness of it, the pathos of the ruin, the incompleteness, and voiceless yet appealing need. Was it possible that there was no need at all or vacancy there but what Miss Herbert, with her smiles and dimples, her laughing insinuations, her claim upon him from

the past, and the first preference of youth, could supply?
Ouna felt a great sadness take the place of her indignation as she turned away. If that was so, how poor
and small it all was—how different from what she had
thought!

CHAPTER III.

THIS was not the only danger that once more over-shadowed the path of Lord Erradeen. Underwood had been left alone in one of those foreign centres of "pleasure," so called, whither he had led his so often impatient and unruly pupil. He had been left, without notice, by a sudden impulse, such as he was now sufficiently acquainted with in Walter—who had always the air of obeying angrily and against his will the temptations with which he was surrounded: a sort of moral indignation against himself and all that aided in his degradation curiously mingling with the follies and vices into which he was led. You never knew when you had him, was Captain Underwood's own description. He would dart aside at a tangent, go off at the most unlikely moment, dash down the cup when it was at the sweetest, and abandon with disgust the things that had seemed to please him most. And Underwood knew that the moment was coming when his patron and *protégé* must return home: but notwithstanding he was left, without warning, as by a sudden caprice; the young man, who scorned while he yielded to his influence, having neither respect nor regard enough for his companion to leave a word of explanation. Underwood was astonished and angry as a matter of course, but his anger soon subsided, and the sense of Lord Erradeen's importance to him was too strong to leave room for lasting resentment, or at least for anything in the shape of relinquishment. He was not at all disposed to give the young victim up. Already he had tasted many of what to him were the sweets of life by Walter's means, and there were endless capabilities in Lord Erradeen's fortune and in his unsettled mind, which made a companion like Underwood too wise ever to take offence, necessary to him—which that worthy would not let slip. After the shock of finding himself deserted, he took two or three days to consider the matter, and then he made his plan. It was bold, yet he thought not too bold. He followed in the very track of his young patron, passing through Edinburgh and reaching Auchnasheen on the same momentous day which had witnessed Julia Herbert's visit to the isle. Captain Underwood was very well known at Auchnasheen. He had filled in many ways the position of manager and steward to the last lord. He had not been loved, but yet he had not been actively disliked. If there was some surprise and a little resistance on the part of the household there was at least no open revolt. They received him coldly, and required considerable explanation of the many things which he required to be done. They were all aware, as well as he was, that

Lord Erradeen was to be expected from day to day, and they had made such preparations for his arrival as suggested themselves : but these were not many, and did not at all please the zealous captain. His affairs, he felt, were at a critical point. It was very necessary that the young man should feel the pleasure of being expected, the surprise of finding everything arranged according to his tastes.

"You know very well that he will come here exhausted, that he will want to have everything comfortable," he said to the housekeeper and the servants. " No one would like after a fatiguing journey to come into a bare sort of a miserable place like this."

"My lord is no so hard to please," said the housekeeper, standing her ground. " Last year he just took no notice. Whatever was done he was not heeding."

"Because he was unused to everything : now it is different ; and I mean to have things comfortable for him."

"Well, captain! I am sure it's none of my wish to keep the poor young gentleman from his bits of little comforts. Ye'll have *his* authority ? "

"Oh, yes, I have his authority. It will be for your advantage to mind what I tell you ; even more than with the late lord. I've been abroad with him. He left me but a short time ago ; I was to follow him, and look after everything."

At this the housekeeper looked at the under-factor Mr. Shaw's subordinate, who had come to intimate to

her her master's return. "Will that be all right, Mr.
Adamson?" Adamson put his shaggy head on one side
like an intelligent dog and looked at the stranger. But
they all knew Captain Underwood well enough, and
no one was courageous enough to contradict him.

'It will, maybe, be as ye say," said the under-factor
cautiously. "Anyway it will do us no harm to take
his orders," he added, in an undertone to the woman.
"He was always very far ben with the old lord."

"The worse for him," said that important functionary
under her breath. But she agreed with Adamson
afterwards that as long as it was my lord's comfort he
was looking after and not his own, his orders should be
obeyed. As with every such person, the household
distrusted this confident and unpaid major domo. But
Underwood had not been tyrannical in his previous
reign, and young Lord Erradeen during his last re-
sidence at Auchnasheen had frightened them all. He
had been like a man beside himself. If the captain
could manage him better, they would be grateful to the
captain; and thus Underwood, though by no means
confident of a good reception, had no serious hindrances
to encounter. He strolled forth when he had arranged
everything to "look about him." He saw the Birkenbraes boat pass in the evening light, returning from the
castle, with a surprise which took away his breath. The
boat was near enough to the shore as it passed to be
recognised and its occupants; but not even Katie, whose
eyesight was so keen, recognised the observer on the

beach. He remarked that the party were in earnest
conversation, consulting with each other over something,
which seemed to secure everybody's attention, so that
the ordinary quick notice of a stranger, which is common
to country people, was not called forth by his own
appearance. It surprised him mightily to see that such
visitors had ventured to Kinloch Houran. They never
would have done so in the time of the last lord. Had
Walter all at once become more friendly, more open-
hearted, perhaps feeling in the company of his neighbours a certain safety? Underwood was confounded by
this new suggestion. It did not please him. Nothing
could be worse for himself than that Lord Erradeen
should find amusement in the society of the neighbourhood. There would be no more riot if this was the case,
no "pleasure," no play; but perhaps a wife—most
terrible of all anticipations. Underwood had been
deeply alarmed before by Katie Williamson's ascendancy; but when Lord Erradeen returned to his own
influence, he had believed that risk to be over. If,
however, it recurred again, and, in this moment while
undefended by his, Underwood's, protection, if the young
fellow had rushed into the snare once more, the captain
felt that the incident would acquire new significance.

There were women whom he might have tolerated if
better could not be. Julia Herbert was one whom he
could perhaps—it was possible—have "got on with,"
though possibly she would have changed after her
marriage; but with Katie, Underwood knew that he

never would get on. If this were so he would have at
once to disappear. All his hopes would be over—his
prospect of gain or pleasure by means of Lord Erradeen.
And he had "put up with" so much! nobody knew
how much he had put up with. He had humoured the
young fellow, and endured his fits of temper, his changes
of purpose, his fantastic inconsistencies of every kind.
What friendship it was on his part, after Erradeen had
deserted him, left him planted there—as if he cared for
the d—— place where he had gone only to please the
young'un! thus to put all his grievances in his pocket
and hurry over land and sea to make sure that all was
comfortable for the ungrateful young man! That was
true friendship, by Jove; what a man would do for a
man! not like a woman that always had to be waited
upon. Captain Underwood felt that his vested rights
were being assailed, and that if it came to this it would
be a thing to be resisted with might and main. A
wife! what did Erradeen want with a wife? Surely it
would be possible to put before him the charms of
liberty once more and prevent the sacrifice. He walked
along the side of the loch almost keeping up with the
boat, hot with righteous indignation, in spite of the
cold wind which had driven Mrs. Forrester into the
house. Presently he heard the sound of salutations on
the water, of oars clanking upon rowlocks from a different quarter, and saw the boat from the isle—Hamish
rowing in his red shirt—meet with the large four-oared
boat from Birkenbraes and pause while the women's

voices exchanged a few sentences, chorused by Mr.
Williamson's bass. Then the smaller boat came on
towards the shore, towards the point near which a
carriage was waiting. Captain Underwood quickened
his steps a little, and he it was who presented himself
to Julia Herbert's eyes as she approached the bit of
rocky beach, and hurrying down, offered his hand to
help her.

"What a strange meeting," cried Julia; "what a
small world, as everybody says! Who could have
thought, Captain Underwood, of seeing you here?"

" I might reply, if the surprise were not so delightful,
who could have thought, Miss Herbert, of seeing you
here? for myself it is a second home to me, and has
been for years."

"My reason for being here is simple. Let me introduce you to my cousin, Lady Herbert. Sir Thomas has
got the shootings lower down. I suppose you are with
Lord Erradeen."

Lady Herbert had given the captain a very distant
bow. She did not like the looks of him, as indeed it
has been stated no ladies did, whether in Sloebury or
elsewhere; but at the name of Erradeen she paid a
more polite attention, though the thought of her horses
waiting so long in the cold was already grievous to
her. "I hope," she said, "that Lord Erradoen does not
lodge his friends in that old ruin, as he does himself,
people say."

" We are at Auchnasheen, a house you may see among

the trees," said the captain. "Feudal remains are captivating, but not to live in. Does our friend Walter know, Miss Herbert, what happiness awaits him in your presence here?"

"What a pretty speech," Julia cried; "far prettier than anything Walter could muster courage to say. No, Captain Underwood, he does not. It was all settled quite suddenly. I did not even know that he was here."

"Julia, the horses have been waiting a long time," said Lady Herbert. "I have no doubt Lord Erradeen is a very interesting subject—but I don't know what Barber (who was the coachman) will say. I shall be glad to see your friends any day at luncheon. Tell Lord Erradeen, please. We are two women alone, Sir Thomas is on the hills all day; all the more we shall be glad to see him—I mean you both—if you will take pity on our loneliness. Now, Julia, we really must not wait any longer."

"Tell Walter I shall look for him," said Julia, kissing her hand as they drove away. Underwood stood and looked after the carriage with varied emotions. As against Katie Williamson, he was overjoyed to have such an auxiliary—a girl who would not stand upon any punctilio—who would pursue her object with any assistance she could pick up, and would not be above an alliance defensive or offensive, a girl who knew the advantage of an influential friend. So far as that went he was glad: but, heavens! what a neighbourhood, bristling with women; a girl at every corner ready to decoy his prey out of his hands. He was rueful, even though he was in a measure satisfied. If he could play his cards sufficiently well to detach Walter from both one and the other, to show the bondage which was veiled under Julia's smiles and complacency, as well as under Katie's uncompromising code, and to carry him off under their very eyes, that would indeed be a triumph; but failing that, it was better for him to make an ally of Julia, and push her cause, than to suffer himself to be ousted by the other, the little parvenue, with her cool impertinence, who had been the first, he thought, to set Walter against him.

He walked back to Auchnasheen, full of these thoughts, and of plans to recover his old ascendancy. He had expedients for doing this which would not bear recording, and a hundred hopes of awakening the passions, the jealousies, the vanity of the young man whom already he had been able to sway beyond his expectations. He believed that he had led Walter by the nose, as he said, and had a mastery over him which would be easily recovered if he but got him for a day or two to himself. It was a matter of fact that he had done him much, if not fatal harm; and if the captain had been clever enough to know that he had no mastery whatever over his victim, and that Walter was the slave of his own shifting and uneasy moods, of his indolences and sudden impulses, and immediate abandonment of himself to the moment, but not of Captain Underwood, that tempter might have done him still more harm. But he did not possess this finer perception, and thus lost a portion of his power.

He went back to Auchnasheen to find a comfortable dinner, a good fire, a cheerful room, full of light and comfort, which reminded him of "old days," which he gave a regretful yet comfortable thought to in passing —the time when he had waited, not knowing what moment the old lord, his former patron, should return from Kinloch Houran. And now he was waiting for the other—who was so unlike the old lord—and yet had already been of more use to Underwood, and served him better in his own way, than the old lord had ever done. He was much softened, and even perhaps a little maudlin in his thoughts of Walter as he sat over that comfortable fire. What was he about, poor boy? Not so comfortable as this friend and retainer, who was drinking his wine and thinking of him. But he should find some one to welcome him when he returned. He should find a comfortable meal and good company, which was more than the foolish fellow would expect. It was foolish of him, in his temper, to dart away from those who really cared for him, who really could be of use to him ; but by this time the young lord would be too glad, after his loneliness, to come back and find a faithful friend ready to make allowances for him, and so well acquainted with his circumstances here.

So well acquainted with his circumstances ! Under-wood, in his time, had no doubt wondered over these as

much as any one; but that was long ago, and he had
in the mean time become quite familiar with them, and
did not any longer speculate on the subject. He had
no supernatural curiosity for his part. He could understand that one would not like to see a ghost: and he
believed in ghosts—in a fine, healthy, vulgar, natural
apparition, with dragging chains and hollow groans.
But as for anything else, he had never entered into the
question, nor had he any thought of doing so now.
However, as he sat by the fire with all these comfortable accessories round him, and listened now and then
to hear if any one was coming, and sometimes was
deceived by the wind in the chimneys, or the sound of
the trees in the fresh breeze which had become keener
and sharper since he came indoors, it happened, how he
could not tell, that questions arose in the captain's
mind such as he had never known before.

The house was very still, the servants' apartments
were at a considerable distance from the sitting-rooms,
and all was very quiet. Two or three times in the
course of the evening, old Symington, who had also
come to see that everything was in order for his master,
walked all the way from these retired regions through
a long passage running from one end of the house to
the other, to the great door, which he opened cautiously,
then shut again, finding nobody in sight, and retired
the same way as he came, his shoes creaking all the way.
This interruption occurring at intervals had a remarkable effect upon Underwood. He began to wait for its

recurrence, to count the steps, to feel a thrill of alarm as they passed the door of the room in which he was sitting. Oh, yes, no doubt it was Symington, who always wore creaking shoes, confound him ! But what if it were not Symington ? What if it might be some one else, some mysterious being who might suddenly open the door, and freeze into stone the warm, palpitating, somewhat unsteady person of a man who had eaten a very good dinner and drunk a considerable quantity of wine ? This thought so penetrated his mind, that gradually all his thoughts were concentrated on the old servant's perambulation, watching for it before it came, thinking of it after it had passed. The steady and solemn march at intervals, which seemed calculated and regular, was enough to have impressed the imagination of any solitary person. And the captain was of a primitive simplicity of mind in some respects. His fears paralysed him; he was afraid to get up, to open the door, to make sure what it was. How could he tell that he might not be seized by the hair of the head by some ghastly apparition, and dragged into a chamber of horrors ! He tried to fortify himself with more wine, but that only made his tremor worse. Finally the panic came to a crisis, when Symington, pausing, knocked at the library door. Underwood remembered to have heard that no spirit could enter without invitation, and he shut his mouth firmly that no habitual "come in" might lay him open to the assault of the enemy. He sat breathless through the ensuing moment of suspense, while Symington waited outside. The captain's hair stood up on his head; his face was covered with a profuse dew; he held by the table in an agony of apprehension when he saw the door begin to turn slowly upon its hinges.

"My lord will not be home the night," said Symington, slowly.

The sight of the old servant scarcely quieted the perturbation of Underwood. It had been a terrible day for Symington. He was ashy pale or grey, as old men become when the blood is driven from their faces. He had not been able to get rid of the scared and terror-stricken sensation with which he had watched the Birkenbraes party climbing the old stairs, and wandering as he thought at the peril of their lives upon the unsafe battlements. He had been almost violent in his calls to them to come down: but nobody had taken any notice, and they had talked about their guide and about the gentleman who was living with Lord Erradeen, till it seemed to Symington that he must go distracted. "Where there ever such fools—such idiots! since there is nobody staying with Lord Erradeen but me, his body servant," the old man had said tremulously to himself. At Symington's voice the captain gave a start and a cry. Even in the relief of discovering who it was, he could not quiet the excitement of his nerves.

".It's you, old Truepenny," he cried, yet looked at him across the table with a tremor, and a very forced and uncomfortable smile.

"That's not my name," said Symington, with, on his side, the irritation of a disturbed mind. "I'm saying that it's getting late, and my lord will no be home to-night."

"By Jove!" cried Captain Underwood, "when I heard you passing from one end of the house to the other, I thought it might be—the old fellow over there, coming himself——"

"I cannot tell, sir, what you are meaning by the old fellow over there. There's no old fellow I know of but old Macalister; and it was not for him you took me."

"If you could have heard how your steps sounded through the house! By Jove! I could fancy I hear them now."

"Where?" Symington cried, coming in and shutting the door, which he held with his hand behind him, as if to bar all possible comers. And then the two men looked at each other, both breathless and pale.

"Sit down," said Underwood. "The house feels chilly and dreary, nobody living in it for so long. Have a glass of wine. One wants company in a damp, dreary old hole like this."

"You are very kind, captain," said the old man; "but Auchnasheen, though only my lord's shooting-box, is a modern mansion, and full of every convenience. It would ill become me to raise an ill name on it."

" I wonder what Erradeen's about?" said the captain.
" I bet he's worse off than we are. How he must
wish he was off with me on the other side of the
Channel."

"Captain! you will, maybe, think little of me, being
nothing but a servant; but it is little good you do my
young lord on the ither side of the Channel."

Underwood laughed, but not with his usual vigour.

"What can I do with your young lord," he said.
"He takes the bit in his teeth, and goes—to the devil
his own way."

"Captain, there are some that think the like of you
sore to blame."

Underwood said nothing for a moment. When he
spoke there was a quiver in his voice.

"Let me see the way to my room, Symington. Oh
yes, I suppose it is the old room; but I've forgotten.
I was there before? well, so I suppose; but I have
forgotten. Take the candle as I tell you, and show me
the way."

He had not the least idea what he feared, and he did
not remember ever having feared anything before; but
to-night he hung close to Symington, following at his
very heels. The old man was anxious and alarmed,
but not in this ignoble way. He deposited the captain
in his room with composure, who would but for very
shame have implored him to stay. And then his footsteps sounded through the vacant house, going further

and further off till they died away in the distance.
Captain Underwood locked his door, though he felt it
was a vain precaution, and hastened to hide his head
under the bed-clothes: but he was well aware that this
was a vain precaution too.

CHAPTER IV.

It was on the evening of the day after Captain
Underwood's arrival that Lord Erradeen left Kinloch
Houran for Auchnasheen. After labour, rest. He could
not but compare as he walked along in the early falling
autumnal twilight the difference between himself now,
and the same self a year ago, when he had fled from
the place of torture to the house of peace, a man nearly
frantic with the consciousness of all the new bonds
upon him, the uncomprehended powers against which
he had to struggle, the sense of panic and impotence,
yet of mad excitement and resistance, with which his
brain was on flame. The recollection of the ensuing
time spent at Auchnasheen, when he saw no one, heard
no voice but his own, yet lived through day after day
of bewildering mental conflict, without knowing who it
was against whom he contended, was burned in upon
his recollection. All through that time he had been
conscious of such a desire to flee as hurried the pace of
his thoughts, and made the intolerable still more intolerable. His heart had sickened of the unbearable
fight into which he was compelled like an unwilling

soldier with death behind him. To resist had always been Walter's natural impulse; but the impulse of flight had so mingled with it that his soul had been in a fever, counting no passage of days, but feeling the whole period long or short, he did not know which, as one monstrous uninterrupted day or night, in which the processes of thought were never intermitted. His mind was in a very different condition now. He had got over the early panic of nature. The blinding mists of terror had melted away from his eyes, and the novelty and horror of his position, contending with unseen dominations and powers, had almost ceased for the moment to affect his mind, so profoundly exhausted was he by the renewed struggle in which he had been engaged.

The loch was veiled in mist, through which it glimmered faintly with broken reflections, the wooded banks presenting on every side a sort of ghostly outline, with the colour no more than indicated against the dreary confusion of air and vapour. At some points there was the glimpse of a blurred light, looking larger and more distant than it really was, the ruddy spot made by the open door of the little inn, the whiter and smaller twinkle of the manse window, the far-off point, looking no more than a taper light in the distance, that shone from the isle. There was in Walter's mind a darkness and confusion not unlike the landscape. He was worn out: there was in him none of that vivid feeling which had separated between his human soul in its despair and the keen sweetness of the morning. Now all was night within him and around. His arms had fallen from his hands. He moved along, scarcely aware that he was moving, feeling everything blurred, confused, indistinct in the earth about him and in the secret places of his soul. Desire for flight he had none : he had come to see that it was impossible : and he had not energy enough to wish it. And fear had died out of him. He was not afraid. Had he been joined on the darkling way by the personage of whom he had of late seen so much, it would scarcely have quickened his pulses. All such superficial emotion had died out of him : the real question was so much superior, so infinitely important in comparison with any such transitory tremors as these. But at the present moment he was not thinking at all, scarcely living, any more than the world around him was living, hushed into a cessation of all energy and almost of consciousness, looking forward to night and darkness and repose.

It was somewhat surprising to him to see the lighted windows at Auchnasheen, and the air of inhabitation about the house with which he had no agreeable associations, but only those which are apt to hang about a place in which one has gone through a fever, full of miserable visions, and the burning restlessness of disease. But when he stepped into the hall, the door being opened to him by Symington as soon as his foot was heard on the gravel, and turning round to go into the library found himself suddenly in the presence of

Captain Underwood, his astonishment and dismay were beyond expression. The dismay came even before the flush of anger, which was the first emotion that showed itself. Underwood stood holding open the library door, with a smile that was meant to be ingratiating and conciliatory. He held out his hand, as Walter, with a start and exclamation, recognised him.

" Yes," he said, " I'm here, you see. Not so easy to get rid of when once I form a friendship. Welcome to your own house, Erradeen."

Walter did not say anything till he had entered the room and shut the door. He walked to the fire, which was blazing brightly, and placed himself with his back to it, in that attitude in which the master of a house defies all comers.

" I did not expect to find you here," he said. " You take me entirely by surprise."

" I had hoped it would be an agreeable surprise," said the captain, still with his most amiable smile. " I thought to have a friend's face waiting for you when you came back from that confounded place would be a relief."

" What do you call a confounded place?" said Walter, testily. " You know nothing about it, as far as I am aware. No, Underwood, it is as well to speak plainly. It is not an agreeable surprise. I am sorry you have taken the trouble to come so far for me."

" It was no trouble. If you are a little out of sorts,

never mind. I am not a man to be discouraged for a hasty word. You want a little cheerful society——"

"Is that what you call yourself?" Walter said with a harsh laugh. He was aware that there was a certain brutality in what he said; but the sudden sight of the man who had disgusted him even while he had most influenced him, and of whom he had never thought but with a movement of resentment and secret rage, affected him to a sort of delirium. He could have seized him with the force of passion and flung him into the loch at the door. It would have been no crime, he thought, to destroy such vermin off the face of the earth—to make an end of such a source of evil would be no crime. This was the thought in his mind while he stood upon his own hearth, looking at the man who was his guest and therefore sacred. As for Captain Underwood, he took no offence; it was not in his *rôle* to do so, whatever happened. What he had to do was to regain, if possible, his position with the young man upon whom he had lived and enriched himself for the greater part of the year, to render himself indispensable to him as he had done to his predecessor. For this object he was prepared to bear everything, and laugh at all that was too strong to be ignored. He laughed now, and did his best, not very gracefully, to carry out the joke. He exerted himself to talk and please throughout the dinner, which Walter went through in silence, drinking largely, though scarcely eating at all—for Kinloch Houran was not a place which encouraged an appetite.

After dinner, in the midst of one of Underwood's
stories, Walter lighted a candle abruptly, and saying
he was going to bed, left his companion without apology
or reason given. It was impossible to be more rude.
The captain felt the check, for he had a considerable
development of vanity, and was in the habit of amusing
the people to whom he chose to make himself agreeable. But this affront, too, he swallowed. " He will have
come to himself by morning," he said. In the morning,
however, Walter was only more gloomy and unwilling
to listen, and determined not to respond. It was only
when in the middle of the breakfast he received a note
brought by a mounted messenger who waited for an
answer, that he spoke. He flung it open across the
table to Underwood with a harsh laugh.

" Is this your doing, too ? " he cried.

" My doing, Erradeen ! "

Underwood knew very well what it was before he
looked at it. It was from Lady Herbert, explaining
that she had only just heard that Lord Erradeen was
so near a neighbour, and begging him, if he was not,
like all the other gentlemen, on the hills, that he
would come ("and your friend Captain Underwood") to
luncheon that day to cheer two forlorn ladies left all by
themselves in this wilderness. "And you will meet an
old friend," it concluded playfully. The composition
was Julia's, and had not been produced without careful
study.

"My doing!" said Captain Underwood. "Can you suppose that *I* want you to marry, Erradeen?"

It was a case, he thought, in which truth was best.

Walter started up from his seat.

"Marry!" he cried, with a half-shout of rage and dismay.

"Well, my dear fellow, I don't suppose you are such a fool; but, of course, that is what *she* means. The fair Julia——"

"Oblige me," cried Lord Erradeen, taking up once more his position on the hearth, "by speaking civilly when you speak of ladies in my house."

"Why, bless me, Erradeen, you gave me the note——"

"I was a fool—that is nothing new. I have been a fool since the first day when I met you and took you for something more than mortal. Oh, and before that!" cried Walter bitterly. "Do not flatter yourself that you did it. It is of older date than you."

"The fair Julia——" Underwood began; but he stopped when his companion advanced upon him threatening, with so gloomy a look and so tightly strained an arm that the captain judged it wise to change his tone. "I should have said, since we are on punctilio, that Miss Herbert and you are older acquaintances than you and I, Erradeen."

"Fortunately you have nothing to do with that," Walter said, perceiving the absurdity of his rage.

Then he walked to the window and looked out so long and silently that the anxious watcher began to think the incident over. But it was not till Walter, after this period of reflection, had written a note and sent it to the messenger, that he ventured to speak.

"You have accepted, of course. In the circumstances it would be uncivil——"

Walter looked at him for a moment, breaking off his sentence as if he had spoken.

"I have something to tell you," he said. "My mother is coming to Auchnasheen."

"Your mother!" Underwood's voice ran into a quaver of dismay.

"You will see that in the circumstances, as you say, I am forced to be uncivil. When my mother is here she will, of course, be the mistress of the house; and she, as you know——"

"Will not ask me to prolong my visit," said the captain, with an attempt at rueful humour. "I think we may say as much as that, Erradeen."

"I fear it is not likely," Walter said.

Captain Underwood gave vent to his feelings in a prolonged whistle.

"You will be bored to death. Mark my words, I know you well enough. You will never be able to put up with it. You will be ready to hang yourself in a week. You will come off to me. It is the best thing that could happen so far as I am concerned—wishing to preserve your friendship as I do——"

"Is it friendship, then, that has bound us together?" said Lord Erradeen.

E 2

"What else? Disinterested friendship on my part. I take your laugh rather ill, Erradeen. What have I gained by it, I should like to know? I've liked you, and I liked the last man before you. I have put up with a great deal from you—tempers like a silly woman, vagaries of all sorts, discontent and abuse. Why have I put up with all that?"

"Why indeed? I wish you had not," said the young man scornfully. "Yes, you have put up with it, and made your pupil think the worse of you with every fresh exercise of patience. I should like to pay you for all that dirty work."

"Pay me!" the captain said, faltering a little. He was not a very brave man, though he could hold his own; and there was a force of passion and youth in his "pupil"—with what bitterness that word was said!—that alarmed him a little. Besides, Walter had a household of servants behind him—grooms, keepers, all sorts of people—who held Captain Underwood in no favour. "Pay me! I don't know how you could pay me," he said.

"I should like to do it—in one way; and I shall do it—in another," said Walter still somewhat fiercely. Then once more he laughed. He took out a pocket-book from his coat, and out of that a cheque. "You have been at some expense on my account," he said; "your journey has been long and rapid. I consider myself your debtor for that, and for the—good intention. Will this be enough?"

In the bitter force of his ridicule and dislike, Walter held out the piece of paper as one holds a sweetmeat to a child. The other gave a succession of rapid glances at it to make out what it was. When he succeeded in doing so a flush of excitement and eagerness covered his face. He put out his hand nervously to clutch it with the excited look of the child before whom a prize is held out, and who catches at it before it is snatched away. But he would not acknowledge this feeling.

"My lord," he said, with an appearance of dignity offended, "you are generous; but to pay me, as you say, and offer money in place of your friendship——"

"It is an excellent exchange, Underwood. This is worth something, if not very much—the other," said Walter with a laugh, "nothing at all."

Perhaps this was something like what Captain Underwood himself thought, as he found himself, a few hours later, driving along the country roads towards the railway station, retracing the path which he had travelled two days before with many hopes and yet a tremor. His hopes were now over, and the tremor too; but there was something in his breast pocket better, for the moment at least, than any hopes, which kept him warm, even though the wind was cold. He had failed in his attempt to fix himself once more permanently on Lord Erradeen's shoulders—an attempt in which he had not been very sanguine. It was a desperate venture, he knew, and it had failed; but, at the same time, circumstances might arise which would justify

another attempt, and that one might not fail : and, in
the mean time, his heart rose with a certain elation
when he thought of that signature in his breast pocket.
That was worth an effort, and nothing could diminish
its value.   Friendship might fail, but a cheque is
substantial.   He had something of the dizzy feeling of
one who has fallen from a great height, and has not yet
got the giddiness of the movement out of his head.
And yet he was not altogether discouraged.   Who
could tell what turn the wheel of fortune might take ?
and, in the mean time, there was that bit of paper.
The horse was fresh, and flew along the road, up and
down, at a pace very different from that of Big John's
steeds, which had brought Captain Underwood to Auchnasheen.   About half-way along he came up to the
waggonette from Birkenbraes, in which was Mr. Braithwaite and his luggage, along with two other guests,
ladies, bound for the station, and escorted by Mr.
Williamson and Katie, as was their way.

"Dear me, is that Underwood?" cried Mr. Williamson with the lively and simple curiosity of
rural use and wont.   "So you're there, captain," he
said, as the dog-cart came up behind the heavier
carriage.

"No, I'm not here—I'm going," said Underwood,
quickly, " hurrying to catch the train."

" Oh, there is plenty of time ; we are going too
(Bless me," he said aside, " how many visitors think
you they can have had in yon old place ?)   I am

thinking ye have been with our young neighbour, Lord Erradeen."

"That is an easy guess. I am leaving him, you mean. Erradeen is a reformed character. He is turning over a new leaf—and full time too," Captain Underwood cried, raising his voice that he might be heard over the rattle of the two carriages. Notwithstanding the cheque which kept him so warm, he had various grudges against Walter, and did not choose to lose the opportunity for a little mischief.

"It is always a good thing," said Mr. Williamson, "to turn over a new leaf. We have all great occasion to do that."

"Especially when there are so many of them," the captain cried, as his light cart passed the other. He met the party again at the station, where they had to wait for the train. Katie stood by herself in a thoughtful mood while the departing guests consulted over their several boxes, and Captain Underwood seized the moment: "I am sorry to lose the fun," he said, in a confidential tone, "but I must tell you, Miss Williamson, what is going to happen. Erradeen has been pursued up here into his stronghold by one of the many ladies —— I expect to hear she has clutched hold of him before long, and then you'll have a wedding."

"Is that why you are going away, Captain Underwood?"

"He has gone a little too far, you know, that is the

truth," said the captain. "I am glad he is not going
to take in any nice girl. I couldn't have stood by and
seen that. I should have had to warn her people.
Even Miss Julia, by Jove! I'm sorry for Miss Julia, if
she gets him. But she is an old campaigner; she will
know how to take care of herself."

"Is it because Lord Erradeen is so bad that you are
leaving him, or because he is going to be good?" Katie
asked. Captain Underwood on ordinary occasions was
a little afraid of her; but his virtuous object fortified
him now.

"Oh, by Jove! he goes too far," said Underwood.
"I am not squeamish, heaven knows, but he goes too
far. I can speak now that it's all over between him
and me. I never could bear to see him with nice girls;
but he's got his match in Miss Julia. The fair Julia—
that is another pair of shoes."

"Who was he meaning with his fair Julias?" said
Mr. Williamson as they drove away. "Yon's a scoun-
drel, if there ever was one, and young Erradeen is well
rid of him. But when thieves cast out, honest folk get
their ain. Would yon be true?"

Katie was in what her father called "a brown study,"
and did not care to talk. She only shook her head—a
gesture which could be interpreted as any one pleased.

"I am not sure," said Mr. Williamson, in reply.
"He knows more about Lord Erradeen than any person
on the loch. But who is the fair Julia, and is he really
to be married to her? I would like fine to hear all

about it. I will call at Auchnasheen in the afternoon
and see what he has to say."

But Katie remained in her brown study, letting her
father talk. She knew very well who the fair Julia
was. She remembered distinctly the scene at Burlington House. She saw with the clearest perception what
the tactics were of the ladies at the Lodge. Katie had
been somewhat excited by the prospect of being Oona's
rival, which was like something in a book. It was like
the universal story of the young man's choice, not
between Venus and Minerva, or between good and evil,
but perhaps, Katie thought, between poetry and prose,
between the ideal and the practical. She was interested
in that conflict and not unwilling in all kindness and
honour to play her part in it. Oona would be the ideal
bride for him, but she herself, Katie felt, would be
better in a great many ways, and she did not feel that
she would have any objection to marry Lord Erradeen.
But here was another rival with whom she did not
choose to enter the lists. It is to be feared that Katie
in her heart classified Miss Herbert as Vice, as the
sinner against whom every man is to be warned, and
turned with some scorn from any comparison with her
meretricious attractions. But she was fair and just, and
her heart had nothing particular to do with the matter;
so that she was able calmly to wait for information,
which was not Oona's case.

It had been entirely at random that Lord Erradeen
had announced his mother's approaching arrival to

Underwood. The idea had come into his mind the moment before he made use of it, and he had felt a certain amusement in the complete success of this hastily-assumed weapon. It had been so effectual that he began to think it might be available in other conflicts as well as this: and in any case he felt himself pledged to make it a matter of fact. He walked to the village when Underwood had gone, to carry at once his intention into effect. Though it was only a cluster of some half-dozen houses, it had a telegraph-office—as is so general in the Highlands—and Walter sent a brief, emphatic message, which he felt would carry wild excitement into Sloebury. "You will do me a great favour if you will come at once, alone," was Walter's message. He was himself slightly excited by it. He began to think over all those primitive relationships of his youth as he walked along the quiet road. There was sweetness in them, but how much conflict, trouble, embarrassment!—claims on one side to which the other could not respond—a sort of authority, which was no authority—a duty which did nothing but establish grievances and mutual reproach. His mind was still in the state of exhaustion which Captain Underwood had only temporarily disturbed; and a certain softening was in the weakened faculties, which were worn out with too much conflict. Poor mother, after all! He could remember, looking back, when it was his greatest pleasure to go home to her, to talk to her, pouring every sort of revelation into her never-wearied ears; all his

school successes and tribulations, all about the other
fellows, the injustices that were done, the triumphs that
were gained. Could women interest themselves in all
that as she had seemed to interest herself? or had she
sometimes found it a bore to have all these schoolboy
experiences poured forth upon her? Miss Merivale
had very plainly thought it a bore; his voice had given
her a headache. But Mrs. Methven never had any
headaches, or anything that could cloud her attention.
He remembered now that his mother was not a mere
nursery woman—that she read a great deal more than
he himself did, knew many things he did not know, was
not silly, or a fool, or narrow-minded, as so many women
are. Was it not a little hard, after all, that she should
have nothing of her son but the schoolboy prattle?
She had been everything to him when he was a boy,
and now she was nothing to him; perhaps all the time
she might have been looking forward to the period
when he should be a man, and have something more
interesting to talk over with her than a cricket-match
—for, to be sure, when one came to think of it, she
could have no personal interest in a cricket-match. A
momentary *serrement* of compunction came to Walter's
heart. Poor mother! he said to himself; perhaps it
was a little hard upon her. And she must have the
feeling, to make it worse, that she had a right to something better. He could not even now get his mind
clear about that right.

As he returned from the telegraph-office he too met

the waggonette from Birkenbraes, which was stopped
at sight of him with much energy on the part of Mr.
Williamson.

"We've just met your friend Captain Underwood.
If you'll not take it amiss, Lord Erradeen, I will say
that I'm very glad you're not keeping a man like that
about you. But what is this about—a lady? I hear
there's a lady—the fair——What did he call her, Katie?
I am not good at remembering names."

"It is of no consequence," said Katie, with a little
rising colour, "what such a man said."

"That's true, that's true," said her father; "but still,
Erradeen, you must mind we are old friends now, and
let us know what's coming. The fair——Toots, I
thought of it a minute ago? It's ridiculous to forget
names."

"You may be sure I shall let you know what's
coming. My mother is coming," Walter said.

And this piece of news was so unexpected and start-
ling that the Williamsons drove off with energy to
spread it far and near. Mr. Williamson himself was as
much excited as if it had been of personal importance
to him.

"Now that will settle the young man," he said; "that
will put many things right. There has not been a lady
at Auchnasheen since ever I have been here. A mother
is the next best thing to a wife, and very likely the one
is in preparation for the other, and ye will all have to
put on your prettiest frocks for her approval." He

followed this with one of his big laughs, looking round
upon a circle in which there were various young persons
who were very marriageable. "But I put no faith in
Underwood's fair—what was it he called her?" Mr.
Williamson said.

CHAPTER V.

Two days after, Mrs. Methven arrived at Kinloch Houran by the afternoon coach, alone.

She had interpreted very literally the telegram which had brought such a tremor yet such a movement of joy to her heart. Her son wanted her. Perhaps he might be ill, certainly it must be for something serious and painful that she was called; yet he wanted her! She had been very quiet and patient, waiting if perhaps his heart might be touched and he might recall the tie of nature and his own promises, feeling with a sad pride that she wanted nothing of him but his love, and that without that the fine houses and the new wealth were nothing to her. She was pleased even to stand aloof, to be conscious of having in no way profited by Walter's advancement. She had gained nothing by it, she wished to gain nothing by it. If Walter were well, then there was no need for more. She had enough for herself without troubling him. So long as all was well! But this is at the best a forlorn line of argument, and it cannot be doubted that Mrs. Methven's bosom throbbed with a great pang of disappointment

when she sat and smiled to conceal it, and answered
questions about Walter, yet could not say that she
had seen him or any of his "places in Scotland," cr
knew much more than her questioners did. When
his message arrived her heart leapt in her breast.
There were no explanations, no reason given, but that
imperative call, such as mothers love to have addressed
to them: "Come;" all considerations of her own
comfort set aside in the necessity for her which had
arisen at last. Another might have resented so complete an indifference to what might happen to suit
herself. But there are connections and relationships
in which this is the highest compliment. He knew
that it did not matter to her what her own convenience
was, as long as he wanted her. She got up from her
chair at once, and proceeded to put her things together
to get ready for the journey. With a smiling countenance she prepared herself for the night train. She
would not even take a maid. "He says, alone. He
must have some reason for it, I suppose," she said to
Miss Merivale. "I am the reason," said Cousin Sophy:
"He doesn't want me. You can tell him, with my
love, that to travel all night is not at all in my way,
and he need have had no fear on that subject." But
Mrs. Methven would not agree to this, and departed
hurriedly without any maid. She was surprised a
little, yet would not allow herself to be displeased,
that no one came to meet her: but it was somewhat
forlorn to be set down on the side of the loch in the

wintry afternoon, with the cold, gleaming water before her, and no apparent way of getting to the end of her journey.

"Oh yes, mem, you might drive round the head of the loch: but it's a long way," the landlady of the little inn said, smoothing down her apron at the door, "and far simpler just crossing the water, as everybody does in these parts."

Mrs. Methven was a little nervous about crossing the water. She was tired and disappointed, and a chill had crept to her heart. While she stood hesitating a young lady came up, whose boat waited for her on the beach, a man in a red shirt standing at the bow.

"It is a lady for Auchnasheen, Miss Oona," said the landlady, "and no boat. Duncan is away, and for the moment I have not a person to send: and his lordship will maybe be out on the hill, or he will have forgotten, or maybe he wasna sure when to expect you, mem?"

"No, he did not know when to expect me. I hope there is no illness," said Mrs. Methven, with a thrill of apprehension.

At this the young lady came forward with a shy yet frank grace.

"If you will let me take you across," she said, "my boat is ready. I am Oona Forrester. Lord Erradeen is quite well I think, and I heard that he expected— his mother."

"Yes," said Mrs. Methven. She gave the young stranger a penetrating look. Her own aspect was

perhaps a little severe, for her heart had been starved
and repressed, and she wore it very warm and low
down in her bosom, never upon her sleeve. There
rose over Oona's countenance a soft and delicate flush
under the eyes of Walter's mother. She had nothing
in the world to blush for, and probably that was why
the colour rose. They were of infinite interest to each
other, two souls meeting, as it were, in the dark, quite
unknown to each other and yet—who could tell?—to
be very near perhaps in times to come. The look they
interchanged was a mutual question. Then Mrs.
Methven felt herself bound to take up her invariable
defence of her son.

"He did not, most likely, think that I could arrive
so soon. I was wrong not to let him know. If I
accept your kindness will it be an inconvenience to
you?"

This question was drowned in Oona's immediate
response and in the louder protest of Mrs. Macfarlane.
"Bless me, mem, you canna know the loch! for there
is nobody but would put themselves about to help a
traveller: and above all Miss Oona, that just has no
other thought. Colin, put in the lady's box intill the
boat, and Hamish, he will give ye a hand."

Thus it was settled without further delay. It seemed
to the elder lady like a dream when she found herself
afloat upon this unknown water, the mountains standing
round, with their heads all clear and pale in the wonderful atmosphere from which the last rays of the sunset

had but lately faded, while down below in this twilight scene the colour had begun to go out of the autumn trees and red walls of the ruined castle, at which she looked with a curiosity full of excitement. "That is ——?" she said pointing with a strange sensation of eagerness.

"That is Kinloch Houran," said Oona, to whose sympathetic mind, she could not tell how, there came a tender, pitying comprehension of the feelings of the mother, thus thrust alone and without any guide into the other life of her son.

"It is very strange to me—to see the place where Walter——You know perhaps that neither my son nor I were ever here until he——"

"Oh yes," Oona said hastily, interrupting the embarrassed speech; and she added, "My mother and I have been here always, and everybody on the loch knows everybody else. We were aware——"

And then she paused too; but her companion took no notice, her mind being fully occupied. "I feel," she said, "like a woman in a dream."

It was very still on the loch, scarcely a breath stirring (which was very fortunate, for Mrs. Methven, unaccustomed, had a little tremor for the dark water even though so smooth). The autumnal trees alone, not quite put out by the falling darkness, seemed to lend a little light as they hung, reflected, over the loch—a redder cluster here and there looking like a fairy lamp below the water. A thousand suggestions were in the

air, and previsions of she knew not what, a hidden life
surrounding her on every side. Her brain was giddy,
her heart full. By-and-by she turned to her young
companion, who was so sympathetically silent, and
whose soft voice when she spoke, with the little cadence
of an accent unfamiliar yet sweet, had a half-caressing
sound which touched the solitary woman. "You say
your mother and you," she said. "Are you too an
only child?"

"Oh no! there are eight of us: but I am the
youngest, the only one left. All the boys are away.
We live on the isle. I hope you will come and see
us. My mother will be glad——"

"And she is not afraid to trust you—by yourself?
It must be a happy thing for a woman to have a
daughter," Mrs. Methven said, with a sigh. "The
boys, as you say, go away."

"Nobody here is afraid of the loch," said Oona.
"Accidents happen—oh, very rarely. Mamma is a
little nervous about yachting, for the winds come down
from the hills in gusts; but Hamish is the steadiest
oar, and there is no fear. Do you see now the lights
at Auchnasheen? There is some one waiting, at the
landing-place. It will be Lord Erradeen, or some one
from the house. Hamish, mind the current. You
know how it sweeps the boat up the loch?"

"It will just be the wash of that confounded steam-
boat," Hamish said.

The voices sounded in the air without conveying

F 2

any sense to her mind. Was that Walter, the vague
line of darker shadow upon the shade? Was it his
house she was going to, his life that she was entering
once more? All doubts were put to an end speedily
by Walter's voice.

"Is it Hamish?" he cried out.

"Oh, Lord Erradeen, it is me," cried Oona, in
her soft Scotch. "And I am bringing you your
mother."

The boat grated on the bank as she spoke, and this
disguised the tremor in her voice, which Mrs. Methven,
quite incapable of distinguishing anything else, was
yet fully sensible of. She stepped out tremulously
into her son's arms.

"Mother," he cried, "what must you think of me
for not coming to meet you? I never thought you
could be here so soon."

"I should have come by telegraph if I could," she
said, with an agitated laugh : so tired, so tremulous,
so happy, the strangest combination of feelings over-
whelming her. But still she was aware of a something,
a tremor, a tingle in Oona's voice. The boat receded
over the water almost without a pause, Hamish under
impulsion of a whispered word, having pushed off again
as soon as the traveller and her box were landed.
Walter paused to call out his thanks over the water,
and then he drew his mother's arm within his, and led
her up the bank.

"Where is Jane?" he said. "Have you no one

with you? Have you travelled all night, and alone, mother, for me?"

"For whom should I do it, but for you? And did you think I would lose a minute after your message, Walter? But you are well, there is nothing wrong with your health?"

"Nothing wrong with my health," he said, with a half-laugh. "No, that is safe enough. I have not deserved that you should come to me, mother——"

"There is no such word as deserving between mother and son," she said tremulously, "so long as you want me, Walter."

"Take care of those steps," was all he said. "We are close now to the house. I hope you will find your rooms comfortable. I fear they have not been occupied for some time. But what shall you do without a maid? Perhaps the housekeeper——"

"You said to come alone, Walter."

"Oh yes. I was afraid of Cousin Sophy; but you could not think I wanted to impair your comfort, mother? Here we are at the door, and here is Symington, very glad to receive his lady."

"But you must not let him call me so."

"Why not? You are our lady to all of us. You are the lady of the house, and I bid you welcome to it, mother," he said, pausing to kiss her. She had a thousand things to forgive, but in that moment they were as though they had not been.

And there was not much more said until she had

settled down into possession of the library, which answered instead of a drawing-room: had dined, and been brought back to the glowing peat fire which gave an aromatic breath of warmth and character to a Highland house. When all the business of the arrival had thus been gone through, there came a moment when it was apparent that subjects of more importance must be entered upon. There was a pause, and an interval of complete silence which seemed much longer than it really was. Walter stood before the fire for some time, while she sat close by, her hands clasped in her lap, ready to attend. Then he began to move about uneasily, feeling the compulsion of the moment, yet unprepared with anything to say. At length it was she who began.

"You sent for me, Walter?" she said.

"Yes, mother."

Was there nothing more to tell her? He threw into disorder the books on the table, and then he came back again, and once more faced her, standing with his back to the fire.

"My dear," she said hesitating, "it is with no reproach I speak, but only——There was some reason for sending for me?"

He gave once more a nervous laugh.

"You have good reason to be angry if you will; but I'll tell you the truth, mother. I made use of you to get rid of Underwood. He followed me here, and I told him you were coming, and that he could not stay against the will of the mistress of the house. Then I was bound to ask you——"

The poor lady drew back a little, and instinctively put her hand to her heart, in which there was a hot thrill of sensation, as if an arrow had gone in. And then, in the pang of it, she laughed too, and cried—

"You were bound, to be sure, to fulfil your threat. And this is why—this is why, Walter——"

She could not say more without being hysterical, and departing from every rule she had made for herself.

Meanwhile, Walter stood before her, feeling in his own heart the twang of that arrow which had gone through hers, and the pity of it and wonder of it, with a poignant realisation of all; and yet found nothing to say.

After a while Mrs. Methven regained her composure, and spoke with a smile that was almost more pathetic than tears.

"After all, it was a very good reason. I am glad you used me to get rid of that man."

"I always told you, mother," he said, "that you had a most absurd prejudice against that man. There is no particular harm in the man. I had got tired of him. He is well enough in his own way, but he was out of place here."

"Well, Walter, we need not discuss Captain Underwood. But don't you see it is natural that I should exaggerate his importance by way of giving myself the better reason for having come?"

The touch of bitterness and sarcasm that was in her words made Walter start from his place again, and once more turn over the books on the table. She was not a perfect woman to dismiss all feeling from what she said, and her heart was wrung.

After a while he returned to her again.

"Mother, I acknowledge you have a good right to be displeased. But that is not all. I am glad, anyhow— heartily glad to have you here."

She looked up at him with her eyes full, and quivering lips. Everything went by impulse in the young man's mind, and this look—in which for once in his life he read the truth, the eagerness to forgive, the willingness to forget, the possibility, even in the moment of her deepest pain, of giving her happiness—went to his heart. After all it is a wonderful thing to have a human creature thus altogether dependent upon your words, your smile, ready to encounter all things for you, without hesitation, without a grudge. And why should she? What had he ever done for her? And she was no fool. These thoughts had already passed through his mind with a realisation of the wonder of it all, which seldom strikes the young at sight of the devotion of the old. All these things flashed back upon him at the sight of the dumb anguish yet forgiveness in her eyes.

"Mother," he cried, "there's enough of this between you and me. I want you not for Underwood, but for everything. Why should you care for a cad like me? but you do——"

" Care for you ?   Oh, my boy ! "

" I know; there you sit that have travelled night
and day because I held up my finger : and would give
me your life if you could, and bear everything, and
never change and never tire.   Why, in the name of
God, why ? " he cried with an outburst.   " What have
I ever done that you should do this for me ?   You
are worth a score of such as I am, and yet you make
yourself a slave—"

" Oh, Walter, my dear ! how vain are all these words.
I am your mother," she said.

Presently he drew a chair close to her and sat down
beside her.

" All these things have been put before me," he said,
" to drive me to despair.   I have tried to say that it
was this vile lordship, and the burden of the family,
that has made me bad, mother.   But you know better
than that," he said, looking up at her with a stormy
gleam in his face that could not be called a smile, " and
so do I."

" Walter, God forbid that I should ever have thought
you bad.   You have been led astray."

" To do—what I wanted to do," he said with another
smile, " that is what is called leading astray between
a man and those who stand between him and the devil ;
but I have talked with one who thinks of no such
punctilios.   Mother, vice deserves damnation; isn't that
your creed ? "

" Walter ! "

"Oh, I know; but listen to me. If that were so, would a woman like you stand by the wretch still?"

"My dearest boy! you are talking wildly. There are no circumstances, none! in which I should not stand by you."

"That is what I thought," he said, "you and— But they say that you don't know, you women, how bad a man can be: and that if you knew—And then as for God——"

"God knows everything, Walter."

"Ay: and knows that never in my life did I care for or appeal to Him, till in despair. If you think of it, these are not things a man can do, mother: take refuge with women who would loathe him if they knew; or with God, who does know that only in desperation, only when nothing else is left to him, he calls out that name like a spell. Yes, that is all; like an incantation, to get rid of the fiend."

The veins were swollen on Walter's forehead; great drops of moisture hung upon it; on the other hand his lips were parched and dry, his eyes gleaming with a hot treacherous lustre. Mrs. Methven, as she looked at him, grew sick with terror. She began to think that his brain was giving way.

"What am I to say to you?" she cried; "who has been speaking so? It cannot be a friend, Walter. That is not the way to bring back a soul."

He laughed, and the sound alarmed her still more.

"There was no friendship intended," he said, "nor

reformation either. It was intended—to make me a slave."

"To whom, oh! to whom?"

He had relieved his mind by talking thus; but it was by putting his burden upon her. She was agitated beyond measure by these partial confidences. She took his hands in hers, and pleaded with him—

"Oh, Walter, my darling, what has happened to you? Tell me what you mean."

"I am not mad, mother, if that is what you think."

"I don't think so, Walter. I don't know what to think. Tell me. Oh, my boy, have pity upon me; tell me."

"You will do me more good, mother, if you will tell me—how I am to get this burden off, and be a free man."

"The burden of—what? Sin? Oh, my son!" she cried, rising to her feet, with tears of joy streaming from her eyes. She put her hands upon his head and bade God bless him. God bless him! "There is no doubt about that; no difficulty about that," she said; "for everything else in the world there may be uncertainty, but for this none. God is more ready to forgive than we are to ask. If you wish it sincerely with all your heart, it is done. He is never far from any of us. He is here, Walter—here, ready to pardon!"

He took her hands which she had put upon him, and looked at her, shaking his head.

"Mother, you are going too fast," he said. "I want deliverance, it is true; but I don't know if it is *that* I mean."

"That is at the bottom of all, Walter."

He put her softly into her chair, and calmed her agitation; then he began to walk up and down the room.

"That is religion," he said. "I suppose it is at the bottom of all. What was it you used to teach me, mother, about a new heart? Can a man enter a second time—and be born? That seems all so visionary when one is living one's life. You think of hundreds of expedients first. To thrust it away from you, and forget all about it; but that does not answer; to defy it and go the other way out of misery and spite. Then to try compromises; marriage, for instance, with a wife perhaps, one thinks——"

"My dear," said Mrs. Methven, with a sad sinking of disappointment in her heart after her previous exultation, yet determined that her sympathy should not fail, "if you had a good wife no one would be so happy as I—a good girl who would help you to live a good life."

Here he came up to her again, and, leaning against the table, burst into a laugh. But there was no mirth in it. A sense of the ludicrous is not always mirthful.

"A girl," he said, "mother, who would bring another fortune to the family: who would deluge us with money, and fill out the lines of the estates, and make peace—

peace between me and— And not a bad girl either," he added with a softening tone, "far too good for me. An honest, upright little soul, only not—the best; only not the one who — would hate me if she knew——"

"Walter," said Mrs. Methven, trembling, "I don't understand you. Your words seem very wild to me. I am all confused with them, and my brain seems to be going. What is it you mean? Oh, if you would tell me all you mean and not only a part which I cannot understand!"

There never happens in any house a conversation of a vital kind, which is not interrupted at a critical moment by the entrance of the servants, those legitimate intruders who can never be staved off. It was Symington now who came in with tea, which, with a woman's natural desire to prevent any suspicion of agitation in the family, she accepted. When he had gone the whole atmosphere was changed. Walter had seated himself by the fire with the newspapers which had just come in, and all the emotion and *attendrissement* were over. He said to her, looking up from his reading—

"By-the-bye, mother, Julia Herbert is here with some cousins; they will be sure to call on you. But I don't want to have any more to do with them than we can help. You will manage that?"

"Julia Herbert," she said. The countenance which had melted into so much softness, froze again and grew

severe. "Here! why should she be here? Indeed,
I hope I shall be able to manage that, as you say."

But oh, what ignoble offices for a woman who would
have given her life for him as he knew! To frighten
away Underwood, to "manage" Julia. Patience! so
long as it was for her boy.

CHAPTER VI.

ON the next morning after his mother's arrival, Lord Erradeen set out early for Birkenbraes. Everything pushed him towards a decision; even her prompt arrival, which he had not anticipated, and the clearing away from his path of the simpler and more easy difficulties that beset him, by her means. But what was far more than this was the tug at his heart, the necessity that lay before him to satisfy, one way or the other, the demands of his tyrant. He could not send away that spiritual enemy, who held him in his grip, as he did the vulgar influence of Underwood. *That* had disgusted him almost from the first; he had never tolerated it, even when he yielded to it; and the effort he had made in throwing it over had been exhilarating to him, and gave a certain satisfaction to his mind. But now that was over, and he had returned again to the original question, and found himself once more confronted by that opponent who could not be shaken off— who, one way or other, must be satisfied or vanquished, if life were to be possible. Vanquished? How was he to be vanquished?—by a pure man and a strong—by a

pure woman and her love—by the help of God against
a spiritual tyranny. He smiled to himself as he hurried
along the road, thinking of the hopelessness of all this
—himself neither pure nor strong; and Oona, who, if
she knew—and God, whom, as his tempter had said, he
had never sought nor thought of till now. He hurried
along to try if the second best was within his reach;
perhaps even that might fail him for anything he knew.
The thought of meeting the usual party in the house of
the Williamsons was so abhorrent to him, and such a
disgust had risen in his mind of all the cheerful circumstances of the big, shining house, that he set out early
with the intention of formally seeking an interview with
Katie, and thus committing himself from the beginning.
The morning was bright and fair, with a little shrill
wind about, which brought the yellow leaves fluttering
to his feet, and carried them across him as he walked—
now detached and solitary, now in little drifts and heaps.
He hurried along, absorbed in his own thoughts, shutting his eyes to the vision of the isle, as it lay all
golden, russet, and brown upon the surface of the water
which gave its colours back; Walter would not look nor
see the boat pushing round the corner, with the back of
Hamish's red shirt alone showing, as the prow came
beyond the shade of the trees. He did not see the
boat, and yet he knew it was there, and hurried, hurried
on to escape all reminders. The great door at Birkenbraes stood open, as was its wont—the great stone steps
lying vacant in the sunshine, and everything still about.

It was the only hour at which the place was quiet. The men were out on the hill, the ladies following such rational occupations as they might have to resort to, and the house had an air of relief and repose. Walter felt that he pronounced his own fate when he asked to see Miss Williamson.

"Mr. Williamson is out, my lord," the solemn functionary said, who was far more important and dignified than the master of the house. "I asked to see Miss Williamson," Lord Erradeen repeated, with a little impatience; and he saw the man's eyebrows raised.

So far as the servants were concerned, and through them the whole district, Walter's "intentions" stood revealed.

Katie Williamson was alone. She was in her favourite room—the room especially given over to her amusements and occupations. It was not a small room, for such a thing scarcely existed in Birkenbraes. It was full of windows, great expanses of plate glass, through which the mountains and the loch appeared uninterrupted, save by a line of framework here and there, with a curious open-air effect. It was in one of the corners of the house, and the windows formed two sides of the brilliant place; on the others were mirrors reflecting the mountains back again. She sat between them, her little fair head the only solid thing which the light encountered. When she rose, with a somewhat astonished air, to receive her visitor, her trim figure, neat and alert, stood out against the background of the trees and rocks on the lower slopes of the hills. A curious transparency, distinctness, and absence of privacy and mystery were in the scene. The two seemed to stand together there in the sight of all the world.

"Lord Erradeen!" Katie said, with surprise, almost consternation. "But if I had been told, I should have come down-stairs to you. Nobody but my great friends, nobody but women, ever come here."

"I should have thought that any one might come. There are no concealments here," he said, expressing the sentiment of the place unconsciously. Then, seeing that Katie's colour rose: "Your boudoir is not all curtained and shadowy, but open and candid—as you are."

"That last has saved you," said Katie, with a laugh. "I know what you mean—and that is that my room (for it is not a boudoir—I never *boude*) is far too light, too clear for the fashion. But this is my fashion, and people who come to me must put up with it." She added, after a moment: "What did you say to Sanderson, Lord Erradeen, to induce him to bring you here?"

"I said I wanted to see Miss Williamson."

"That was understood," said Katie, once more with an increase of colour, and looking at him with a suppressed question in her eyes. Her heart gave a distinct knock against her breast, but did not jump up and flutter, as hearts less well regulated will do in such circumstances; for she too perceived what Sanderson had perceived, that the interview was not one to take place amid all the interruptions of the drawing-room. Sanderson was a very clever person, and his young mistress agreed with him; but, nevertheless, made a private memorandum that he should have notice, and that she would speak to papa.

"Yes, I think it must be easily understood. I have come to you with a great deal that is very serious to say."

"You look very serious," said Katie; and then she added, hurriedly, "And I want very much to speak to you, Lord Erradeen. I want you to tell me—who was that gentleman at Kinloch Houran? I have never been able to get him out of my mind. Is he paying you a visit? What is his name? Has he been in this country before? But oh, to be sure, he must have been, for he knew everything about the castle. I want to know, Lord Erradeen——"

"After you have heard what I have got to say——"

"No, not after—before. I tremble when I think of him. It is ridiculous, I know; but I never had any such sensation before. I should think he must be a mesmerist, or something of that sort," Katie said, with a pale and nervous smile; "though I don't believe in mesmerism," she added, quickly.

"You believe in nothing of the kind—is it not so? You put no faith in the stories about my family, in the influence of the past on the present, in the despotism— But why say anything on that subject. You laugh."

"I believe in superstition," said Katie somewhat tremulously, "and that it impresses the imagination, and puts you in a condition to believe—things. And

G 2

then there is a pride in having anything of the sort connected with one's own family," she said recovering herself. " If it was our ghost I should believe in it too."

"Ghost—is not a word that means much?" Walter said. And then there was a pause. It seemed to him that his lips were sealed, and that he had no longer command of the ordinary words. He had known what he had meant to say when he came, but the power seemed to have gone from him. He stood and looked out upon the wide atmosphere, and the freedom of the hills, with a blank in his mind, and that sense that nothing is any longer of importance or meaning which comes to those who are baffled in their purpose at the outset. It was Katie who with a certain sarcasm in her tone recalled him to himself. " You came—because you had something serious to say to me, Lord Erradeen." She was aware of what he intended to say; but his sudden pause at the very beginning had raised the mocking spirit in Katie. She was ready to defy and provoke, and silence with ridicule, the man whom she had no objection to accept as her husband— provided he found his voice.

"It is true—I had something very serious to say. I came to ask you whether you could—" All this time he was not so much as looking at her; his eyes were fixed dreamily and rather sadly upon the landscape, which somehow seemed so much more important than the speck of small humanity which he ought to have been addressing. But at this point Walter recollected himself, and came in as it were from the big, silent, observing world, to Katie, sitting expectant, divided between mockery and excitement, with a flush on her cheeks, but a contraction of her brows, and an angry yet smiling mischief in her eyes.

" To ask you," he said, " whether you would—pass your life with me. I am not much worth the taking. There is a poor title, there is a family which we might restore and—emancipate perhaps. You are rich, it would be of no advantage to you. But at all events it would not be like asking you to banish yourself, to leave all you cared for. I have little to say for myself," he went on after a pause with a little more energy, " you know me well enough. Whether I should ever be good for anything would—most likely—rest with you. I am at present under great depression—in trouble and fear—"

Here he came to another pause, and looked out upon the silent mountains and great breadths of vacant air in which there was nothing to help: then with a sigh turned again and held out his hand. " Will you have me—Katie ? " he said.

Katie sat gazing at him with a wonder which had by degrees extinguished the sarcasm, the excitement, the expectation, that were in her face. She was almost awestricken by this strangest of all suits that could be addressed to a girl—a demand for herself which made no account of herself, and missed out love and every usual preliminary. It was serious indeed—as serious

as death : more like that than the beginning of the
most living of all links. She could not answer him
with the indignation which in other circumstances she
might have felt. It was too solemn for any ebullition
of feeling. She felt overawed, little as this mood was
congenial to her.

" Lord Erradeen," she said, "you seem to be in great
trouble."

He made an affirmative movement of his head, but
said no more.

"—Or you would not put such a strange question to
me," she went on. " Why should I have you ? When
a man offers himself to a girl he says it is because he
loves her. You don't love me—"

She made a momentary breathless pause with a half-
hope of being interrupted ; but save by a motion of his
hand, Walter made no sign. " You don't love me," she
went on with some vehemence, " nor do you ask me to
love you. Such a proposal might be an insult. But I
don't think you mean it as an insult."

" Not that. You know better. Anything but
that ! "

" No—I don't think it is that. But what is it then,
Lord Erradeen ? "

Her tone had a certain peremptory sound which
touched the capricious spring by which the young
man's movements were regulated. He came to himself.
" Miss Williamson," he said, " when you ran away from
me in London it was imminent that I should ask you

this question. It was expected on all sides. You went away, I have always believed, to avoid it."

"Why should it have been imminent? I went away," cried Katie, forgetting the contradiction, "because some one came in who seemed to have a prior right. She is here now with the same meaning."

"She has no prior right. She has no right at all, nor does she claim any," he said hurriedly. "It is accident. Katie! had you stayed, all would have been determined then, and one leaf of bitter folly left out of my life."

"Supposing it to be so," she said calmly, "I am not responsible for your life, Lord Erradeen. Why should I be asked to step in and save you from—bitter folly or anything else? And this life that you offer me, are you sure it is fit for an honest girl to take? The old idea that a woman should be sacrificed to reform a man has gone out of fashion. Is that the *rôle* you want me to take up?" Katie cried, rising to her feet in her excitement. "Captain Underwood (whose word I would never take) said you were bad, unworthy a good woman. Is that true?"

"Yes," he said in a low tone, "it is true."

Katie gazed at him for a moment, and then in her excitement sat down and cried, covering her face with her hands. She it was, though she was not emotional, who was overcome with feeling. Walter stood gazing at her with a sort of stupefaction, seeing the scene pass with a sense that he was a spectator rather than an

actor in it, his dark figure swaying slightly against the
clearness of the landscape which took so strange a part
in all that was happening. It had passed now altogether
out of his hands.

As for Katie, it would be impossible to tell what sudden
softening, what pity, mingled with keen vexation and
annoyance, forced these tears from her eyes. Her heart
revolted against him and melted towards him all at
once. Her pride would not let her accept such a proposal; and yet she would have liked to accept him, to
take him in hand, to be his providence, and the moulder
of his fate. A host of hurrying thoughts and sentiments
rushed headlong through her mind. She had it in her
to do it, better than any silly woman of the world,
better than a creature of visionary soul like Oona.
She was practical, she was strong, she could do it. But
then all her pride rose up in arms. She wept a few
hot impatient tears which were irrestrainable: then
raised her head again.

"I am very sorry for you," she said. "If you were
my brother, Lord Erradeen, I would help you with all
my might, or if I—cared for you more than you care for
me. But I don't," she added after a pause.

He made an appealing, deprecating movement with
his hands, but did not speak.

"I almost wish I did," said Katie regretfully; "if I
had been fond of you I should have said yes: for you
are right in thinking I could do it. I should not have
minded what went before. I should have taken you

up and helped you on. I know that I could have done it; but then I am not—fond of you," she said slowly. She did not look at him as she spoke; but had he renewed his claim upon her, even with his eyes, Katie would have seen it, and might have allowed herself to be persuaded still. But Walter said nothing. He stood vaguely in the light, without a movement, accepting whatever she might choose to say. She remained silent for a time, waiting. And then Katie sprang to her feet again, all the more indignant and impatient that she had been so near yielding, had he but known. " Well!" she said, "is it I that am to maintain the conversation? Have you anything more to say, Lord Erradeen ? "

"I suppose not," he answered slowly. "I came to you hoping perhaps for deliverance, at least partial—for deliverance— Now that you will not, there is nothing for it but a struggle to the death."

She looked at him with a sort of vertigo of amazement. Not a word about her, no regret for losing her, not a touch of sentiment, of gratitude, not even any notice of what she had said! The sensation of awe came back to her as she stood before this insensibility which was half sublime. Was he mad ? or a wretch, an egotist, wanting a woman to do something for him, but without a thought for the woman ?

"I am glad," she said, with irrepressible displeasure, " that it affects you so little. And now I suppose the incident is over and we may return to our occupations.

I was busy—with my housekeeping," she said with a laugh. "One might sometimes call a struggle with one's bills a struggle to the death."

He gave her a look which was half-anger, half-remonstrance; and then to Katie's amazement resumed in a moment the tone of easy intercourse which had always existed between them.

"You will find your bills refreshing after this high-flown talk," he said. "Forgive me. You know I am not given to romantic sentiment any more than yourself."

"I don't know," said Katie, offended, "that I am less open to the romantic than other people when the right touch is given."

"But it is not my hand that can give the right touch?" he said. "I accept my answer as there is nothing else for me to do. But I cannot abandon the country," he added after a moment, "and I hope we may still meet as good friends."

"Nothing has happened," said Katie with dignity, "to lessen my friendship for you, Lord Erradeen." She could not help putting a faint emphasis on the pronouns. The man rejected may dislike to meet the woman who has rejected him, but the woman can have no feeling in the matter. She held out her hand with a certain stateliness of dismissal. "Papa need not know," she said, "and so there will be nothing more about it. Good-bye."

Walter took her hand in his, with a momentary

perception that perhaps there had been more than lay
on the surface in this interview, on her side as well as
his. He stooped down and kissed it respectfully, and
even with something like tenderness. "You do not
refuse it to me, in friendship, even after all you have
heard?"

"It shall always be yours in friendship," Katie said,
the colour rising high in her face.

She was glad he went away without looking at her
again. She sat down and listened to his footsteps along
the long corridor and down the stairs with a curious
sensation as if he carried something with him that
would not return to her again. And for long after she
sat in the broad daylight without moving, leaving the
books upon the table—which were not housekeeping
books—untouched—going over this strange interview,
turning over all the past that had any connection with
Lord Erradeen. It seemed all to roll out before her
like a story that had been full of interest: and now
here was the end of it. Such a fit of wistful sadness
had seldom come over the active and practical intelligence of Katie. It gave her for the moment a new
opening in nature. But by degrees her proper moods
came back. She closed this poetical chapter with a
sigh, and her sound mind took up with a more natural
regret the opportunity for congenial effort which she
had been compelled to give up. She said to herself
that she would not have minded that vague badness
which he had owned, and Underwood had accused him

of. She could have brought him back. She had it in
her to take the charge even of a man's life. So she
thought in inexperience, yet with the powerful confidence which so often is the best means of fulfilling
triumphantly what it aims at. She would not have
shrunk from the endeavour. She would have put her
vigorous young will into his feeble one, she thought,
and made him, with her force poured into him, a man
indeed, contemptuous of all miserable temptations, able
to sail over and despise them. As she mused her eyes
took an eager look, her very fingers twitched with the
wish to be doing. Had he come back then it is very
possible that Katie would have announced to him her
change of mind, her determination "to pull him
through." For she could have done it! she repeated
to herself. Whatever his burdens had been, when she
had once set her shoulder to the wheel she would have
done it. Gambling, wine, even the spells of such
women as Katie blushed to think of—she would have
shrunk before none of these. His deliverance would
not have been partial, as he had said, but complete.
She would have fought the very devils for him and
brought him off. What a work it was that she had
missed! not a mere commonplace marriage with nothing
to do. But with a sigh Katie had to acknowledge that
it was over. She could not have accepted him, she
said, excusing herself to herself. It would have been
impossible. A man who asks you like *that*, not even
pretending to care for you—you could not do it! But,

alas! what an opportunity lost! Saying this she gave herself a shake, and smoothed her hair for luncheon, and put the thought away from her resolutely. Katie thought of Dante's nameless sinner who made "the great refusal." She had lost perhaps the one great opportunity of her life.

CHAPTER VII.

LORD ERRADEEN retired very quietly, as became a man defeated. Though Katie heard his retiring steps, he hardly did so himself, as he came down the broad softly-carpeted stair-case. There was a sound of voices and of movement in the great dining-room, where a liveried army were preparing the table for one of the great luncheons, under the orders of the too discreet and understanding Sanderson—but nobody about to see the exit of the rejected suitor, who came out into the sunshine with a sort of dim recognition of the scenery of Katie's boudoir; but the hills did not seem so near as they were in that large-windowed and shining place. Failure has always a subduing effect upon the mind even when success was scarcely desired; and Walter came out of the great house with the sense of being cut off from possibilities that seemed very near, almost certain, that morning. This subduing influence was the first that occupied his mind as he came out, feeling as if he were stealing away from the scene of what had been far from a triumph. Perhaps he was a little ashamed of his own certainty; but at all events he was subdued and silent, refraining almost from thought.

He had got securely out of the immediate neighbourhood, and was safe from the risk of meeting any one belonging to it, and being questioned where he had been, before he began to feel the softening of relief, and a grateful sense of freedom. Then his heart recurred with a bound to the former situation. Expedients or compromises of any kind were no more to be thought of; the battle must be fought out on its natural ground. He must yield to the ignominious yoke, or he must conquer. Last year he had fled, and forced himself to forget, and lived in a fever of impulses which he could not understand, and influences which drew him like—he could not tell like what—mesmerism, Katie had said, and perhaps she was right. It might be mesmerism; or it might be only the action of that uncontrolled and capricious mind which made him do that to-day which he loathed to-morrow. But however it was, the question had again become a primary one, without any compromise possible. He must yield, or he must win the battle. He put the losing first, it seemed so much the most likely, with a dreary sense of all the impossibilities that surrounded him. He had no standing ground upon which to meet his spiritual foe. Refusal, what was that? It filled his life with distraction and confusion, but made no foundation for anything better, and afforded no hope of peace. Peace! The very word seemed a mockery to

Walter. He must never know what it was. His soul
(if he had one) would not be his own; his impulses,
hitherto followed so foolishly, would be impotent for
everything but to follow the will of another. To
abdicate his own judgment altogether, to give up that
power of deciding for himself which is the inheritance
of the poorest, never to be able to help a poor neighbour, to aid a friend: to be a mere puppet in the
hands of another—was it possible that he, a man, was
to give himself up, thus bound hand and foot, to a
slavery harder than that of any negro ever born? It
was this that was impossible he cried within himself.

And then there suddenly came before Walter, like
a vision set before him by the angels, a gleam of the
one way of escape. When a poor wretch has fallen
into a pit, a disused quarry, perhaps, or an old coal-pit,
or a still more eerie dungeon, there shines over him, far
off, yet so authentic, a pure, clear intensity of light
above, a concentrated glory of the day, a sort of opening
of heaven in his sight. This is the spot of light, more
beautiful than any star, which is all that the walls of
his prison permit him to see of the common day, which
above-ground is lavished around us in such a prodigal
way that we make no account of it. There are times
when the common virtues of life, the common calm and
peacefulness, take an aspect like this to the fallen soul:
—the simple goodness which, perhaps, he has scoffed at
and found tame and unprofitable, appearing to the
spirit in prison like heaven itself, so serene and so

secure. To think he himself has fallen from that, might have possessed and dwelt in it, safe from all censure and dishonour, if he had not been a fool! To think that all the penalties to which he has exposed himself might never have existed at all—if he had not been a fool! To think that now if some miracle would but raise him up to it—And then there are moments in which even the most vicious, the most utterly fallen, can feel as if no great miracle would be required, as if a little help, only a little, would do it—when strength is subdued and low, when the sense of dissatisfaction is strong, and all the impulses of the flesh in abeyance, as happens at times. Walter's mind came suddenly to this conviction as he walked and mused. A good life, a pure heart, these were the things which would over-come—better, far better than any gain, than any sop given to fate; and he felt that all his desires went up towards these, and that there was nothing in him but protested against the degradation of the past. He had, he said to himself, never been satisfied, never been but disgusted with the riot and so-called pleasure. While he indulged in them he had loathed them, sinning contemptuously with a bitter scorn of himself and of the indulgences which he professed to find sweet.

Strange paradox of a soul! which perceived the foul-ness of the ruin into which it had sunk, and hated it, yet sank deeper and deeper all the while. And now how willing he was to turn his back upon it all, and how easy it seemed to rise with a leap to the higher

level and be done with everything that was past! The
common goodness of the simple people about seemed
suddenly to him like a paradise in which was all that
was lovely. To live among your own, to do them good,
to be loved and honoured, to have a history pure and
of good report, nothing in it to give you a blush; to
love a pure and good woman, and have her for your
companion all your life—how easy, how simple, how
safe it was! And what tyrant out of the unseen could
rule a man like this, or disturb his quiet mastery of
himself and all that belonged to him? Once upon
that standing ground and who could assail you? And
it seemed at that moment so easy and so near. Everything round was wholesome, invigorating, clear with
the keen purity of nature, fresh winds blowing in his
face, air the purest and clearest, inspiring body and soul,
not a lurking shade of temptation anywhere, everything
tending to goodness, nothing to evil.

"And you think these pettifogging little virtues will
deliver *you*," said some one quietly by his side.

There were two figures walking along in the wintry
sunshine instead of one—that was all. The stone-
cutter on the road who had seen Lord Erradeen pass
and given him a good morning, rubbed his eyes when
next he paused to rest and looked along the road. He
saw two gentlemen where but one had been, though it
was still so early and "no a drap" had crossed his lips.
"And a pretty man!" he said to himself with mingled
amazement and admiration. As for Walter, it was

with an instinctive recoil that he heard the voice so
near to him, but that not because of any supernatural
sensation, though with an annoyance and impatience
inexpressible that any one should be able to intrude
on his privacy and thus fathom his thoughts.

"This is scarcely an honourable advantage you take
of your powers."

The other took no notice of this reproach. "A good
man," he said, "a good husband, a good member of
society, surrounded by comfort on all sides and the
approbation of the world. I admire the character as
much as you do. Shall I tell you what this good man
is? He is the best rewarded of all the sons of men.
Everything smiles upon him : he has the best of life.
Everything he does counts in his favour. And you
think that such a man can stand against a purpose
like mine? But for that he would want a stronger
purpose than mine. Goodness," he continued reflect-
ively, "is the best policy in the world. It never fails.
Craft may fail, and skill and even wisdom, and the
finest calculations ; but the good always get their
reward. A prize falls occasionally to the other quali-
ties, but theirs is the harvest of life. To be successful
you have only to be good. It is far the safest form of
self-seeking, and the best." He had fallen into a
reflective tone, and walked along with a slight smile
upon his lips, delivering with a sort of abstract authority his monologue, while Walter, with an indescribable
rage and mortification and confusion of all his thoughts,

accompanied him like a schoolboy overpowered by an
authority against which his very soul was rebel. Then
the speaker turned upon his companion with a sort
of benevolent cordiality. "Be good!" he said. "I
advise it—it is the easiest course you can pursue : you
will free yourself from by far the worst part of the evils
common to humanity. Nothing is so bad as the self-
contempt under which I have seen you labouring, the
shame of vice for which you have no true instinct, only
a sham appetite invented by the contradictoriness of
your own mind. Be good! it pays better than anything
else in life."

Here Walter interrupted him with an exclamation
of anger irrestrainable. "Stop !" he cried, "you have
tortured me by my sins, and because I had nothing
better to fall back upon. Will you make this more
odious still ? "

"By no means," said the other, calmly. "You think
I want you to be miserable ? You are mistaken—I
don't. Seeking the advantage of my race as I do,
there is nothing I more desire than that you should
have the credit of a spotless life. I love reputation.
Be good! it is the most profitable of all courses. I
repeat that whatever may fail that never does. Your
error is to think that it will free you from me. So
far as concerns me it would probably do you more
injury than good ; for it may well be that I shall have
to enforce measures which will revolt you and make
you unhappy. But then you will have compensations.

The world will believe that only bad advisers or mistaken views could move so good a man to appear on occasions a hard landlord, a tyrannical master. And then your virtue will come in with expedients to modify the secondary effect of my plans and soften suffering. I do not desire suffering. It will be in every way to our advantage that you should smooth down and soften and pour balm into the wounds which in the pursuit of a higher purpose it is necessary to make. Do not interrupt : it is the *rôle* I should have recommended to you, if, instead of flying out like a fool, you had left yourself from the first in my hands."

" I think you must be the devil," Walter said.

" No; nor even of his kind : that is another mistake. I have no pleasure in evil any more than in suffering, unless my object makes it necessary. I should like you to do well. It was I, was it not, that set before you the miserableness of the life you have been leading ? which you had never faced before. Can you suppose that I should wish greatness to the race and misfortune to its individual members ? Certainly not. I wish you to do well. You could have done so, and lived very creditably with the girl whom you have just left, whom you have driven into refusing you. Take my advice—return to her, and all will be well."

" You have a right to despise me," said Walter, quivering with passion and self-restraint. " I did take your advice, and outraged her and myself. But that is over, and I shall take your advice no more."

"You are a fool for your pains," he said. "Go back now and you will find her mind changed. She has thought it over. What! you will not? I said it in your interest, it was your best chance. You could have taken up that good life which I recommend to you with all the more success had there been a boundless purse to begin upon. Poor it is not so easy: but still you can try. Your predecessor was of that kind. There was nothing in him that was bad, poor fellow. He was an agglomeration of small virtues. Underwood was his one vice, a fellow who played cards with him and amused him. No one, you will find, has anything to say against him ; he was thought weak, and so he was—against me. But that did not hinder him from being good."

"In the name of Heaven what do you call yourself, that can speak of good and evil as if they were red and blue!" the young man cried. Passion cannot keep always at a climax. Walter's mind ranged from high indignation, rage, dismay, to a wonder that was almost impersonal, which sometimes reached the intolerable point, and burst out into impatient words. It seemed impossible to endure the calm of him, the reason of him, as he walked along the hilly road like any other man.

"It is not amiss for a comparison," he answered with a smile. His composure was not to be disturbed. He made no further explanations. While he played upon the young man beside him as on an instrument, he himself remained absolutely calm. "But these are abstractions," he resumed, "very important to you in your individual life, not so important to me who have larger affairs in hand. There is something however which will have to be decided almost immediately about the island property. I told you that small business about the cotters in the glen was a bagatelle. On the whole, though I thought it folly at the time, your action in the matter was serviceable. A burst of generosity has a fine effect. It is an example of what I have been saying. It throws dust in the eyes of the world. Now we can proceed with vigour on a larger scale."

"If you mean to injure the poor tenants, never! and whatever you mean, no," cried Walter, "I will not obey you. Claim your rights, if you have any rights, publicly."

"I will not take that trouble. I will enforce them through my descendant."

"No! you can torture me, I am aware, but something I have learned since last year."

"You have learned," said his companion calmly, "that your theatrical benevolence was not an unmixed good, that your *protégés* whom you kept to that barren glen would have been better off had they been dislodged cruelly from their holes. The question in its larger forms is not to be settled from that primitive point of view. I allow," he said with a smile, "that on the whole that was well done. It leaves us much more

free for operations now. It gives a good impression—a
man who in spite of his kind heart feels compelled to
carry out—"

"You are a demon," cried the young man, stung
beyond endurance. "You make even justice a matter
of calculation, even the natural horror of one's mind.
A kind heart! is that like a spade, an instrument in
your hands?"

"The comparison is good again," said his campanion
with a laugh; "your faculty that way is improving.
But we must have no trifling about the matter in
hand. The factor from the isles is not a fool like
this fellow here, whom I tolerate because he has his
uses too. The other will come to you presently, he
will lay before you—"

"I will not hear him—once for all I refuse—"

"What, to receive your own servant?" said the
other. "Come, this is carrying things too far. You
must hear, and see, and consent. There is no alter-
native, except—"

"Except—if it comes to that, what can you do to
me?" asked Walter, ghastly with that rending of the
spirit which had once more begun within him, and with
the host of fierce suggestions that surged into his mind.
He felt as men feel when they are going mad, when the
wild intolerance of all conditions which is the root of
insanity mounts higher and higher in the brain—when
there is nothing that can be endured, nothing supportable, and the impulse to destroy and ravage, to uproot

trees and beat down mountains, to lay violent hands
upon something, sweeps like a fiery blast across the
soul. Even in madness there is always a certain self-
restraint. He knew that it would be vain to seize the
strong and tranquil man who stood before him, distort-
ing everything in heaven and earth with his calm con-
sistency: therefore in'all the maddening rush of impulse
that did not suggest itself. " What can you do to me ? "
How unnecessary was the question ! What he could
do was sensible in every point, in the torrent of excitement that almost blinded, almost deafened the miserable
young man. He saw his enemy's countenance as through
a mist, a serene and almost beautiful face—looking at
him with a sort of benevolent philosophical pity which
quickened the flood of passion. His own voice was
stifled in his throat, he could say no more. Nor could
he hear for the ringing in his ears, what more his
adversary was saying to him—something wildly incoherent he thought, about Prospero, Prospero! " Do
you think I am Prospero to send you aches and
stitches ? " The words seemed to circle about him in
the air, half mockery, half folly. What had that to
do with it ? He walked along mechanically, rapt
in an atmosphere of his own, beating the air like a
drowning man.

How long this horror lasted he could never tell.
While still those incomprehensible syllables were
wavering about him, another voice suddenly made itself
heard, a touch came upon his arm. He gave a violent

start, recoiling from the touch, not knowing what it
was. By degrees, however, as the giddiness went off,
he began to see again, to perceive slowly coming into
sight those mountains that had formed the background
in Katie's room, and to hear the soft wash of the
waters upon the beach. He found himself standing
close to the loch, far below the road upon which he had
been walking. Had he rushed down to throw himself
into the water, and thus end the terrible conflict? He
could never tell. Or whether it was some angel that
had arrested the terrible impulse. When the mist
dispersed from his eyes he saw this angel in a red shirt
standing close to him, looking at him with eyes that
peered out beneath the contraction of a pair of shaggy
sandy eyebrows, from an honest freckled face. " My
lord! you'll maybe no have seen Miss Oona?" Hamish
said. And Walter heard himself burst into a wild
laugh that seemed to fill the whole silent world with
echoes. He caught hold of the boatman's arm with a
grasp that made even Hamish shrink. " Who sent you
here?" he cried; "who sent you here? Do you come
from God?" He did not know what he said.

" My lord! you mustna take that name in vain. I'm
thinking the Almighty has a hand in maist things, and
maybe it was just straight from Him I've come, though
I had no suspicion o' that," Hamish said. He thought
for the first moment it was a madman with whom he
had to do. Walter had appeared with a rush down
the steep bank, falling like some one out of the skies,

scattering the pebbles on the beach, and Hamish had employed Oona's name in the stress of the moment as something to conjure with. He was deeply alarmed still as he felt the quiver in the young man's frame, which communicated itself to Hamish's sturdy arm. Madness frightens the most stout-hearted. Hamish was brave enough, as brave as a Highlander need be, but he was half alarmed for himself, and much more for Oona, who might appear at any moment. "I'll just be waiting about and nothing particular to do," he said in a soothing tone; "if ye'll get into the boat, my lord, I'll just put your lordship hame. Na, it's nae trouble, nae trouble." Hamish did not like the situation; but he would rather have rowed twenty maniacs than put Oona within reach of any risk. He took Lord Erradeen by the elbow and directed him towards the boat, repeating the kindly invitation of his country— "Come away, just come away; I've naething particular to do, and it will just be a pleasure."

"Hamish," said Walter, "you think I am out of my mind: but you are mistaken, my good fellow. *I* think you have saved my life, and I will not forget it. What was that you said about Miss Oona!"

Hamish looked earnestly into the young man's face.

"My lord," he began with hesitation, "you see—if a young gentleman is a thocht out of the way, and just maybe excited about something and no altogether his ain man—what's that to the like of me? Never a

hair o' hairm would that do to Hamish. But when it's
a leddy, and young and real tender-hearted! We maun
aye think o' them, my lord, and spare them—the
weemen. No, it's what we dinna do—they have the
warst in a general way to bear. But atween you and
me, my lord, that though you're far my shuperior, are
just man and man——"

"It is you that are my superior, Hamish," said Lord
Erradeen; "but look at me now and say if you think
I am mad. You have saved me. I am fit to speak to
her now. Do you think I would harm her? Not for
anything in the world."

"No if you were—yoursel'—Lord Erradeen."

"But I am—myself. And the moment has come
when I must know. Take my hand, Hamish; look
at me. Do you think I am not to be trusted with
Oona?"

"My lord, to make Hamish your judge, what's that
but daft too? And what right have ye to call my
young leddy by her name? You're no a drap's blood
to them, nor even a great friend."

Oona's faithful guardian stood lowering his brows
upon the young lord with a mingled sense of the
superiority of his office, and of disapproval, almost contemptuous, of the madman who had given it to him.
That he should make Hamish the judge was mad
indeed. And yet Hamish was the judge, standing on
his right to defend his mistress. They stood looking at
each other, the boatman holding his shaggy head high,

reading the other's face with the keenest scrutiny. But just then there came a soft sound into the air, a call from the bank, clear, with that tone, not loud but penetrating, which mountaineers use everywhere.

"Are you there, Hamish?" Oona cried.

CHAPTER VIII.

Oona's mind had been much disturbed, yet in no painful way, by the meeting with Mrs. Methven. The service which she had done to Walter's mother, the contact with her, although almost in the dark, the sense of approach to another woman whose mind was full of anxiety and thought for him, agitated her, yet seemed to heal and soften away the pain which other encounters had given her. It gave her pleasure to think of the half-seen face, made softer by the twilight, and of the tremor of expectation and anxiety that had been in it. There was somehow in this a kind of excuse to herself for her involuntary preoccupation with all that concerned him. She had felt that there was an unspoken sympathy between her and the stranger, and that it was something more than chance which brought them together. As the boat pushed off into the loch, and she felt she had left the mother to a certain happiness in her son, her heart beat with a subdued excitement. She felt with them both, divining the soul of the mother who came to him with trembling, not approving perhaps, not fully trusting, but loving; and of the son

who was at fault, who had not shown her the tenderness which her love merited in return. The sense of
that union so incomplete in fact, and so close in nature,
filled Oona with emotion. As the boat glided along
the glittering pathway of the lake between the reflected
banks, her mind was full of the two who had gone away
together arm and arm into the soft darkness. How
mysterious was that twilight world, the eye incapable
in the dimness of perceiving which was the substance
and which the shadow of those floating woods and
islands! Sometimes the boat would glide into the
tangled reflections of the trees, sometimes strike through
what seemed a headland, a wall of rock, a long projecting promontory in this little world of water, where
nothing was as it seemed. But it was not half so
mysterious as life. It was but lately that this aspect
of existence had struck the healthful soul of the Highland girl. Till the last year all had been open and
sweet as the day about her ways and thoughts. If she
had any secrets at all they had been those which even
the angels guard between themselves and God, those
sacred enthusiasms for the one Love that is above all:
those aspirations towards the infinite which are the
higher breath of gentle souls; or perhaps a visionary
opening into the romance of life in its present form,
which was scarcely less visionary and pure. But
nothing else, nothing more worldly, nothing that her
namesake, "heavenly Una with her milkwhite lamb,"
need have hesitated to avow.

But since then Oona had gone far and wandered
wide in a shadowy world which she shared with no one,
and in which there were mystic forces beyond her
fathoming, influences which caught the wanderer all
unwitting, and drew her hither or thither unawares,
against her will. She was no longer the princess and
sovereign of life as she had been in the earlier portion
of it, but rather its subject or possible victim, moved by
powers which she could not understand nor resist, and
which overcame her before she was aware of their
existence. She thought of all this as her boat made its
way, propelled by the long, strong strokes of Hamish,
amid the shadows; but not angrily, not miserably as
she had sometimes done, with a sadness which (if it was
sadness at all) was sweet, and a secret exhilaration for
which she could not account. The mother seemed
somehow to step into the visionary conflict which was
going on, a half-seen, unknown, but powerful champion
on the side of—— Was it on the side of Oona? She
shrank a little from that identification, and said to
herself, on the side of good. For that there was a
struggle going on between good and evil, which in some
mysterious way centred in Lord Erradeen, she was
mysteriously aware, she could not tell how.

"Yon young lord will be the better of his mother,'
Hamish was saying, his voice coming to her vaguely,
running on without any thought of reply, mingled with
the larger sound of the oars upon the rowlocks, the long
sweep of them through the loch, the gurgle and tinkle

of the water as the boat cut through. Hamish was
faintly visible and even retained till it grew quite dark
some trace of colour in his favourite garment. "He'll
be the better of his mother," he said; "there will aye
be a want when there's no a leddy in the house.
Weeman servants are no to lippen to. A young man
when he has not a wife, he will be muckle the better
for his mother."

Oona heard the words vaguely like a chant amid all
those sounds of the loch which were the music and
accompaniment of her own being. She ran up the
slope when they landed, and burst into the little drawing-room which was so bright after the darkness of the
evening world, with a pleasure in her little adventure,
and in having something to tell which is only known in
the deep recesses, the unbroken quiet of rural life.
Mrs. Forrester was just beginning, as she herself said,
to "weary" for Oona's return. She had put down her
knitting and taken a book. Again she had put aside
her book and taken the knitting. Oona was late.
Oona meant the world and life to the solitary lady on
the crest of the isle. The house, the little retired nest
amid the trees, was full and cheerful when she was
there, and though Mysie and the cook, "ben the
house," gave now and then a sign of life, yet nothing
was complete until the sound of the boat drawn
up on the shingle, the unshipping oars, the light
firm foot on the path, followed by the heavier tread,
scattering the gravel, of Hamish, gave token that all the

little population were gathered within the circle of their rocks and waters. Then Mrs. Forrester brightened and turned her face towards the door with cheerful expectation: for it became a little too cold now to go down to the beach to meet the boat, even with the fur cloak upon her shoulders, which had been her wont on summer nights, and even on wintry days.

"His mother, poor young man! Dear me, that is very interesting, Oona. I was not sure he had a mother. That's good news: for I always took an interest in Lord Erradeen, like one of our own boys. Indeed, you know, Oona, I always thought him like Rob, though their complexions are different. Dear me! I am very glad you were on the spot, and able to show her a little civility. But he should have been there, oh! he should have been there, to meet her. If any of the boys were to do that to me, I would not know what to think—to leave me to the civility of any person that might be passing. Oh, fie! no, I would not know what to think."

"I know what you would think," said Oona, "that there must have been some mistake, that they did not know the hour of the train, or did not know which train, or that they had been too late of starting, or—something. You would be sure to find a good reason, mamma."

"Well, that's true, Oona; no doubt it would be something of that kind, for it is impossible that a nice lad (and Lord Erradeen was always that) would show himself neglectful of his mother. Poor lady! and she would be tired after her journey. I am very glad you were there to show her a little attention. She will perhaps think, as so many of those English do, that we're cold and distant in the north. My dear, you can just ring for the tea: and we'll go and call upon her to-morrow, Oona. Well, perhaps not to-morrow; but wait till she is well rested. We'll go on Thursday, and you can just mention it about, wherever you are to-morrow, that everybody may know. It is such a fine thing for a young man to have his mother with him (when he has not a wife), that we must give her a warm welcome, poor lady," Mrs. Forrester said. She had no reason to call Mrs. Methven poor, but did it as a child does, with a meaning of kindness. She was in fact much pleased and excited by the news. It seemed to throw a gleam of possible comfort over the head of the loch. "The late lord had no woman about him," she said to herself after Oona had left the room. She had quite forgotten that she was beginning to "weary." "Did you hear, Mysie," she went on when "the tea" appeared with all its wealth of scones, "that Lord Erradeen was expecting his mother? I am almost as glad to hear it as if one of our own boys had come home."

"It is a real good thing for the young lord, mem," said Mysie; "and no doubt you'll be going to see her, being such near neighbours, and my lord such great friends with the isle."

I 2

"I would not say very great friends, oh no," said Mrs. Forrester, deprecatory, but with a smile of pleasure on her face. "There is little to tempt a young gentleman here. But no doubt we will call as soon as she is rested —Miss Oona and me."

This formed the staple of their conversation all the evening, and made the little room cheerful with a sentiment of expectation.

"And what kind of a person did you find her, Oona? And do you think she will be a pleasant neighbour? And he was at the water-side to meet her, when he saw the boat? And was he kind? and did he show a right feeling?"

These questions Mrs. Forrester asked over and over again. She put herself in the place of the mother who had arrived so unexpectedly without any one to meet her.

"And you will be sure to mention it, whoever you see to-morrow," she repeated several times, "that she may see we have all a regard for him. I know by myself that is the first thing you think of," Mrs. Forrester added with a pleasant smile. "The boys" were everything they ought to be. There were no eccentricities, nothing out of the way, about them to make public opinion doubtful. Wherever they went, their mother, pleased, but not surprised, heard everything that was pleasant of them. She "knew by herself" that this was what Walter's mother would want to hear.

And Oona "mentioned it" to the Ellermore Camp-
bells, with whom she had some engagement next
morning, and where she met Miss Herbert from the
Lodge. Julia was already popular with her nearest
neighbours, and had an attendant at her side in the
shape of a friend invited by Sir Thomas as an ardent
sportsman, but of whom Julia had taken the command
from his first appearance. She was in high spirits,
finding everything go well with her, and slightly off her
balance with the opening up of new prosperity. She
threw herself into the discussion with all the certainty
of an old acquaintance.

"I don't understand why you should be so pleased,"
said Julia. "Are you pleased? or is it only a make-
believe? Oh, no, dear Oona; I do not suppose you are
so naughty as that. You never were naughty in your
life—was she? Never tore her pinafore, or dirtied her
frock? It is pretty of you, all you girls, to take an
interest in Walter's mother; but for my part I like
young men best without their mothers," Miss Herbert
said, with a laugh, and a glance towards the attendant squire, who said to himself that here was a
girl above all pretences, who knew better than to
attempt to throw dust in the eyes of wise men like
himself.

Some of the Ellermore girls laughed, for there is
nothing that girls and boys are more afraid of than this
reputation of never having dirtied their pinafores;
while their mother, with the easy conviction of a

woman so full of sons and daughters that she is glad, whenever she can, to shirk her responsibilities, said :

"Well, that is true enough : a young man should not be encumbered with an old woman ; and if I were Mrs. Methven——"

"But thank Heaven, you are not at all like Mrs. Methven," said Julia. "She is always after that unfortunate boy. It did not matter where he went, he was never free of her. Sitting up for him, fancy ! making him give her an account of everything. He had to count up how many times he came to see me."

"Which perhaps would be difficult," some one said.

Julia laughed—that laugh of triumph which disturbs feminine nerves.

"He did come pretty often," she said, "poor fellow. Oh, most innocently ! to get me to play his accompaniments. Don't you know he sings ? Oh, yes, very tolerably : if he would but open his mouth, I used to tell him ; but some people like to be scolded, I think."

"By you," said the attendant in an undertone.

Julia gave him a look which repaid him.

"I always had to take his part. Poor Walter !" she said with a sigh. "And then when I had him by myself I scolded him. Isn't that the right way ? I used to get into great trouble about that boy," she added. "When one has known a person all one's life one can't help taking an interest—— And he was so mismanaged in his youth."

"Here is a Daniel come to judgment," said Jeanie Campbell: "so much wiser than the rest of us. Lord Erradeen must be years older than you are. Let us call, mother, all the same, and see what sort of a dragon she is."

"I shall call, of cousre," the mother said; "and I don't want to hear anything about dragons. I am one too, I suppose. Thank you, Oona, for telling me. I should not like to be wanting in politeness. Your mother will be going to-morrow, I shouldn't wonder? Well, we shall go the next day, girls. Erradeen marches with Ellermore, and I know your father wishes to pay every respect."

"I suppose when you're a lord," said Tom, who was very far down in the family, and of no account, "you can go upon a rule of your own ; but it would be far greater fun for Erradeen if he would mix himself up more with other people. Did anybody ever find out who that fellow was that was staying with him ? Braithwaite thought he must be something very fine indeed—a foreign prince, or that sort. He said such a fellow couldn't be English without being well known. It seems he knew everybody, and everything you could think of. A tremendous swell, according to Braithwaite. Oona, who was he? you ought to know."

At this all eyes turned to Oona, who grew red in spite of herself.

"I have no way of knowing," she said. "I saw such a person once — but I never heard who he was."

"I am not superstitious," said Mrs. Campbell, "but there are people seen about that old castle that—make your blood run cold. No, I never saw anything myself; but your father says——"

"My father never met this fellow," cried Tom. "He wasn't a fellow to make any mistake about. Neither old nor young—oh, yes, oldish : between forty and fifty; as straight as a rod, with eyes that go through and through you; and a voice—I think Erradeen himself funks him. Yes, I do. He turned quite white when he heard his voice."

"There are all kinds of strange stories about that old castle," said one of the Campbell sisters in an explanatory tone, addressing Julia. "You must not be astonished if you hear of unearthly lights, and some dreadful ordeal the heir has to go through, and ghosts of every description."

"I wish, Jeanie," said Tom, "when a fellow asks a question, that you would not break in with your nonsense. Who is talking of ghosts? I am asking who a fellow was—a very fine gentleman, I can tell you; something you don't see the like of often——"
The young man was much offended by his sister's profanity. He went to the door with Oona, fuming.

'These girls never understand," he said; "they make a joke of everything. This was one of the grandest fellows I ever saw—and then they come in with their rubbish about ghosts!"

"Never mind," Oona said, giving him her hand. The conversation somehow had been more than she herself could bear, and she had come away with a sense of perplexity and indignation. Tom, who was hot and indignant too, was more in sympathy with her than the others who talked about ghosts, which made her angry she could scarcely tell why.

"Let me walk with you," said Julia Herbert, following. "I have sent Major Antrobus to look after the carriage. He is a friend of my cousin Sir Thomas, and supposed to be a great sportsman, but not so devoted to slaughter as was hoped. Instead of slaughtering, he is slaughtered, Lady Herbert says. I am sure I don't know by whom. Do let me walk with you a little way. It is so nice to be with you." Julia looked into Oona's face with something of the ingratiating air which she assumed to her victims of the other sex. "Dear Miss Forrester——" and then she stopped with a laugh. "I don't dare to call you by your Christian name."

"It must be I then that am the dragon, though I did not know it," Oona said; but she did not ask to be called by her Christian name.

"I see—you are angry with me for what I said of Mrs. Methven. It is quite true, however; that is the

kind of woman she is.   But I don't excuse Walter, for
all that.   He was very wicked to her.   Ever since he
was a boy at school he has been nasty to his mother.
Everybody says it is her own fault, but still it was not
nice of him, do you think?   Oh, *I* think him very nice,
in many ways.   I have known him so long.   He has
always been most agreeable to me—sometimes *too*
agreeable," said Julia with a smile, pausing, dwelling
upon the recollection.   "But his mother and he never
got on.   Sometimes those that are the very nicest out
of doors are rather disagreeable at home.   Haven't you
seen that?   Oh, I have, a hundred times.   Of course
the mother is sure to be to blame.   She ought to have
made a cheerful home for him, you know, and asked
young people, and cheerful people, instead of a set of
fogies.   But she never would do that.   She expected
him to put up with her old-fashioned ways.

Oona made no reply.   She was disturbed in the ideal
that had been rising within her—an ideal not all made
up of sunshine and virtue, but where at least the darker
shades were of a more elevated description than petty
disobediences on one hand and exactions on the other.
Life becomes mean and small when dragged down to
this prosaic level, which was the natural level in Julia's
mind, not pitiful and debasing, as it appeared to Oona.
As there was no response to what she had said, Julia
resumed, putting her hand with a great show of affection
within Oona's arm.

"I want you to let me be your friend," she said,

"and I don't want you to be deceived. I fear you think too well of people; and when you hear anything against them, then you feel displeased. Oh, yes, I know. You are not pleased with me for telling the truth about the Methvens."

"I wonder rather," said Oona, somewhat coldly, "that being so much a friend of Lord Erradeen you should—betray him; for we should never have known this without you."

"Oh, betray him; what hard words!" cried Julia, making believe to shrink and hide her face. "I would not betray him for worlds, poor dear Walter, if I had a secret of his. But this is no secret at all," she added, with a laugh; "everybody knows they never got on. And between ourselves, Walter has been a sad bad boy. Oh, yes, there is no doubt about it. I know more of the world than a gentle creature like you, and I know that no man is very good. Oh, don't say a word, for you don't understand. There are none of them very good. What goes on when they are knocking about the world—we don't know what it is: but it is no good. Everybody that knows human nature knows that. But Walter has gone further, you know, than the ordinary. Oh, he has been a bad boy. He took up with Captain Underwood before he knew anything about Kinloch Houran, while he was not much more than a boy: and everybody knows what Captain Underwood is. He has gambled and betted, and done a great many still more dreadful things. And poor

Mrs. Methven scolded and cried and nagged : and that
has made everything worse."

Oona's countenance changed very much during this
conversation. It flushed and paled, and grew stern
with indignation, and quivered with pity. It seemed
to her that all that was said must be true : it
had not the air of an invention. She asked, with a
trembling voice, "If this is so, how is it that you still
care for him ? still——" she would have said—pursue
him ; but Oona's womanly instincts were too strong for
this, and she faltered and paused, and said, feebly, "still
—keep him in your thoughts ? "

"Oh, we must not be too hard, you know," said
Julia, smiling ; "a man must sow his wild oats. Oh,
I should myself had I been a man. I should not have
been content with your humdrum life. I should have
stormed all over the place and had a taste of everything. Don't you think it is better for them when
they have been downright bad ? I do ; it makes
them more humble. They know, if you came to
inquire into them, there would not be a word to say
for them. I think it is a good thing, for my part ; I
don't mind. I am not afraid of it. But still it must
be confessed that Walter has been, oh ! very bad ! and
unkind to his mother ; not what people call a good son.
And what is the use of her coming here ? She is
coming only to spoil sport, to poke her nose into everything. I have no patience with that kind of woman.
Now I can see in your face you are quite shocked with

me. You think it is I who am bad. But you know
I have taken a great fancy to you, and I want you to
know."

"I have no wish to know," said Oona. She had
grown very pale—with the feeling of having been out
in a storm and exposed to the beating of remorseless
rain, the fierce hail that sometimes sweeps the hills.
She heard Julia's laugh ringing through like something
fiendish in the midst of her suffering. She was glad to
escape, though beaten down and penetrated by the
bitter storm. The silence was grateful to her, and to
feel herself alone. She scarcely doubted that it was
all true. There was something in Miss Herbert's tone
which brought conviction with it : the levity and in-
dulgence were abhorrent to Oona, but they sounded
true. Julia pressed her hand as she turned back, saying something about Major Antrobus and the carriage,
with a laugh at Oona's startled looks, "Don't look so
pale ; you are too sensitive. It is nothing more than
all of them do. Good-bye, dear," Julia said. She
bent forward with a half-offer of a kiss, from which
Oona shrank : and then went away laughing, calling
out, "People will think you have seen one of those
ghosts."

A ghost ! Oona went upon her way, silent, aching
in heart and spirit. What was a ghost, as they said,
in comparison ? No ghost but must know secrets that
would at the least make levity and irreverence impossible. Nothing but a human voice could mock and

jibe at that horror and mystery of evil before which Oona's spirit trembled. She had walked some way alone upon the daylight road, with the wholesome wind blowing in her face, and the calm of nature restoring her to composure, but not relieving the ache in her heart, before she came to the edge of the bank, and called in her clear voice to Hamish in the boat.

CHAPTER IX.

"LORD ERRADEEN!" His appearance was so unexpected, so curiously appropriate and inappropriate, that Oona felt as if she must be under some hallucination, and was beholding an incarnation of her own thoughts instead of an actual man.

And Walter was himself at so high a strain of excitement that the agitation of her surprise seemed natural to him. It scarcely seemed possible that everybody around, and specially that she, did not know the crisis at which he stood. He took the hand which she instinctively put forward, into both his, and held fast by it as if it had been an anchor of salvation.

"I am a fugitive," he said. "Will you receive me, will you take me with you? Have pity upon me, for you are my last hope."

"Lord Erradeen—has anything—happened? What —have you done?"

She trembled, standing by him, gazing in his face, not withdrawing her hand, yet not giving it, lost in wonder; yet having come to feel that something he had done, some guilt of his, must be the cause.

"I have done— I will tell you everything. I wish to tell you everything: let me come with you, Oona."

All this time Hamish, standing behind Walter, was making signs to his young mistress, which seemed to no purpose but to increase her perplexity. Hamish shook his shaggy head, and his eyebrows worked up and down. He gesticulated with his arm pointing along the loch. Finally he stepped forward with a sort of desperation.

"I'm saying, Miss Oona, that we're in no hurry. There will always be somebody about that would be glad, real glad, of a visit from you. And as his lordship is a wee disturbed in his mind, and keen to get home, I could just put him up to Auchnasheen—it would take me very little time—and syne come back for you."

Oona stood startled, undecided between the two— alarmed a little by Walter's looks, and much by the significance of the gestures of Hamish, and his eagerness and anxiety.

"I will no be keeping you waiting long at all—oh, not at all. And my lord will be best at home, being a wee disturbed in his mind—and we're in no hurry— no hurry," Hamish insisted, doing his best to place himself between the two.

"Hamish thinks I am mad," said Walter. "I do not wonder. But I am not mad. I want neither home nor anything else—but you. It is come to that

—that nobody can help me but you. First one tries expedients," he cried, "anything to tide over; but at last one comes—one comes to the only true—"

"You are speaking very wildly," said Oona. "I don't know what you mean, Lord Erradeen; and Hamish is afraid of you. What is it? We are only simple people—we do not understand."

He dropped her hand which he had held all the time, half, yet only half against her will, for there was something in the way he held it which forbade all idea of levity. She looked at him very wistfully, anxious, not with any offence, endeavouring to put away all prepossession out of her mind—the prejudice in his favour which moved her heart in spite of herself—the prejudice against him, and indignant wonder whether all was true that she had heard, which had arisen from Julia's words. Her eyelids had formed into anxious curves of uncertainty, out of which her soul looked wistfully, unable to refuse help, perplexed, not knowing what to do.

"If you refuse to hear me," he said, "I have no other help to turn to. I know I have no right to use such an argument, and yet if you knew—I will urge no more. It is death or life—but it is in your hands."

Oona's eyes searched into his very soul.

"What can I do?" she said, wondering. "What power have I? How can I tell if it is—true—" she faltered, and begged his pardon hastily when she had said that word. "I mean—I do not mean—" she said confusedly. "But oh, what can I do? it is not possible that I——"

It is cruel to have the burden put upon you of another's fate. Sometimes that is done to a woman lightly in the moment of disappointment by a mortified lover. Was this the sort of threat he meant, or was it perhaps—true? Oona, who had no guile, was shaken to the very soul by that doubt. Better to risk an affront in her own person than perhaps to fail of an occasion in which sincere help was wanted and could be given. She had not taken her eyes from him, but searched his face with a profound uncertainty and eagerness. At last, with the sigh of relief which accompanies a decision, she said to Hamish,

"Push off the boat. Lord Erradeen will help me in," with something peremptory in her tone against which her faithful servant could make no further protest.

Hamish proceeded accordingly to push off the boat into the water, and presently they were afloat, steering out for the centre of the loch. They were at some distance from the isle on the other side of the low, green island with its little fringe of trees, so different from the rocky and crested isles about, which is known on Loch Houran as the Isle of Rest. The low wall round about the scattered tombs, the scanty ruins of its little chapel, were all that broke the soft greenness of those low slopes. There was nothing like it all around in its solemn vacancy and stillness, and nothing

could be more unlike that chill and pathetic calm than
the freight of life which approached it in Oona's boat :
she herself full of tremulous visionary excitement—the
young man in his passion and desperation; even the
watchful attendant, who never took his eyes from Lord
Erradeen, and rowed on with all his senses on the alert,
ready to throw himself upon the supposed maniac at a
moment's notice, or without it did the occasion require.
There was a pause till they found themselves separated
by a widening interval of water from the shore, where
at any moment a chance passenger might have disturbed their interview. Here no one could disturb
them. Walter placed himself in front of Hamish facing
Oona : but perhaps the very attitude, the freedom and
isolation in which he found himself with her, closed
his lips. For a minute he sat gazing at her, and did
not speak.

"You wished — to say something to me, Lord
Erradeen ? "

It was she again, as Katie had done before, who
recalled to him his purpose—with a delicate flush
colouring the paleness of her face, half in shame that
after all she had to interfere to bring the confession
forth.

"So much," he said, "so much that I scarcely know
where to begin." And then he added, "I feel safe
with you near me. Do you know what it means to
feel safe ? But you never were in deadly danger.
How could you be ? "

K 2

"Lord Erradeen, do not mystify me with these strange sayings," she cried. "Do they mean anything? What has happened to you? or is it only—is it nothing but——"

"A pretence, do you think, to get myself a hearing—to beguile you into a little interest? That might have been. But it is more serious, far more serious. I told you it was life or death." He paused for a moment and then resumed. "Do you remember last year when you saved me?"

"I remember—last year," she said with an unsteady voice, feeling the flush grow hotter and hotter on her cheek, for she did not desire to be reminded of that self-surrender, that strange merging of her being in another's which was her secret, of which she had been aware, but no one else. "I never understood it," she added, with one meaning for herself and one for him. The hidden sense was to her more important than the other. "It has always been—a mystery——"

"It was the beginning of the struggle," he said. "I came here, you know—don't you know?—out of poverty to take possession of my kingdom—that was what I thought. I found myself instead at the beginning of a dreary battle. I was not fit for it, to begin with. Do you remember the old knights had to prepare themselves for their chivalry with fasting, and watching of arms, and all that—folly——" A gleam of self-derision went over his face, and yet it was deadly serious underneath.

"It was no folly," she said.

"Oh, do you think I don't know that? The devil laughs in me, now and then, but I don't mean it. Oona—let me call you Oona, now, if never again—I had neither watched nor prayed——"

He made a pause, looking at her pitifully; and she, drawn, she knew not how, answered, with tears in her eyes, "I have heard that you—had strayed——"

"That means accidentally, innocently," he said. "It was not so. I had thought only of myself: when I was caught in the grip of a will stronger than mine, unprepared. There was set before me—no, not good and evil as in the books, but subjection to one—who cared neither for good nor evil. I was bidden to give up my own will, I who had cared for nothing else : to give up even such good as was in me. I was not cruel. I cared nothing about worldly advantages; but these were henceforward to be the rule of my life— pleasant, was it not?" he said with a laugh, "to a man who expected to be the master—of everything round."

At the sound of his laugh, which was harsh and wild, Hamish, raising himself so as to catch the eye of his mistress, gave her a questioning, anxious look. Oona was very pale, but she made an impatient gesture with her hand to her humble guardian. She was not herself at ease ; an agonizing doubt lest Walter's mind should have given way had taken possession of her. She answered him as calmly as she could, but with a tremor

in her voice, " Who could ask that, Lord Erradeen ?
Oh no, no—you have been deceived."

" You ask me who ! you who gave me your hand—
your hand that was like snow—that had never done
but kindness all your life—and saved me—so that I
defied him. And you ask me who ? "

He put out his hand as he spoke and touched hers
as it lay in her lap. His face was full of emotion,
working and quivering. "Give it to me, Oona !—will
you give it to me ? I am not worthy that you should
touch me. It has been said to me that you would turn
from me—ah, with disgust !—*if you knew*. And I
want you to know everything. For you gave it then
without pausing to think. Oona ! I am going to tell
you everything. Give it to me," he said, holding out
his hands one over the other to receive and clasp hers,
his eyes moist, his lips appealing with a quivering
smile of entreaty. And how may it be told what was
in Oona's heart ? Her whole being was moved through
and through with tenderness, wonder, pity. Her hand
seemed to move of itself towards him. The impulse
was upon her almost too strong to be resisted, to throw
her arms around him, like a mother with a child—to
identify herself with him whatever might follow. The
womanly instinct that held her back—that kept all
these impulses in check and restrained the heart that
seemed leaping out of her bosom towards this man
whom she loved in spite of herself, and who had need
of her, most sacred of all claims—was like a frame of

iron round her, against which she struggled, but from which she could not get free. Tears filled her eyes— she clasped her hands together in an involuntary appeal. "What can I do? What can I do?" she cried.

"You shall hear all," said he. "I have tried every-thing before coming back to that which I always knew was my only hope. I fled away after that night. Do you remember?" (She almost smiled at this, for she remembered far better than he, and the wonder and despair of it, and his boat going away over the silent loch, and his face eager to be gone, and she indignant, astonished, feeling that her life went with him; but of all this he knew nothing.) "I fled—thinking I could escape and forget. There seemed no better way. There was no one to help me, only to mar and waste—what was all wasted and spoilt already. I want to tell you everything," he said faltering, drooping his head, with-drawing his eyes from her, "but I have not the courage —you would not understand me. Nothing that you could imagine could reach to a hundredth part of the evil I have known." He covered his face with his hands. The bitterness of the confession he dared not make seemed to stifle his voice and every hope.

And Oona's heart quivered and beat against the strong bondage that held it in, and her hands fluttered with longing to clasp him and console him. What woman can bear to hear out such a confession, not to interrupt it with pardon, with absolution, with cries to bring

forth the fairest robe? She touched his head with her
hands for a moment, a trembling touch upon his hair,
and said, "God forgive you. God will forgive you,"
with a voice almost choked with tears.

He raised his head and looked at her with an eager
cry. "I want—not forgiveness. I want life," he cried,
"life, new life. I want to be born again. Is not that
in the Bible? To be born again, to begin again from
the beginning, everything new. Help me, Oona! I
am not thinking of the past. It is *now* I am thinking
of. I am not thinking of forgiveness—punishment if you
please, anything!—but a new life. He knew man who
said that," Walter cried, raising his head. "What
use is it to me to forgive me? I want to be born
again."

When he thus delivered himself of his exceeding
bitter cry, this woman too, like his mother, answered
him with a shining face, with eyes swimming in tears,
and brilliant with celestial certainty. She put out her
hands to him without a moment's hesitation, and
grasped his and smiled.

"Oh, that is all provided for!" she said. "Yes, He
knew! It is all ready for you—waiting—waiting.
Don't you know our Lord stands at the door and
knocks, till you are ready to let Him in? And now
you are ready. There is nothing more."

He received the soft hands within his with feelings
indescribable, at such a height of emotion that all th
lesser shades and degrees were lost. He twined her

fingers among his own, clasping them with an entire appropriation.

"Oona," he said, "the house is yours, and all in it. Open the door to your Lord, whom I am not worthy to come near—and to everything that is good. It is yours to do it. Open the door!"

They had forgotten Hamish who sat behind, pulling his long, even strokes, with his anxious shaggy countenance fixed like that of a faithful dog upon his mistress, whom he had to guard. He saw the two heads draw very close together, and the murmur of the voices.

"What will she be saying to him? She will be winning him out of yon transport. She will be puttin' peace in his hairt. She has a voice that would wile the bird from the tree," said Hamish to himself. "But oh hon!—my bonnie Miss Oona," Hamish cried aloud.

This disturbed them and made them conscious of the spectator, who was there with them, separate from all the world. Oona, with a woman's readiness to throw her veil over and hide from the eye of day all that is too sacred for the vulgar gaze, raised her face, still quivering with tender and holy passion.

"Why do you say 'oh hon?' There is nothing to say 'oh hon' for, Hamish. No, no; but the other way."

Hamish looked across the young lord, whose head was bowed down still over Oona's hands, which he held. The boatman gave him a glance in which there was doubt and trouble, and then raised his shaggy eyebrows, and addressed a look of entreaty and warning to the fair inspired face that hovered over Walter like a protecting angel. "Ye will not be doing the like of that," he said, "without thought ?"

And all the time the boat swept on over the reflections in the water, by the low shore of the Isle of Rest where death had easy landing, away among the feathery islets, all tufted brown and crimson to the water's edge, where nothing but the wild life of the woods could find footing :— nothing near them but the one anxious, humble retainer, watching over Oona, for whom no one in heaven or earth, save himself, entertained any fear. He quickened those long strokes in the excitement of his soul, but neither did Walter take any account of where he was going, nor Oona awake out of the excitement of the moment to think of the descent into common life which was so near. Hamish only, having the entire conduct of them, hastened their progress back to ordinary existence—if perhaps there might be some aid of reason and common judgment (as he said to himself) there, to see that the man was in his right senses before Oona should be bound for life.

There was no excitement about the isle. It lay as calm in the sunshine as if nothing but peace had ever passed by that piece of solid earth, with its rocks and trees, that little human world amid the waters; every jagged edge of rock, every red-tinted tree against the background of tall firs, and the firs themselves in their dark motionless green, all shining inverted in the liquid

clearness around. The two were still afloat, though
their feet were on solid ground; and still apart from all
the world, though the winding way led direct to the
little centre of common life in which Oona was all in
all. But they did not immediately ascend to that gentle
height. They paused first on the little platform, from
which Kinloch Houran was the chief object. One of
those flying shadows that make the poetry of the hills,
was over it for a moment, arrested as by some consciousness of nature, while they stood and gazed. There
Walter stood and told to Oona the story of Miss
Milnathort, and how she had said that two, set upon all
good things, would hold the secret in their hands.
Two—and here were the two. It seemed to him that
every cloud had fled from his soul from the moment
when he felt her hands in his, and had bidden her
"open the door." Oh, fling wide the door to the Christ
who waits outside, the Anointed, the Deliverer of men :
to peace and truth, that wait upon Him, and mercy and
kindness, and love supreme that saves the world!
Fling wide the doors! Not a bolt or bar but that soft
hand shall unloose them, throw them wide, that the
Lord may come in. Not a crevice, or corner, or dark
hiding-place of evil but shall open to the light. He
said so standing there, holding her hand still, not only
as a lover caressing, protecting, holds the soft hand he
loves, but as a man drowning will hold by the hand held
out to save him. It was both to Walter. He told her,
and it was true, that from the day when she had put it

into his a year ago, he had never lost the consciousness
that in this hand was his hope.

Oona was penetrated by all these words to the depths
of her heart. What girl could be told that in her hands
was the saving of one she loved, without such a movement of the soul to the highest heroism and devotion
as raises human nature above itself? Her soul seemed
to soar, drawing his with it, into heights above. She
felt capable of everything—of the highest effort and the
humblest service. That union of the spiritual being
above his, and the human longing beneath, came back
to her in all the joy of a permitted and befitting mood.
She was his to raise him above all those soils of life of
which he was sick and weary; and his to sweep away
the thorns and briars out of his path; to lead him and
to serve him, to mingle her being in his life so that no
one henceforward should think of Oona save as his
second and helpmeet: yet so to guide his uncertain way
as that it should henceforward follow the track of light
by which the best of all ages has gone. Even to understand that office of glory and humility demands an
enlightenment, such as those who do not love can never
attain. To Oona it seemed that life itself became
glorious in this service. It raised her above all earthly
things. She looked at him with the pity of an angel,
with something of the tenderness of a mother, with an
identification and willingness to submit which was pure
woman. All was justified to her—the love that she had

given unsought, the service which she was willing and ready to give.

He stopped before they had reached the height upon which stood home and the sweet and simple existence which embraced these mysteries without comprehending them. A darker shadow, a premonition of evil, came over him.

"And yet," he said, "I have not told you all. I have something more still to say."

CHAPTER X.

WHAT did there remain to say?

He had made his confession, which, after all, was no confession, and she had stopped his mouth with pardon. His cry for new life had overcome every reluctance in her. Her delicate reserve, the instinct that restrained her, had no more power after that. She had stood no longer behind any barrier—at that touch she had thrown her heart wide open and taken him within.

"What more?" she said. "There can be no more."

"Much more: and you were to hear all: not only the wretched folly into which I fled, to try if I could forget, but something meaner, nearer——something for which you will despise me. Oh, do not smile; it is past smiling for you and me—for you as well as me now, Oona. God forgive me that have tangled your life in mine!"

"What is it?" she said, giving him an open look of trust and confidence. "I am not afraid."

He was. Far worse than the general avowal of sins which she did not understand was the avowal he had to make of something which she could understand.

He perceived that it would wound her to the heart—
He had no fear now that Oona would throw him off.
She had put her hand into his, and was ready to pour
the fresh and spotless stream of her life into his. It
was no more possible for her to separate herself, to
withdraw from him, whatever might happen. He
perceived this with a keen pang of remorse, for the first
time entering with all his heart into the soul of another,
and understanding what it meant. She could not now
turn her back upon him, go away from him; and he
was about to give her a sharp, profound, intolerable
wound.

"Oona," he said, with great humility, "it occurred
to-day. I cannot tell whether you will be able to see
why I did it, or how I did it. This morning——" He
paused here, feeling that the words hung in his throat
and stifled him. "This morning—I went—and insulted
Katie Williamson, and asked her—to marry me."

She had been listening with her sweet look of pity and
tenderness—sorry, sorry to the depths of her heart, for
the evil he had done—sorry beyond tears; but yet ready
with her pardon, and not afraid. At the name of Katie
Williamson there came up over her clear face the shadow
of a cloud—not more than the shadow. When such
words as these are said they are not to be understood all
at once. But they woke in her a startled curiosity—a
strange surprise.

"This morning—it is still morning," she said, bewildered; "and Katie——"

"Oona! you do not understand."

"No. I do not quite—understand. What is it? This morning? And Katie——"

"I asked her this morning to join her land to my land and her money to my money: to be—my wife."

She drew her hand slowly out of his, looking at him with eyes that grew larger as they gazed. For some time she could not say a word, but only got paler and paler, and looked at him.

"Then what place—have I?—what am—I?" she said, slowly. Afterwards a sudden flush lighted up her face. "She would not: and then you came—to me?" she said.

A faint smile of pain came to her mouth. Walter had seen that look very recently before—when he told his mother why it was that he had sent for her. Was he capable of giving nothing but pain to those he loved? If he had tried to explain or apologise, it is doubtful whether Oona's faculties, so suddenly and strangely strained, could have borne it. But he said nothing. What was there to say?—the fact which he had thus avowed was beyond explanation. He met her eyes for a moment, then drooped his head. There was nothing—nothing to be said. It was true. He had gone to another woman first, and then, when that failed, as a last resource had come to her. The anguish was so sharp that it brought that smile. It was incredible in the midst of her happiness. Her heart seemed wrung and crushed in some gigantic grasp. She looked at him with wondering, incredulous misery.

" You thought then, I suppose," she said, "that one —was as good as another ? "

" I did not do that, Oona; it is, perhaps, impossible that you should understand. I told you—I had tried —every expedient: not daring to come to the one and only—the one, the only——"

She waved her hand as if putting this aside, and stood for a moment looking out vaguely upon the loch —upon the sheen of the water, the castle lying darkly in shadow, the banks stretching upward and downward in reflection. They had been glorified a moment since in the new union; now they were blurred over, and conveyed no meaning. Then she said drearily—

" My mother — will wonder why we do not come in—"

" May I speak to her—at once ? Let me speak."

" Oh no !" she cried. " Say nothing—nothing ! I could not bear it."

And then he seized upon her hand, the hand she had taken from him, and cried out—

" You are not going to forsake me, Oona ! You will not cast me away ? "

" I cannot," she said very low, with her eyes upon the landscape, " I cannot !" Then, turning to him, " You have my word, and I have but one word : only everything is changed. Let us say no more of it just now. A little time—I must have a little time."

And she turned and walked before him to the house. They went in silence, not a word passing between them.

Mysie, startled, came out to the door to ascertain who it could be who were preceded by the sound of footsteps only, not of voices. It was "no canny," she said. And to think this was Miss Oona, whose cheerful voice always came home before her to warn the house that its pride and joy was approaching! Mysie, confounded, went to open the door of the drawing-room that her mistress might be made to share her uneasiness.

"It will just be Miss Oona, mem, and my lord," Mysie said, "but very down, as if something had happened and not saying a word."

"Bless me!" cried Mrs. Forrester. Her heart naturally leapt to the only source of danger that could affect her deeply. "It is not a mail day, Mysie," she said; "there can be no ill news."

"The Lord be thanked for that!" Mysie said: and then stood aside to give admittance to those footsteps which came one after the other without any talking or cheerful note of sound. Mrs. Forrester rose to meet them with a certain anxiety, although her mind was at rest on the subject of the mails. It might be something wrong at Eaglescairn: it might be——

"Dear me! what is the matter, Oona? You are white, as if you had seen a ghost," she said, with a more tangible reason for her alarm.

"I am quite well, mamma. Perhaps I may have seen a ghost—but nothing more," she said with a half-laugh. "And here is Lord Erradeen whom we picked up, Hamish and I."

"And Lord Erradeen, you are just very whitefaced too," cried Mrs. Forrester. "Bless me, I hope you have not both taken a chill. That will sometimes happen when the winter is wearing on, and ye are tempted out on a fine morning with not enough of clothes. I have some cherry brandy in my private press, and I will just give you a little to bring back the blood to your cheeks : and come in to the fire. Dear me, Oona, do not shiver like that ! and you not one that feels the cold. You have just taken a chill upon the water, though it is such a beautiful morning. And so you have got your mother with you, Lord Erradeen ? "

"She came yesterday. She was so fortunate as to meet—Miss Forrester."

It seemed to him a wrong against which he was ready to cry out to earth and heaven that he should have to call her by that formal name. He paused before he said it, and looked at her with passionate reproach in his eyes. And Oona saw the look, though her eyes were averted, and trembled, with what her mother took for cold.

"You may be sure Oona was very content to be of use : and I hope now you have got her you will keep her, Lord Erradeen. It will be fine for your house and the servants, and all, to have a lady at Auchnasheen. There has not been a lady since the last lord but one, who married the last of the Glen Oriel family, a person that brought a great deal of property with her. I remember her very well. They said she was not his

L 2

first love, but she was a most creditable person, and
well thought upon, and kind to the poor. We were
saying to ourselves, Oona and me, that we would go up
the loch to-morrow and call, if you are sure Mrs. Methven is rested from her journey, and will like to see such
near neighbours."

" But, mother—" Oona said.

" But what? There is no but, that I know of. You
know that it was all settled between us. We thought
to-day she would be tired, and want repose rather than
company. But by to-morrow she would be rested, and
willing to see what like persons we are in this place.
That would be very natural. And I am proud Oona
was in the way, to take her across the loch. People
that come from flat countries where there is little
water, they are sometimes a little timid of the loch, and
in the dark too. But she will have got over all that
by to-morrow, and to call will be a real pleasure. Did
you mention, Oona, at Ellermore and other places that
Mrs. Methven had arrived?—for everybody will be keen
to see your mother, Lord Erradeen."

" It is very kind. She will rather see you than any
one."

" Hoots," said Mrs. Forrester with a smile and a
shake of her head, " that is just flattery; for we have
very little in our power except good-will and kindness:
but it will give me great pleasure to make your mother's
acquaintance, and if she likes mine, that will be a
double advantage. But you are not going away, Lord

Erradeen? You have this moment come! and Mysie will be reckoning upon you for lunch, and I have no doubt a bird has been put to the fire. Well, I will not say a word, for Mrs. Methven's sake, for no doubt she will be a little strange the first day or two. Oona, will you see that Hamish is ready? And we will have the pleasure of calling to-morrow," Mrs. Forrester said, following to the door. Her easy smiles, the little movements of her hands, the fluttering of the pretty ribbons in her cap, added to the calm and tranquil stream of her talk so many additional details of the softest quietude of common life. She stood and looked after the young pair as they went down together to the beach, waving her hand to them when they turned towards her, as unconscious of any disturbing influence as were the trees that waved their branches too. Passion had never been in her little composed and cheerful world. By-and-by she felt the chill of the wind, and turned and went back to her fireside. "No doubt that winter is coming now," she said to herself, " and no wonder if Oona, poor thing, was just frozen with the cold on the water. I wish she may not have taken a chill." This was the greatest danger Mrs. Forrester anticipated, and she did not doubt that a hot drink when Oona went to bed would make all right.

It was very strange to both of the young wayfarers to find themselves alone again in the fresh air and stillness. Since the moment when they had landed in an ecstasy of union, until this moment when they went

down again to the same spot, years might have passed
for anything they knew. They did not seem to have a
word to say to each other. Oona was a step or two in
advance leading the way, while behind her came Walter,
his head drooping, his courage gone, not even the
despair in him which had given him a wild and fiery
energy. Despair itself seemed hopeful in comparison
with this. He had risen into another life, come to
fresh hopes, received beyond all expectation the help
which he had sought for elsewhere in vain, but which
here alone he could ever find; but now the soul had
gone out of it all, and he stood bewildered, deprived of
any power to say or do. All through his other miseries
there had been the thought of this, like a distant stronghold in which if he ever reached it there would be
deliverance. If he ever reached it! and now he had
reached it, but too late. Was it too late? He followed
her helplessly, not able to think of anything he could
say to her, though he had pleaded so eagerly, so
earnestly, a little while ago. There comes a time after
we have poured out our whole soul in entreaties,
whether to God or man, when exhaustion overpowers
the mind, and utterance is taken from us, and even
desire seems to fail—not that what we long for is less
to be desired, but that every effort is exhausted and a
dreary discouragement has paralysed the soul. Walter
felt not less, but more than ever, that in Oona was his
every hope. But he was dumb and could say no more,
following her with a weight upon his heart that allowed

him no further possibility, no power to raise either voice
or hand. They walked thus as in a mournful procession
following the funeral of their brief joy, half way down
the bank. Then Oona who was foremost paused for a
moment, looking out wistfully upon that familiar prospect, upon which she had looked all her life. The
scene had changed, the sky had clouded over, as if in
harmony with their minds; only over Kinloch Houran
a watery ray of sunshine, penetrating through the
quickly gathering clouds, threw a weird light. The
ruinous walls stood out red under this gleam askance of
the retreating sun. It was like an indication—a pointing out, to the executioner of some deadly harm or
punishment, of the victim. Oona paused, and he
behind her, vaguely turning as she turned, gazing at
this strange significant light, which seemed to point
out, "This is the spot"—was that what was meant?—
" the place to be destroyed."

" It was in shadow a moment since," Oona said, and
her voice seemed to thrill the air that had been brooding
over them in a heavy chill, as if under the same influence that made them voiceless. What did she mean?
and why should she care——

" The shadow was better," he said, but he did not
know what he himself meant more than what she
could mean.

" It has come here," said Oona, " between you and
me. You said you insulted Katie. I cannot think that
it was your meaning to—insult me."

"Insult—*you !*" his mind was so clear of that, and his own meaning in respect to the other so evident to him, that the dead quietude of his discouragement yielded to a momentary impatience. But how was he to make that clear ?

"No, I cannot think it. Whatever you meant, whether it was in levity, whether it was—— I do not believe *that.*"

"Oona," he cried, waking to the desperation of the position, "will you give me up, after all we have said ?"

She shook her head sadly.

"I will never now deny you what help I can give you, Lord Erradeen."

He turned from her with a cry of bitterness.

"Help without love is no help. Alms and pity will do nothing for me. It must be two—who are one."

She answered him with a faint laugh which was more bitter still; but restrained the jest of pain which rose to her lips, something about three who could not be one. It was the impulse of keen anguish, but it would not have become a discussion that was as serious as life and death.

"It is all a confusion," she said; "what to say or do I know not. It is such a thing—as could not have been foreseen. Some would think it made me free, but I do not feel that I can ever be free." She spoke without looking at him, gazing blankly out upon the landscape. "You said it was no smiling matter to you or me—to you and me. Perhaps," she interrupted herself as if a new light had come upon her, "that is the true meaning of what you say—two that are one; but it is not the usual creed. Two for misery——"

"Oh not for misery, Oona! there is no misery for me where you are."

"Or—any other," she said with a smile of unimaginable suffering, and ridicule, and indignation.

He answered nothing. What could he say to defend himself? "If you could see into my heart," he said after a time, "you would understand. One who is in despair will clutch at anything. Can you imagine a man trying like a coward to escape the conflict, rather than facing it, and bringing the woman he loved into it?"

"Yes," she said, "I can imagine that; but not in the man who is me." Then she moved away towards the beach, saying, "Hamish is waiting," with a sigh of weariness.

"Oona," said Walter, "you will give me your hand again before we part?"

"What does it matter if I give it or hold it back? It is yours whether I will or not. You should have told me before. I should have understood. Oh, I am ashamed, ashamed! to think of all I have said to you. How could you betray me first before you told me? In the same morning! It is more than a woman can bear!" she cried.

Perhaps this outburst of passion relieved her, for she turned and held out her hand to him with a smile of

pain which was heartrending. "It did not seem like
this when we landed," she said.

"And it would not seem like this, oh, Oona! if you
could see my heart."

She shook her head, looking at him all the while
with that strange smile, and then drew away her hand
and repeated, "Hamish is waiting." Hamish in the
background, standing up against the shining of the
water, with his oar in his hand, waited with his anxious
eyes upon his young lady, not knowing how it was. He
would have pitched Lord Erradeen into the loch, or laid
him at his feet with Highland passion, had she given
him a sign. He held the boat for him instead to step
in, with an anxious countenance. Love or hate, or
madness or good meaning, Hamish could not make out
what it was.

"To-morrow!" Walter said, "if I can live till to-
morrow in this suspense——"

She waved her hand to him, and Hamish pushed off.
And Oona stood as in a dream, seeing over again the
scene which had been in her mind for so long—but
changed. She had watched him go away before, eager
to be gone, carrying her life with him without knowing
it, without desiring it: he unaware of what he was
doing, she watching surprised, bereaved of herself, innocently and unaware. How poignant had that parting
been! But now it was different. He gazed back at
her now, as she stood on the beach, leaving his life
with her, all that was in him straining towards her,

gazing till they were each to the other but a speck in the distance. Two that were one! Oh, not perhaps for mutual joy, not for the happiness that love on the surface seems to mean—rather for the burden, the disappointment, the shame. She waved her hand once more over the cold water, and then turned away. Till to-morrow—"if I can live till to-morrow"—as he had said.

CHAPTER XI.

THE rest of this day passed over Walter like a dream in a fever. Through a kind of hot mist full of strange reflections, all painful, terrible, lurid, with confusion and suffering he saw the people and things about him—his mother questioning him with anxious words, with still more anxious eyes; his servants looking at him wondering, compassionate; and heard now and then a phrase which came to his consciousness and thereafter continued to rise before him from time to time, like a straw cast into a whirlpool and boiling up as the bubbles went and came—something about seeing a doctor, something about sending for Mr. Cameron, with now and then an imploring entreaty, "Oh, my boy! what ails you? what is wrong?" from Mrs. Methven. These were the words that came back to his ears in a kind of refrain. He answered, too, somehow, he was aware, that there was nothing the matter with him, that he wanted no doctor, no counsellor, in a voice which seemed to come from any point of the compass rather than from his own lips. It was not because of the breach which had so rapidly followed the transport of his complete union with Oona. That, too, had become secondary, a detail scarcely important in the presence of the vague tempest which was raging within him, and which he felt must come to some outburst more terrible than anything he had yet known when he was left to himself. He had come back to Auchnasheen under the guidance of Hamish, distracted, yet scarcely unhappy, feeling that at the end, whatever misunderstanding there might be, he was assured of Oona, her companionship, her help, and, what was greatest of all, her love. She had not hesitated to let him see that he had that; and with that must not all obstacles, however miserable, disappear at the last? But when he landed, the misery that fell upon him was different from the pain of the temporary misunderstanding. He became conscious at once that it was the beginning of the last struggle, a conflict which might end in—he knew not what: death, downfall, flight, even shame, for aught he knew. The impulse was strong upon him to speed away to the hillside and deliver himself over to the chances of this battle, which had a fierce attraction for him on one hand, while on the other it filled him with a mad terror which reason could not subdue.

So strong was this impulse that he hurried past the gate of Auchnasheen and took the path that led up to the moors, with a sense of flying from, yet flying to, his spiritual enemies. He was met there by the gamekeeper, who began to talk to him about the game, and the expediency of inviting "twa-three" gentlemen to

shoot the coverts down by Corrieden, an interruption
which seemed to his preoccupied soul too trivial, too
miserable, to be borne with. He turned from the
astonished speaker in the midst of his explanations,
and rushed back with the impatience which was part
of his character, exaggerated into a sort of mad intolerance of any interruption. Not there, not there—he
began to remember the wild and mad contest which
last year had gone on upon those hills, and with an
instantaneous change of plan retraced his steps to the
house, and burst into his mother's presence, so pale, so
wild, with eyes almost mad in their fire, looking out
from the curves of his eyelids like those of a maniac.
Her terror was great. She came up to him and laid her
hands upon him, and cried out, What was it? what was
it? After this the active frenzy that had possessed him
seemed to sink into a maze of feverish confusion which
was less violent, less terrible, more like the operations
of nature. He was not aware that he looked at her
piteously, and said, "I want to stay with you, mother"
—childlike words, which penetrated with a misery that
was almost sweet to Mrs. Methven's very heart. She
put her arms round him, drawing down his head upon
her bosom, kissing his forehead with trembling lips,
holding him fast, as when he was a child and came to
her for consolation. He was scarcely aware of all this,
and yet it soothed him. The excitement of his brain
was calmed. That uneasy haze of fever which confuses
everything, the half-delirium of the senses through

which the mind looks as through a mist, uneasy, yet
with visions that are not all miserable, was a sort of
paradise in comparison with the frenzy of a conflict in
which every expedient of torture was exercised upon
him. He was grateful for the relief. That he did not
know what he said or what she said, but heard the
answering voices far off, like something musical, was
nothing. There was a kind of safety in that society : the
enemy could not show himself there. He had to stand
off baffled and wait—ah, wait ! that was certain. He had
not gone away—not Oona, not the mother, could save the
victim altogether. They protected him for the moment,
they held the foe at arm's length : but that could not
be always. Sooner or later the last struggle must come.

Walter remained within-doors all day. It was contrary to all his habits, and this of itself added to the
alarm of all about him; but it was not inconsist-
ent with the capricious impatient constitution of his
mind, always ready to turn upon itself at a moment's
notice, and do that which no one expected. During
every moment of this long day he had to resist the
strong impulse which was upon him—more than an
impulse, a tearing and rending of his spirit, sometimes
rising into sudden energy almost inconceivable—to go
out and meet his enemy. But he held his ground so
far with a dumb obstinacy which also was part of his
character, and which was strengthened by the sensation
of comparative exemption so long as he had the protection of others around him, and specially of his

mother's presence. It was with reluctance that he saw
her go out of the room even for a moment; and his
eager look of inquiry when she left him, his attempts
to retain her, his strained gaze towards the door till
she returned, gave Mrs. Methven a sort of anguish of
pleasure, if those contradictory words can be put together. To feel that she was something, much to him,
could not but warm her heart; but with that was the
misery of knowing that something must indeed be very
far wrong with Walter to make him thus, after so many
years of independence, cling to his mother.

"It is like a fever coming on," she said to Symington, with whom alone she could take any counsel. "He
is ill, very ill, I am sure of it. The doctor must be
sent for. Have you ever seen him like this before?"

"My lady," said old Symington, "them that have the
Methvens to deal with have need of much gumption.
Have I seen him like that before? Oh, yes, I have
seen him like that before. It is just their hour and the
power o' darkness. Let him be for two-three days——"

"But in two or three days the fever may have taken
sure hold of him. It may be losing precious time: it
may get—fatal force——"

"There is no fears of his life," said old Symington;
"there is enough fear of other things."

"Of what? Oh, for God's sake! tell me; don't leave
me in ignorance!" the mother cried.

"But that's just what I cannot do," Symington said.
"By the same taken that I ken nothing mysel'."

While this conversation was going on, Walter, through his fever, saw them conspiring, plotting, talking about him as he would have divined and resented in other moods, but knew vaguely now in his mist of being that they meant him no harm, but good.

And thus the day went on. He prolonged it as long as he could, keeping his mother with him till long after the hour when the household was usually at rest. But, however late, the moment came at last when he could detain her no longer. She, terrified, ignorant, fearing a dangerous illness, was still more reluctant to leave him, if possible, than he was to let her go, and would have sat up all night watching him had she ventured to make such a proposal. But at last Walter summoned up all his courage with a desperate effort, an effort of despair which restored him to himself and made a clear spot amid all the mist and confusion of the day.

" Mother," he said, as he lighted her candle, "you have been very good to me to-day ! Oh I know you have always been good—and I always ungrateful ; but I am not ungrateful now."

" Oh, Walter ! what does that word mean between you and me ? If I could but do anything. It breaks my heart to see you like this."

" Yes, mother," he said, "and it may break my heart. I don't know what may come of it—if I can stand, or if I must fall. Go and pray for me, mother."

" Yes, my dearest—yes, my own boy ! as I have done

every day, almost every hour, since ever you were born."

"And so will Oona," he said. He made no response of affection to this brief record of a life devoted to him, which Mrs. Methven uttered with eyes full of tears and every line of her countenance quivering with emotion. He was abstracted into a world beyond all such expressions and responses, on the verge of an ordeal too terrible for him, more terrible than any he had yet sustained—like a man about to face fearful odds, and counting up what aids he could depend upon. "And so will Oona," he repeated to himself, aloud but unawares: and looked up at his mother with a sad glimmer of a smile and kissed her, and said, "That should help me." Then, without waiting for her to go first, he walked out of the room, like a blind man, feeling with his hand before him, and not seeing where he went.

For already there had begun within him that clanging of the pulses, that mounting of every faculty of the nerves and blood to his head, the seat of thought, which throbbed as though it would burst, and to his heart, which thundered and laboured and filled his ears with billows of sound. All his fears, half quiescent in the feverish pause of the day, were suddenly roused to action, ranging themselves to meet the last, the decisive, the most terrible assault of all. He went into his room and closed the door upon all mortal succour. The room was large and heavily furnished in the clumsy fashion of the last generation—heavy curtains, huge articles of furniture looming dark in the partial light, a gloomy expanse of space, dim mirrors glimmering here and there, the windows closely shut up and shrouded, every communication of the fresh air without, or such succour of light as might linger in the heavens, excluded. The old castle, with its ruined battlements, seemed a more fit scene for spiritual conflict than the dull comfort of this gloomy chamber, shut in from all human communication. But Walter made no attempt to throw open the closed windows. No help from without could avail him, and he had no thought or time to spare for any exertion. He put his candle on the table and sat down to await what should befall.

The night passed like other nights to most men, even to the greater number of the inhabitants in this house. Mrs. Methven after a while, worn out, and capable of nothing that could help him, dozed and slept, half dressed, murmuring familiar prayers in her sleep, ready to start up at the faintest call. But there came no call. Two or three times in the night there was a faint stir, and once old Symington, who was also on the alert, and whose room was near that of his master, saw Lord Erradeen come out of his chamber with a candle in his hand, the light of which showed his countenance all ghastly and furrowed as with the action of years, and go down-stairs. The old man, watching from the gallery above, saw his master go to the door, which he opened, admitting a blast of night wind which seemed to bring in the darkness as well as cold. Symington waited trembling to hear it clang behind the unfortunate young man. Where was he going to in the middle of the night? But after a few minutes, the door, instead of clanging, closed softly, and Walter came back. It might be that this happened more than once while the slow hours crept on, for the watcher, hearing more than there was to hear, thought that there were steps about the house, and vague sounds of voices. But this was all vanity and superstition. No one came in—with none, save with his own thoughts, did Walter speak. Had his enemy entered bodily, and even with maddening words maintained a personal conflict, the sufferer would have been less harshly treated. Once, as Symington had seen, he was so broken down by the conflict that he was on the eve of a shameful flight which would have been ruin. When he came down-stairs with his candle in the dead of the night and opened the great hall door, he had all but thrown down his arms and consented that nothing remained for him but to escape while he could, as long as he could, to break all ties and abandon all succour, and only flee, flee from the intolerable moment. He had said to himself that he could bear it no longer, that he must escape anyhow, at any cost, leaving love and honour, and duty and every higher thought—for what could help him— nothing—nothing—in earth or heaven.

That which touched him to the quick was not any new menace, it was not the horror of the struggles through which he had already passed, it was the mad-

dening derision with which his impulses were represented
to him as the last expedients of the most refined selfishness. When his tormentor in the morning had bidden
him, with a smile, " Be good ! " as the height of policy,
it had seemed to Walter that the point of the intolerable
was reached, and that life itself under such an inter-
pretation became insupportable, a miserable jest, a
mockery hateful to God and man; but there was yet a
lower depth, a more hateful derision still. Love ! what
was his love ? a way of securing help, a means of
obtaining, under pretences of the finest sentiment,
some one who would supremely help him, stand by
him always, protect him with the presence of a nature
purer than his own. Nothing was said to the unhappy
young man. It was in the course of his own thoughts
that this suggestion arose like a light of hell illumin-
ating all the dark corners of his being. Had he ever
said to Oona that he loved her ? Did he love her ?
Was it for any motive but his own safety that he
sought her ? Katie he had sought for her wealth, for
the increase of importance she could bring, for the
relief from torture she could secure to him. And
Oona, Oona whom he loved ! Was it for love he fled
to her ? Oh, no, but for safety ! All was miserable,
all was self, all was for his own interest, to save *him*, to
emancipate him, to make life possible for him. He
had started to his feet when this intolerable consciousness (for was it not true ?) took possession of him. It
was true. She was sweet and fair, and good and lovely,

a creature like the angels; but he, miserable, had thought only that in her company was safety—that she could deliver him. He sent forth a cry which at the same time sounded like the laughter of despair, and seemed to shake the house; and took up his candle, and opened his door and hurried forth to escape, where he did not know, how he did not know nor care, to escape from the ridicule of this life, the horror of this travestie and parody of everything good and fair. Heaven and earth! to seek goodness because it was the most profitable of all things; to seek love because it was safety; to profane everything dear and sacred to his own advantage! Can a man know this, and recognise it with all the masks and pretences torn off, and yet consent to live, and better himself by that last desecration of all! He went down with hurried steps through the silence of his house, that silence through which was rising the prayers of the mother in whose love too he had taken refuge when in despair, whom he had bidden to go and pray, for his advantage, solely for him, that he might steal from God a help he did not deserve, by means of her cries and tears. "And so would Oona," he had said. Oh, mockery of everything sacred!—all for him, for his self-interest, who deserved nothing, who made use of all.

He opened the door, and stood bare-headed, solitary, on the edge of the black and lonely night; behind him life and hope, and torture and misery—before the void, the blank into which the wretched may escape and lose

—if not themselves, that inalienable heritage of woe,
yet their power to harm those who love them. He
loved nobody, it seemed, but for himself—prized nothing
but for himself; held love, honour, goodness, purity,
only as safeguards for his miserable life. Let it go
then, that wretched contemner of all good—disappear
into the blackness of darkness, where God nor man
should be disturbed by its exactions more!

The night was wild with a raving wind that dashed
the tree-tops against the sky, and swept the clouds
before it in flying masses; no moon, no light, gloom
impenetrable below, a pale glimpse of heaven above,
swept by black billows of tumultuous clouds; somewhere in the great gloom, the loch, all invisible, waited
for the steps that might stumble upon its margin; the
profound world of darkness closed over every secret
that might be cast into it. He stood on the threshold
in a momentary pause, forlorn, alone, loosing his hold
of all that he had clung to, to save him. Why should
he be saved who was unworthy? Why trouble earth
or heaven? The passion and the struggle died out of
Walter's soul: a profound sadness took possession of
him; he felt his heart turn trembling within him, now
that he had given up the instinct of self-preservation
which had driven him to her feet—to Oona whom he
loved. God bless her! not for him would be that sweet
companionship, and yet of all things the world con-
tained, was not that the best? Two that should be one.
All that was external died away from him in his despair.

He forgot for the first time since it had been revealed to him, that he had an enemy, a tyrant waiting for his submission. His heart turned to the love which he had thought he dishonoured, without even recollecting that cursed suggestion. It seemed to him now that he was giving it up for Oona's sake, and that only now all the beauty of it, the sweetness of it, was clear to him. Oh, the pity! to see all this so lovely, so fair, and yet have to resign it! What was everything else in comparison with that? But for her sake, for her dear sake!

How dark it was, impenetrable, closing like a door upon the mortal eyes which had in themselves no power to penetrate that gloom! He stepped across the threshold of life, and stood outside, in the dark. He turned his eyes—for once more, for the last time, in the great calm of renunciation, his heart in a hush of supreme anguish, without conflict or struggle—to where she was, separated from him only by silent space and atmosphere, soon to be separated by more perfect barriers; only to turn his head that way, not even to see where she was hidden in the night—so small a satisfaction, so little consolation, yet something before the reign of nothingness began.

All dark; but no, half way between heaven and earth, what was that, shining steady through the gloom? Not a star; it was too warm, too large, too near; the light in Oona's window shining in the middle of the night when all was asleep around. Then she was not

asleep, though everything else was, but watching—and
if watching, then for him. The little light, which was
but a candle in a window, suddenly, brilliantly lighted
up the whole heavens and earth to Walter. Watching,
and for him; praying for him, not because of any appeal
of his, but out of her own heart, and because she so
willed it—out of the prodigality, the generous, un-
measured love which it was her choice to give him—not
forced but freely, because she so pleased. He stood for
a moment with awe in his heart, arrested, not able to
make another step, pale with the revolution, the revelation, the change of all things. His own dark thoughts
died away; he stood astonished, perceiving for the first
time what it was. To have become part of him had
brought no joy to Oona, but it was done, and never
could be undone; and to be part of her, what was that
to Walter? He had said it without knowing what it
meant, without any real sense of the great thing he
said. Now it fell upon him in a great wonder, full of
awe. He was hers, he was *her*, not himself henceforward, but a portion of another, and that other portion
of him standing for him at the gates of heaven. His
whole being fell into silence, overawed. He stepped
back out of the night and closed softly the great door,
and returned to his room, in which everything was
stilled by a spell before which all evil things fly—the
apprehension of that love which is unmerited, unex-
torted, unalterable. When he reached his room, and
had closed the door, Walter, with trembling hands

undid the window, and flung it open to the night, which was no more night or darkness, but part of the everlasting day, so tempered that feeble eyes might perceive those lights which hide themselves in the sunshine. What was it he saw? Up in the heavens, where the clouds swept over them, stars shining, undisturbed, though hidden by moments as the masses of earthly vapour rolled across the sky; near him stealing out of his mother's window a slender ray of light that never wavered; further off, held up as in the very hand of love, the little lamp of Oona. The young man was silent in a great awe; his heart stirring softly in him, hushed, like the heart of a child. For him! unworthy! for him who had never sought the love of God, who had disregarded the love of his mother, who had profaned the love of woman: down, down on his knees—down to the dust, hiding his face in gratitude unutterable. He ceased to think of what it was he had been struggling and contending for; he forgot his enemy, his danger, himself altogether, and, overawed, sank at the feet of love, which alone can save.

CHAPTER XII.

LORD ERRADEEN was found next morning lying on his bed full dressed sleeping like a child. A man in his evening dress in the clear air of morning is at all times a curious spectacle, and suggestive of many uncomfortable thoughts, but there was about Walter as he lay there fast asleep an extreme youthfulness not characteristic of his appearance on ordinary occasions, which made the curious and anxious spectator who bent over him, think instinctively of a child who had cried itself to sleep, and a convalescent recovering from a long illness. Symington did not know which his young master resembled the most. The old man stood and looked at him, with great and almost tender compassion. One of the windows stood wide open admitting the air and sunshine. But it had evidently been open all night, and must have chilled the sleeper through and through. Symington had come at his usual hour to wake Lord Erradeen. But as he looked at him the water came into his eyes. Instead of calling him he covered him carefully with a warm covering, softly closed the window, and left all his usual morning preparations untouched. This done, he went down-stairs to the breakfast-room where Mrs. Methven, too anxious to rest, was already waiting for her son. Symington closed the door behind him and came up to the table which was spread for breakfast.

"My lady," he said, "my lord will no be veesible for some time. I found him sleeping like a bairn, and I had not the heart to disturb him. No doubt he's had a bad night, but if I'm any judge of the human countenance he will wake another man."

"Oh, my poor boy! You did well to let him rest, Symington. I will go up and sit by him."

"If ye will take my advice, my lady, ye will just take a little breakfast; a good cup of tea, and one of our fine fresh eggs, or a bit of trout from the loch; or I would find ye a bonnie bit of the breast of a bird."

"I can eat nothing," she said, "when my son is in trouble."

"Oh, canny, canny, my lady. I am but a servant, but I am one that takes a great interest. He's in no trouble at this present moment; he's just sleeping like a baby, maybe a wee bit worn out, but not a line o' care in his face; just sleepin'—sleepin' like a little bairn. It will do you mair harm than him if I may mak' so bold as to speak. A cup of tea, my lady, just a cup of this fine tea, if nothing else—it will do ye good. And I'll answer for him," said Symington. "I'm well acquaint with all the ways of them," the old servant

added, "if I might venture, madam, to offer a word of
advice, it would be this, just to let him bee."

A year ago Mrs. Methven would have considered this
an extraordinary liberty for a servant to take, and perhaps would have resented the advice; but at that time
she did not know Symington, nor was she involved in
the mysterious circumstances of this strange life. She
received it with a meekness which was not characteristic, and took the cup of tea, which he poured out for
her, with a lump of sugar too much, by way of consolation, and a liberal supply of cream, almost with humility.
"If he is not better when he comes down-stairs, I
think I must send for the doctor, Symington."

"I would not, my lady, if I were you. I would just
watch over him, but let him bee. I would wait for
two or three days and just put up with everything.
The Methvens are no just a race like other folk. Ye
require great judgment to deal with the Methvens.
Ye have not been brought up to it, my lady, like
me."

All this Mrs. Methven received very meekly, and
only gratified herself with a cup of tea which was
palatable to her, after Symington, having done everything he could for her comfort, had withdrawn. She
was very much subdued by the new circumstances in
which she found herself, and felt very lonely and cast
away, as in a strange land where everything was unknown. She sat for a long time by herself, trying to
calm her thoughts by what Symington had said. She

consented that he knew a great deal more than she
did, even of her son in his new position, and had come
to put a sort of infinite faith in him as in an oracle.
But how hard it was to sit still, or to content herself
with looking out upon that unfamiliar prospect, when
her heart was longing to be by her son's bedside !
Better to let him bee !—alas, she knew very well and
had known for long that it was better to let him bee.
But what was there so hard to do as that was ? The
shrubberies that surrounded the window allowed a
glimpse at one side of the loch, cold, but gleaming in
the morning sunshine. It made her shiver, yet it was
beautiful : and as with the landscape, so it was with
her position here. To be with Walter, ready to be of
use to him, whatever happened, that was well; but all
was cold, and solitary, and unknown. Poor mother !
She had loved, and cherished, and cared for him all the
days of his life, and a year since he had scarcely seen
Oona; yet it was Oona's love, and not his mother's,
which had made him understand what love was.
Strange injustice, yet the injustice of nature, against
which it is vain to rebel.

While Mrs. Methven, sad and anxious and perplexed,
sat in the unfamiliar room, and looked on the strange
landscape in which she found no point of sympathy,
Oona in the solitude of the isle, was full of similar
thoughts. The day which had passed so miserably to
Walter had gone over her in that self-repression which
is one of the chief endowments of women, in her

mother's cheerful society, and amid all the little occupations of her ordinary life. She had not ventured to
indulge herself even in thought, unless she had been
prepared, as she was not, to open everything to Mrs.
Forrester—and thus went through the hours in that
active putting aside of herself and her own concerns,
which is sometimes called hypocrisy and sometimes self-
renunciation. She smiled, and talked, and even ate
against her will, that her mother might not take fright
and search into the cause, so that it was not till she
had retired into the refuge of her own room that she
was at liberty to throw herself down in all the abandonment of solitude and weep out the tears which made
her brow heavy, and think out the thoughts with which
her mind was charged almost to bursting. Her candle
burned almost all the night long, until long after the
moment in which the sight of it held Walter back from
the wild flight from her and everything to which his
maddening thoughts had almost driven him.

The conflict in Oona's mind was longer, if not so
violent. With an effort she was able to dismiss herself
from the consideration, and with that entire sympathy
which may mistake the facts but never the intention,
to enter into the mind of her lover. There was much
that she could not understand, and did not attempt to
fathom, and the process was not one of those that bring
happiness, as when a woman, half-adoring, follows in
her own exalted imagination the high career of the
hero whom she loves. Walter was no hero, and Oona

no simple worshipper to be beguiled into that deification. She had to account to herself for the wanderings, the contradictions, the downfalls of a man of whom she could not think, as had been the first impulse of pain, that any woman would satisfy him, that Katie or Oona, it did not matter which—but who it was yet true had offered himself to Katie first, had given himself to vice (as she remembered with a shudder) first of all, and had been roaming wildly through life without purpose or hope. In all the absolutism of youth to know this, and yet to recognise that the soul within may not be corrupt, and that there may be still an agony of longing for the true even in the midst of the false, is difficult indeed. She achieved it, but it was not a happy effort. Bit by bit it became clearer to her. Had she known the character of the interview with Katie, which gave her grievous pain even when she reasoned it out and said to herself that she understood it, the task would have been a little less hard : but it was hard and very bitter, by moments almost more than she could bear. As she sat by the dying fire, with her light shining so steadily, like a little Pharos of love and steadfastness, her mind went through many faintings and moments of darkness. To have to perceive and acknowledge that you have given your heart and joined your life to that of a man who is no hero, one in whom you cannot always trust that his impulses will be right, is a discovery which is often made in after life, but by degrees, and so gently, so imperceptibly, that love suffers but little shock. But to make this discovery at the very outset is far more terrible than any other obstacle that can stand in the way. Oona was compelled to face it from the first moment almost of a union which she felt in herself no possibility of breaking. She had given herself, and she could not withdraw the gift any more than she could separate from him the love which long before she had been betrayed, she knew not how, into bestowing upon him unasked, undesired, to her own pain and shame.

As she sat all through the night and felt the cold steal upon her, into her very heart, and the desolation of the darkness cover her while she pondered, she was aware that this love had never failed, and knew that to abandon him was no more possible to her than if she had been his wife for years. The girl had come suddenly, without warning, without any fault of hers, out of her innocence and lightheartedness, into the midst of the most terrible problem of life. To love yet not approve, to know that the being who is part of you is not like you, has tendencies which are hateful to you, and a hundred imperfections which the subtlest casuistry of love cannot justify—what terrible fate is this, that a woman should fall into it unawares and be unable to free herself? Oona did not think of freeing herself at all. It did not occur to her as a possibility. How she was to bear his burden which was hers, how she was to reconcile herself to his being as it was, or help the good in him to development, and struggle with him against the evil, that was her problem. Love is often tested in

song and story by the ordeal of a horrible accusation
brought against the innocent, whom those who love
him, knowing his nature, stand by through all disgrace,
knowing that he cannot be guilty, and maintaining his
cause in the face of all seeming proof. How light, how
easy, what an elementary lesson of affection! But to
have no such confidence, to take up the defence of the
sinner who offends no one so much as yourself, to know
that the accusations are true—that is the ordeal by fire,
which the foolish believe to be abolished in our mild
and easy days. Oona saw it before her, realised it, and
made up her mind to it solemnly during that night of
awe and pain. This was her portion in the world : not
simple life and happiness, chequered only with shadows
from terrible death and misfortune, such as may befall
the righteous, but miseries far other, far different, to
which misfortune and death are but easy experiments
in the way of suffering. This was to be her lot.

And yet love is so sweet ! She slept towards morning, as Walter did, and when she woke, woke to a sense
of happiness so exquisite and tender that her soul was
astonished and asked why in an outburst of gratitude
and praise to God. And it was not till afterwards that
the burden and all the darkness came back to her. But
that moment perhaps was worth the pain of the other
—one of those compensations, invisible to men, with
which God still comforts His martyrs. She rose from her
bed and came back to life with a face full of new gravity
and thoughtfulness, yet lit up with smiles. Even Mrs.

Forrester, who had seen nothing and suspected nothing on the previous night except that Oona had perhaps taken a chill, felt, though she scarcely understood, a something in her face which was beyond the ordinary level of life. She remarked to Mysie, after breakfast, that she was much relieved to see that Miss Oona's cold was to have no bad result. " For I think she is looking just bonnier than usual this morning—if it is not my partiality—like a spring morning," Mrs. Forrester said.

" Ah mem, and mair than that," said Mysie. " God bless her ! She is looking as I have seen her look the Sabbath of the Sacrament ; for she's no like the like of us, just hardened baith to good and evil, but a' in a tremble for sorrow and joy, when the occasion comes round."

" I hope we are not hardened," said Mrs. Forrester ; " but I know what you mean, Mysie, though you cannot perhaps express it like an educated person ; and I was afraid that she was taking one of her bad colds, and that we should be obliged to put off our visit to Mrs. Methven—which would have been a great pity, for I had promised to Lord Erradeen."

" Do ye not think, mem," said Mysie, " that yon young lord he is very much taken up with—the isle and those that are on it ? "

" Hoots," said Mrs. Forrester, with a smile, " with you and me, Mysie, do you think ? But that might well be after all, for I would not wonder but he felt more at home with the like of us, that have had so much to do with boys and young men, and all the ways of them. And you know I have always said he was like Mr. Rob, which has warmed my heart to him from the very first day."

Perhaps the mother was, no more than Mysie, inclined to think that she and her old maid won the young lord's attention to the isle: but a woman who is a girl's mother, however simple she may be, has certain innocent wiles in this particular. Lord Erradeen would be a great match for any other young lady on the loch, no doubt: but for Oona what prince was good enough? They both thought so, yet not without a little flutter of their hearts at the new idea which began to dawn.

It was once more a perfectly serene and beautiful day, a day that was like Oona's face, adapted to that "Sabbath of the Sacrament" which is so great a festival in rural Scotland, and brings all the distant dwellers out of the glens and villages. About noon, when the sun was at its height, and the last leaves on the trees seemed to reflect in their red and yellow, and return, a dazzling response to his shining, Hamish, busy about his fishing tackle on the beach, perceived a boat with a solitary rower, slowly rounding the leafy corners, making a circuit of the isle. Hamish was in no doubt as to the rower; he knew everything as well as the two who were most closely concerned. His brow, which for the last twenty-four hours had been full of furrows, gradually began to melt out of those deep-drawn lines, his shaggy

eyebrows smoothed out, his mouth began to soften at
the corners. There was much that was mysterious in
the whole matter, and Hamish had not been able to
account to himself for the change in the young pair
who had stepped out of his boat on to the isle in an
ecstacy of happiness, and had returned sombre, under
the shadow of some sudden estrangement which he
could not understand. Neither could he understand
why it was that the young lord hovered about without
attempting to land at the isle. This was so unlike the
usual custom of lovers, that not even the easy explanation, half-contemptuous, half-respectful, which the
habits of the masters furnish to their servants, of every
eccentricity, answered the occasion—and Hamish could
not but feel that there was something "out of the
ordinary" in the proceeding. But his perplexity on
this subject did not diminish his satisfaction in perceiving that the young lord was perfectly capable of
managing his boat, and that no trace of the excitement
of the previous day was visible in its regular motion,
impelled now and then by a single stroke, floating on
the sunny surface of the water within sight of the red
roofs and shining windows of the house, and kept in its
course out of the way of all rocks and projecting corners
by a skill which could not, Hamish felt sure, be
possessed by a disordered brain. This solaced him
beyond telling, for though he had not said a word to
any one, not even to Mysie, it had lain heavily upon his
heart that Miss Oona might be about to link her life to

that of a daft man.   She that was good enough for any
king ! and what were the Erradeens to make so muckle
work about, but just a mad race that nobody could
understand ?   And the late lord had been one that
could not hold an oar to save his life, nor yet yon Under-
wood-man that was his chosen crony.   But this lad was
different !   Oh ! there was no doubt that there was a
great difference ; just one easy touch and he was clear
of the stanes yonder, that made so little show under the
water—and there was that shallow bit where he would
get aground if he didna mind ; but again a touch and
that difficulty too was cleared.   It was so well done
that the heart of Hamish melted altogether into softness.   And then he began to take pity upon this
modest lover.   He put his hands to his mouth and
gave forth a mild roar which was not more than a
whisper in kind intention.

" The leddies are at home, and will ye no land, my
lord ? " Hamish cried.

Lord Erradeen shook his head, and sent his boat soft
gliding into a little bay under the overhanging trees.

" Hamish," he said, " you can tell me.   Are they
coming to-day to Auchnasheen ? "

" At half-past two, my lord," breathed Hamish through
his curved hands, " they'll be taking the water : and it's
just Miss Oona herself that has given me my orders :
and as I was saying, they could not have a bonnier day."

It seemed to Hamish that the young lord said
" Thank God ! " which was perhaps too much for the

occasion, and just a thocht profane in the circumstances; but a lord that is in love, no doubt there will be much forgiven to him so long as he has a true heart. The sunshine caught Hamish as he stood watching the boat which floated along the shining surface of the water like something beatified, an emblem of divine ease, and pleasure, and calm, and made his face shine too like the loch, and his red shirt glow. His good heart glowed too with humble and generous joy; they were going to be happy then, these Two; no that he was good enough for Miss Oona; but who was good enough for Miss Oona? The faithful fellow drew his rough hand across his eyes. He who had rowed her about the loch since she was a child, and attended every coming and going —he knew it would be "a sair loss," a loss never to be made up. But then so long as she was pleased!

At half-past two they started, punctual as Mrs. Forrester always was. Every event of this day was so important that it was remembered after how exact they were to the minute, and in what a glory of sunshine Loch Houran lay as they pushed out, Mysie standing on the beach to watch them, and lending a hand herself to launch the boat. Mrs. Forrester was well wrapped in her fur cloak with a white "cloud" about her head and shoulders, which she declared was not at all necessary in the sunshine which was like summer.

"It is just a June day come astray," she said, nodding and smiling to Mysie on the beach, who thought once more of the Sacrament-day with its subdued glory and awe, and all the pacifying influence that dwelt in it. And Oona turned back to make a little friendly sign with hand and head to Mysie, as the first stroke of the oars carried the boat away.

How sweet her face was; how tender her smile and bright! more sorrowful than mirthful, like one who has been thinking of life and death, but full of celestial and tender cheer, and a subdued happiness. Mysie stood long looking after them, and listening to their voices which came soft and musical over the water. She could not have told why the tears came to her eyes. Something was about to happen, which would be joyful yet would be sad. "None of us will stand in her way," said Mysie to herself, unconscious of any possibility that she, the faithful servant of the house, might be supposed to have no say in the matter; "oh, not one of us! but what will the isle be with Miss Oona away!"

CHAPTER XIII.

MRS. METHVEN had time to recover from the agitation and trouble of the morning before her visitors' arrival. Walter's aspect had so much changed when he appeared that her fears were calmed, though not dispelled. He was very pale, and had an air of exhaustion, to which his softened manners and evident endeavour to please her gave an almost pathetic aspect. Her heart was touched, as it is easy to touch the heart of a mother. She had watched him go out in his boat with a faint awakening of that pleasure with which in ordinary circumstances a woman in the retirement of age sees her children go out to their pleasure. It gave her a satisfaction full of relief, and a sense of escape from evils which she had feared, without knowing what she feared, to watch the lessening speck of the boat, and to feel that her son was finding consolation in natural and uncontaminated pleasures, in the pure air and sky and sunshine of the morning. When he came back he was a little less pale, though still strangely subdued and softened. He told her that she was about to receive a visit from his nearest neighbours—"the young lady," he added, after a pause, "who brought you across the loch."

"Miss Forrester—and her mother, no doubt? I shall be glad to see them, Walter."

"I hope so, mother—for there is no way in which you can do me so much good."

"You mean—this is the lady of whom you spoke to me—" Her countenance fell a little, for what he had said to her was not reassuring; he had spoken of one who would bring money with her, but who was not the best.

"No, mother; I have never told you what I did yesterday. I asked that—lady of whom I spoke—to give me her money and her lands to add to mine, and she would not. She was very right. I approved of her with all my heart."

"Walter! my dear, you have been so—well—and so —like yourself this morning. Do not fall into that wild way of speaking again."

"No," he said, "if all goes well—never again if all goes well;" and with this strange speech he left her not knowing what to think. She endeavoured to recall to her memory the half-seen face which had been by her side crossing the dark water: but all the circumstances had been so strange, and the loch itself had given such a sensation of alarm and trouble to the traveller, that everything was dim like the twilight in her recollection. A soft voice, with the unfamiliar

accent of the north, a courteous and pleasant frankness
of accost, a strange sense of thus encountering, half-
unseen, some one who was no stranger, nor unimportant
in her life—these were the impressions she had brought
out of the meeting. In all things this poor lady was
like a stranger suddenly introduced into a world unknown to her, where great matters, concerning her
happiness and very existence, were hanging upon
mysterious decisions of others, unknown, and but to be
guessed at faintly through a strange language and
amidst allusions which conveyed no meaning to her
mind. Thus she sat wondering, waiting for the coming
of—she could scarcely tell whom—of some one with
whom she could do more good for Walter than by anything else, yet who was not the lady to whom he had
offered himself only yesterday. Could there be any
combination more confusing? And when, amid all this
mystery, as she sat with her heart full of tremulous
questions and fears, there came suddenly into this
darkling, uncomprehended world of hers the soft and
smiling certainty of Mrs. Forrester, kind and simple,
and full of innocent affectations, with her little airs of
an old beauty, and her amiable confidence in everybody's
knowledge and interest, Mrs. Methven had nearly
laughed aloud with that keen sense of mingled disappointment and relief which throws a certain ridicule
upon such a scene. The sweet gravity of Oona behind
was but a second impression. The first was of this
simple, easy flood of kind and courteous commonplace,

which changed at once the atmosphere and meaning of
the scene.

"We are all very glad upon the loch to hear that
Lord Erradeen has got his mother with him," said the
guileless visitor, "for everything is the better of a lady
in the house. Oh, yes, you will say, that is a woman's
opinion, making the most of her own side : but you
just know very well it is true. We have not seen half
so much of Lord Erradeen as we would have liked—for
in my circumstances we have very little in our power.
No gentleman in the house ; and what can two ladies
do to entertain a young man, unless he will be content
with his tea in the afternoon ? and that is little to ask
a gentleman to. However, I must say all the neighbours are very good-natured, and just accept what we
have got to give."

"Your daughter was most kind to me when I arrived,"
said Mrs. Methven. "I should have felt very lonely
without her help."

"That was nothing. It was just a great pleasure to
Oona, who is on the loch from morning to night," said
Mrs. Forrester. "It was a great chance for her to be
of use. We have little happening here, and the news
was a little bit of excitement for us all. You see,
though I have boys of my own, they are all of them
away—what would they do here ?—one in Canada, and
one in Australia, and three, as I need not say, in India
—that is where all our boys go—and doing very well,
which is just all that heart can desire. It has been a

pleasure from the beginning that Lord Erradeen reminds
me so much of my Rob, who is now up with his regiment in the north-west provinces, and a very promising
young officer, though perhaps it is not me that should
say so. The complexion is different, but I have always
seen a great likeness. And now, Lord Erradeen, I hope
you will bring Mrs. Methven soon, as long as the fine
weather lasts, to the isle ? "

Mrs. Methven made a little civil speech about taking
the first opportunity, but added, " I have seen nothing
yet—not even this old castle of which I have heard so
much."

" It is looking beautiful this afternoon, and I have
not been there myself, I may say, for years," said Mrs.
Forrester. " What would you say, as it is so fine, to
trust yourself to Hamish, who is just the most careful
man with a boat on all the loch, and take a turn as far
as Kinloch Houran with Oona and me ? "

The suggestion was thrown out very lightly, with
that desire to do something for the pleasure of the
stranger, which was always so strong in Mrs. Forrester's
breast. She would have liked to supplement it with a
proposal to " come home by the isle " and take a cup of
tea, but refrained for the moment with great self-denial.
It was caught at eagerly by Walter, who had not known
how to introduce his mother to the sight of the mystic
place which had so much to do with his recent history :
and in a very short time they were all afloat—Mrs.
Methven, half-pleased, half-disappointed with the sudden

changing of all graver thoughts and alarms into the
simplicity of a party of pleasure, so natural, so easy.
The loch was radiant with that glory of the afternoon
which is not like the glory of the morning, a dazzling
world of light, the sunbeams falling lower every moment,
melting into the water, which showed all its ripples
like molten gold. The old tower lay red in the light,
the few green leaves that still fluttered on the ends of
the branches, standing out against the darker background, and the glory of the western illumination beset-
ting every dark corner of the broken walls as if to take
them by joyful assault and triumph over every idea of
gloom. Nothing could have been more peaceful than
the appearance of this group. The two elder ladies sat
in the stern of the boat, carrying on their tranquil
conversation—Mrs. Forrester entering well pleased into
details about "the boys," which Mrs. Methven, surprised, amused, arrested somehow, she could not tell
how, in the midst of the darker, more bewildering
current, responded to now and then with some half-
question, enough to carry on the innocent fulness of the
narrative. Oona, who had scarcely spoken at all, and
who was glad to be left to her own thoughts, sat by her
mother's side, with the eyes of the other mother often
upon her, yet taking no part in the talk; while Walter,
placed behind Hamish at the other end of the boat, felt
this strange pause of all sensation to be something
providential, something beyond all his power of arrang-
ing, the preface to he knew not what, but surely at

least not to any cutting off or separation from Oona.
She had not indeed met his anxious and questioning
looks : but she had not refused to come, and that of
itself was much; nor did there seem to be any anger,
though some sadness, in the face which seemed to him,
as to Mysie, full of sacred light.

"No, I have not been here for long," said Mrs.
Forrester; "not since the late lord's time : but I see
very little change. If you will come this way, Mrs.
Methven, it is here you will get the best view. Yon is
the tower upon which the light is seen, the light, ye
will have heard, that calls every new lord : oh and that
comes many a time when there is no new lord : You
need not bid me whisht, Oona! No doubt there will
be some explanation of it : but it is a thing that all the
world knows."

Mrs. Methven laughed, more at her ease than she
had yet been, and said—

"Walter, what a terrible omission : you have never
told me of this."

Walter did not laugh. His face, on the contrary,
assumed the look of gloom and displeasure which she
knew so well.

"If you will come with me," he said to Mrs. Forrester,
"I will show you my rooms. Old Macalister is more
gracious than usual. You see he has opened the door."

"Oh I will go with great pleasure, Lord Erradeen :
for it is long since I have been inside, and I would like
to see your rooms. Oh how do you do, Macalister ? I

hope your wife and you are quite well, and not suffering with rheumatism. We've come to show Mrs. Methven, that is your master's mother, round the place. Yes, I am sure ye will all be very glad to see her. This is Macalister, a very faithful old servant that has been with the Lords Erradeen as long as I can remember. How long is it—near five and forty years? Dear me, it is just wonderful how time runs on. I was then but lately married, and never thought I would ever live like a pelican in the wilderness in my mother's little bit isle. But your mind just is made to your fortune, and I have had many a happy day there. Dear me, it will be very interesting to see the rooms, we that never thought there were any rooms. Where is Oona? Oh, never take the trouble, Lord Erradeen, your mother is waiting : and Oona, that knows every step of the castle, she will soon find her way."

This was how it was that Oona found herself alone. Walter cast behind him an anxious look, but he could not desert the elder ladies, and Oona was glad to be left behind. Her mind had recovered its calm; but she had much to think of, and his presence disturbed her, with that influence of personal contact which interferes with thought. She knew the old castle, if not every step of it, as her mother said, yet enough to make it perfectly safe for her. Old Macalister had gone first to lead the way, to open doors and windows, that the ladies might see everything, and, save for Hamish in his boat on the beach, there was nobody within sight or call. The shadow of the old house shut out the sunshine from the little platform in front of the door; but at the further side, where the trees grew among the broken masses of the ruin, the sun from the west entered freely. She stood for a moment undecided, then turned towards that wild conjunction of the living and the dead, the relics of the past, and the fresh growth of nature, which give so much charm to every ruin. Oona went slowly, full of thought, up to the battlements, and looked out upon the familiar landscape, full of light and freshness, and·all the natural sounds of the golden afternoon—the lapping of the water upon the rocks, the rustle of the wind in the trees, the far-off murmurs of life, voices cheerful, yet inarticulate, from the village, distant sounds of horses and wheels on the unseen roads, the bark of a dog, all the easy, honest utterance, unthought of, like simple breathing, of common life. For a moment the voice of her own thoughts was hushed within her, replaced by this soft combination of friendly noises. It pleased her better to stand here with the soft air about her, than amid all the agitation of human influences to accompany the others.

But human influence is more strong than the hold of nature; and by-and-by she turned unconsciously from the landscape to the house, the one dark solid mass of habitable walls, repelling the sunshine, while the tower, with its blunted outline above, and all the fantastic breaches and openings in the ruin, gave full play to every level ray. The loch, all golden with the sunset,

the shadows of the trees, the breath and utterance of distant life, gave nothing but refreshment and soothing.
But the walls that were the work of men, and that for
hundreds of years had gathered sombre memories about
them, had an attraction more absorbing. A little
beyond where she was standing, was the spot from
which Miss Milnathort had fallen. She had heard the
story vaguely all her life, and she had heard from
Walter the meaning of it, only the other day. Perhaps
it was the sound of a little crumbling and precipitation
of dust and fragments from the further wall that brought
it so suddenly to her memory; but the circumstances in
which she herself was, were enough to bring those of the
other woman, who had been as herself, before her with
all the vividness of reality. As young as herself, and
more happy, the promised bride of another Walter,
everything before her as before Oona, love and life, the
best that Providence can give, more happy than she,
nothing to disturb the gladness of her betrothal; and
in a moment all over, all ended, and pain and helplessness, and the shadow of death, substituted for her happiness and hope. Oona paused, and thought of that
tragedy with a great awe stealing over her, and pity
which was so intense in her realisation of a story, in
every point save the catastrophe, so like her own, penetrating her very soul. She asked herself which of the
two it was who had suffered most—the faithful woman
who lived to tell her own story, and to smile with celestial patience through her death in life, or the man who

had struggled in vain, who had fallen under the hand of
fate, and obeyed the power of outward circumstances,
and been vanquished, and departed from the higher
meaning of his youth ?   Oona thought with a swelling
and generous throbbing of her heart, of the one—but
with a deeper pang of the other; he who had not failed
at all so far as any one knew, who had lived and been
happy as people say.   She leant against the wall, and
asked herself if anything should befall her, such as
befell Miss Milnathort, whether her Walter would do
the same.   Would he accept his defeat as the other
had done, and throw down his arms and yield?   She
said no in her heart, but faltered, and remembered
Katie.   Yet no !   That had been before, not after their
hearts had met, and he had known what was in hers.
No, he might be beaten down to the dust; he might
rush out into the world, and plunge into the madness
of life, or he might plunge more deeply, more darkly,
into the madness of despairing, and die.   But he would
not yield; he would not throw down his arms and
accept the will of the other.   Faulty as he was, and
stained and prone to evil, this was what he would
never do.

And then her thoughts turned to the immediate
matter before her—the deliverance of the man whose
fate she had pledged herself to share notwithstanding
all his imperfections; he who had found means already,
since she had bound herself to him, to make her heart
bleed; he whom she had loved against her will, against

her judgment, before she was aware. He was to be made free from a bondage, a spiritual persecution, a tyrant who threatened him in every action of his life. Oona had known all her life that there was some mysterious oppression under which the house of Erradeen was bound, and there was no scepticism in her mind in respect to a wonder about which every inhabitant of the district had something to say; but from the moment when it became apparent that she too was to belong to this fated house, it had become insupportable and impossible. She felt, but with less agitation and a calmer certainty than that of Walter, that by whatsoever means it must be brought to an end. Had he been able to bear it, she could not have borne it. And he said that she alone could save him—that with her by his side he was safe; strange words, containing a flattery which was not intended, a claim which could not be resisted. He had said it when as yet he scarcely knew her, he had repeated it when he came to her hot from the presence of the other to whom he had appealed in vain. Strange mixture of the sweet and the bitter! She remembered, however, that he had asked her in the simplicity of desperation to give him her hand to help him, a year ago, and this thought banished all the other circumstances from her mind. She had helped him then, knowing nothing—how was she to help him now? Could she but do it by standing forth in his place and meeting his enemy for him! could she but take his burden on her shoulders and carry it for him!

He who had suffered so much feared with a deadly terror his oppressor; but Oona did not fear him. On her he had no power. In Walter's mind there was the weakness of previous defeat, the tradition of family subjection; but in her there was no such weakness, either personal or traditionary; and what was the use of her innocence, of her courage, if not to be used in his cause? Could she but stand for him, speak for him, take his place!

> " Up and spoke she, Alice Brand,
>   And made the holy sign;
> And if there's blood on Richard's hand,
>   A stainless hand is mine."

Oona's heart was full of this high thought. It drove away from her mind all shadows, all recollections of a less exalting kind. She moved on quietly, not caring nor thinking where she went, forming within herself visions of this substitution, which is in so many cases a woman's warmest desire.

But then she paused, and there became visible to her a still higher eminence of generous love—a higher giddy eminence, more precarious, more dangerous, by which deliverance was less secure; not substitution— that was impossible. In her inward thoughts she blushed to feel that she had thought of a way of escape which for Walter would have been ignoble. It was for him to bear his own part, not to stand by while another did it for him. A noble shame took possession of her that she could for a moment have conceived another way. But with this came back all the anxious thoughts, the questions, the uncertainty. How was she to help him? how pour all the force of her life into him? how transfer to him every needed quality, and give him the strength of two in one?

In the full current of her thoughts Oona was suddenly brought to a pause. It was by the instinct of self-preservation which made her start back on the very edge of the ruin. The sickening sensation with which she felt the crumbling masonry move beneath her foot, drove everything out of her mind for the moment. With a sudden recoil upon herself, Oona set her back against the edge of the parapet that remained, and endeavoured to command and combat the sudden terror that seized hold upon her. She cast a keen wild look round her to find out if there was any way of safety, and called out for help, and upon Walter! Walter! though she felt it was vain. The wind was against her, and caught her voice, carrying it as if in mockery down the loch, from whence it returned only in a vague and distant echo; and she perceived that the hope of any one hearing and reaching her was futile indeed. Above her, on a range of ruin always considered inaccessible, there seemed to Oona a line of masonry solid enough to give her footing. Necessity cannot wait for precedents. She was young and active, and used to exercise, and her nerves were steadied by the strain of actual danger. She made a spring from her insecure standing, feeling the ruin give way under her foot with the impulse, and with the

giddiness of a venture which was almost desperate, flung
herself upon the higher level. When she had got there,
it seemed to her incredible that she could have done it:
and what was to be her next step she knew not, for the
ledge on which she stood was very narrow, and there
was nothing to hold by in case her head or courage
should fail. Everything below and around was shapeless ruin, not to be trusted, all honeycombed, with
hollow places thinly covered over by remains of fallen
roofs and drifted earth and treacherous vegetation.
Only in one direction was there any appearance of
solidity, and that was above her towards the tower
which still stood firmly, the crown of the building,
though no one had climbed up to its mysterious heights
within the memory of man. Round it was a stone
balcony or terrace, which was the spot upon which the
mysterious light, so familiar to her, was periodically
visible. Oona's heart beat as she saw herself within
reach of this spot. She had watched it so often from
the safe and peaceful isle, with that thrill of awe, and
wonder, and half-terror, which gave an additional pleasure to her own complete and perfect safety. She made
a few steps forward, and, putting out her hand with a
quiver of all her nerves, took hold upon the cold roughness of the lower ledge. The touch steadied her, yet
woke an agitation in her frame, the stir of strong excitement; for death lay below her, and her only refuge
was in the very home of mystery, a spot untrodden of
men. For the next few minutes she made her way

instinctively without thought, holding by every projection which presented itself; but when Oona found
herself standing safe within the balustrade, close upon
the wall of the tower, and had drawn breath and recovered a little from the exhaustion and strain—when
her mind got again the upper hand and disentangled
itself from the agitation of the body, the hurry and
whirl of all her thoughts were beyond description. She
paused as upon the threshold of a new world. What
might be about to happen to her? not to perish like
the other, which seemed so likely a few minutes ago,
yet perhaps as tragic a fate ; perhaps the doom of all
connected with the Methvens was here awaiting her.

But there is something in every extreme which dis-
poses the capricious human soul to revolt and recoil.
Oona still spoke to herself, but spoke aloud, as it was
some comfort to do in her utter isolation. She laughed
to herself, nature forcing its way through awe and alarm.
"Doom!" she said to herself, "there is no doom. That
would mean that God was no longer over all. What
He wills let that be done." This calmed her nerves
and imagination. She did not stop to say any prayer
for her own safety. There arose even in her mind upon
the very foundation of her momentary panic, a sudden
new force and hope. She who had so desired to stand
in Walter's place, to be his substitute, might not this,
without any plan or intention of hers, be now placed
within her power ?

In the mean time everything was solid and safe

beneath her feet. The tower stood strong, the pavement of the narrow platform which surrounded it was worn by time and weather, but perfectly secure. Here and there a breach in the balustrade showed like fantastic flamboyant work, but a regiment might have marched round it without disturbing a stone. Oona's excitement was extreme. Her heart beat in her ears like the roaring of a torrent. She went on, raised beyond herself, with a strange conviction that there was some object in her coming, and that this which seemed so accidental was no accident at all, but perhaps —how could she tell?—an ordeal, the first step in that career which she had accepted. She put her hand upon the wall, and guided herself by it, feeling a support in the rough and time-worn surface, the stones which had borne the assault of ages. Daylight was still bright around her, the last rays of the sun dazzling the loch below, which in its turn lent a glory of reflection to the sky above, and sent up a golden sheen through the air from the blaze upon the water. Round the corner of the tower the wind blew freshly in her face from the hills, reviving and encouraging her. Nature was on her side in all its frankness and reality whatever mystery might be elsewhere. When she had turned the corner of the tower, and saw beneath her the roofs of Auchnasheen visible among the trees, Oona suddenly stood still, her heart making, she thought, a pause as well as her feet; then with a bound beginning again in louder and louder pulsation. She had come to a doorway deep set

in the wall, like the entrance of a cavern, with one
broad, much-worn step, and a heavy old door bound
and studded with iron. She stood for a moment uncertain, trembling, with a sense of the unforeseen and
extraordinary which flew to her brain—a bewildering
pang of sensation. For a moment she hesitated what
to do : yet scarcely for a moment, since by this time
she began to feel the force of an impulse which did not
seem her own, and which she had no strength to resist.
The door was slightly ajar, and pushing it open, Oona
found herself, with another suffocating pause, then
bound, of her heart, upon the threshold of a richly
furnished room. She was aware of keeping her hold
upon the door with a terrifying anticipation of hearing
it close upon her, but otherwise seemed to herself to
have passed beyond her own control and consciousness,
and to be aware only of the wonderful scene before her.
The room was lighted from an opening in the roof,
which showed in the upper part the rough stone of the
walls in great blocks, rudely hewn, contrasting strangely
with the heavy curtains with which they were hung
round below. The curtains seemed of velvet, with
panels of tapestry in dim designs here and there : the
floor was covered with thick and soft carpets. A great
telescope occupied a place in the centre of the room,
and various fine instruments, some looking like astro-
nomical models, stood on tables about. The curtained
walls were hung with portraits, one of which she
recognised as that of the last Lord Erradeen. And in

the centre of all supported on a table with a lamp burning in front of it, the light of which (she supposed),
blown about by the sudden entrance of the air, so
flickered upon the face that the features seemed to
change and move, was the portrait of Walter. The cry
which she would have uttered at this sight died in
Oona's throat. She stood speechless, without power to
think, gazing, conscious that this discovery was not for
nothing, that here was something she must do, but
unable to form a thought. The light fell upon the
subdued colours of the hangings and furniture with a
mystic paleness, without warmth; but the atmosphere
was luxurious and soft, with a faint fragrance in it.
Oona held open the door, which seemed in the movement of the air which she had admitted, to struggle
with her, but to which she held with a desperate grasp,
and gazed spellbound. Was it the flickering of the
lamp, or was it possible that the face of the portrait
changed, that anguish came into the features, and that
the eyes turned and looked at her appealing, full of
misery, as Walter's eyes had looked? It seemed to
Oona that her senses began to fail her. There was a
movement in the tapestry, and from the other side of
the room, some one put it aside, and after looking at
her for a moment came slowly out. She had seen him
only in the night and darkness, but there was not
another such that she should mistake who it was. A
thrill ran through her of terror, desperation, and daring.
Whatever might now be done or said, Oona had come
to the crisis of her fate.

He came towards her with the air of courtesy and grace, which seemed his most characteristic aspect. " Come in," he said; " to reach this place requires a stout heart; but you are safe here."

Oona made him no reply. She felt her voice and almost her breathing arrested in her throat, and felt capable of nothing but to hold fast to the heavy door, which seemed to struggle with her like a living thing.

" You are afraid," he said; " but there is no reason to fear. Why should you think I would injure you ? You might have fallen, like others, from the ruin; but you are safe here."

He advanced another step and held out his hand. It seemed to Oona that the door crushed her as she stood against it, but she would not let go her hold; and with all her power she struggled to regain possession of her voice, but could not, paralysed by some force which she did not understand.

He smiled with a slight ridicule in his lofty polite-ness. " I tell you not to fear," he said. " Yours is not a spirit to fear; you who would have put yourself in his place and defied the demon. You find me no demon, and I offer no hostility, yet you are afraid."

Oona was astonished by the sound of her own voice, which burst forth suddenly, by no apparent will of her own, and which was strange to her, an unfamiliar tone, " I am not afraid—I am in—the protection of God—"

He laughed softly. " You mean to exorcise me," he said; " but that is not so easily done; and I warn you that resistance is not the best way. You have trusted yourself to me—"

" No—no—"

" Yes. You fled from the danger to which another in your place succumbed, and you have taken refuge with me. To those who do so I am bound. Come in; there is no danger here."

It seemed to Oona that there were two beings in her —one which ridiculed her distrust, which would have accepted the hand held out; another—not her, surely, not her frank and unsuspicious self—who held back and clung in terror to the door. She stammered, hearing even in her voice the same conflict, some tones that were her own, some shrill that were not hers—" I want no protection—but God's."

" Why then," he said with a smile, " did you not remain among the ruins ? What brought you here ? "

There was an answer—a good answer if she could have found it—but she could not find it, and made no reply.

" You refuse my friendship, then," he said, " which is a pity, for it might have saved you much suffering. All the same, I congratulate you upon your prize."

These last words stopped the current towards him of that natural sentiment of confidence and faith in her fellow-creatures, which was Oona's very atmosphere. Her prize ! What did he mean by her prize ?

" There could not be anything more satisfactory to your friends," he said. " A title—large estates—a

position which leaves nothing to be desired. Your mother
must be fully satisfied, and your brothers at the ends of
the world will all feel the advantage. Other conquests
might have been better for the Erradeens, but for you
nothing could be more brilliant. It was a chance too,
unlikely, almost past hoping for, thus to catch a heart
in the rebound."

She stood aghast, gazing with eyes that were pained
by the strain, but which would not detach themselves from his face. Brilliant! advantages! Was
she in a dream? or what was the meaning of the
words?

"It is against my own policy," he continued, "as
perhaps you know; still I cannot help admiring your
skill, unaided, against every drawback. You have a
strong mind, young lady of the isle, and the antecedents
which would have daunted most women have been allies
and auxiliaries to you." His laugh was quite soft and
pleasant, sounding like gentle amusement, not ridicule.
"I know your family," he continued, "of old. They
were all men of strong stomachs, able to swallow much
so long as their own interest was concerned. With
Highland caterans, that is comprehensible; but one so
young as you—named like you—after—" he laughed
again that low soft laugh of amusement as if at something which tickled him in spite of himself, "the
emblem of purity and innocence—'heavenly Una with
her milk-white lamb.'"

"You want," said Oona, whose voice sounded hoarse

in her throat, and sharp to her own ears, "to make me mad with your taunts; to make me give up—"

"Pardon me, I am only congratulating you," he said, and smiled, looking at her with a penetrating look of amusement and that veiled ridicule which does not infringe the outward forms of politeness. She gazed back at him with eyes wide open, with such a pang of wondering anguish and shame in her heart as left her speechless; for what he said was true. She had thought of her union with Walter in many ways before, but never in this. Now it all flashed upon her as by a sudden light. What he said was true. She who had never given a thought to worldly advantage, had nevertheless secured it as much as if that had been her only thought. Her senses seemed to fail her in the whirl and heart-sickness of the revelation. It was true. She who had believed herself to be giving all, she was taking to herself rank, wealth, and honour, in marrying Walter. And giving to him what?—a woman's empty hand; no more. Oona was very proud though she did not know it, and the blow fell upon her with crushing effect. Every word had truth in it; her mother would be satisfied; the family would profit by it wherever they were scattered; and she would be the first to reap the advantage.

Oona felt everything swim around her as in the whirl and giddiness of a great fall. Her fall was greater than that of Miss Milnathort, for it was the spirit not the body that was crushed and broken. She could not lift

up her head. A horrible doubt even of herself came
into her mind in her sudden and deep humiliation.
Had this been in her thoughts though she did not
know it? No stroke could have been aimed at her so
intolerable as this.

He kept his eyes upon her, as if with a secret enjoyment of her overthrow. "You do not thank me for my
congratulations," he cried.

"Oh!" she cried in the wondering self-abandonment
of pain, "can you be a man, only a man, and strike so
deep?" Then the very anguish of her soul gave her
a sudden inspiration. She looked round her with her
eyes dilating. "When you can do this," she said,
putting with unconscious eloquence her hand to her
heart, "what do you want with things like those?"
The sight of the lamp which burned before Walter's
portrait had given her a painful sense of harm and
danger when she saw it first. It filled her now with a
keen disdain. To be able to pierce the very soul, and
yet to use the aid of *that!* She did not know what its
meaning was, yet suffering in every nerve, she scorned
it, and turned to him with a questioning look which
was full of indignation and contempt.

And he who was so strong, so much above her in
power and knowledge, shrank—almost imperceptibly,
but yet he shrank—startled, from her look and question.
"*That?*" he said, "you who know so little of your own
mind, how can you tell how human nature is affected?
—by what poor methods, as well as by great. You

understand nothing—not yourself—far less the devices of the wise."

"Oh, you are wise," cried Oona, "and cruel. You can make what is best look the worst. You can confuse our souls so that we cannot tell what is good in us, and what evil. I know, I know, you are a great person. Yet you hide and lurk in this place which no man knows; and work by spells and charms like—like—"

"Like what?" a gleam of anger and shame—or of something that might have betrayed these sentiments on any other face—crossed his usually calm and lofty countenance. Oona, opposite to him, returned his look with a passionate face of indignation and disdain. She had forgotten herself altogether, and everything but the thrill and throbbing of the anguish which seemed to have taken the place of her heart in her. She feared nothing now. The blow which she had received had given her the nobleness of desperation.

"Like a poor—witch," she said; "like the wizard they call you; like one who plays upon the ignorant, not like the powerful spirit you are. You that can beat us down to the dust, both him and me. You that can turn sweet into bitter, and good into evil. Oh, how can you for shame take that way too, like a—juggler," she cried in her passion; "like a sorcerer; like——"

"You speak like a fool, though you are no fool," he said, "not knowing the stuff that we are made of." He made a step towards her as he spoke, and though his tone was rather sad than fierce, there came upon

Oona in a moment such a convulsion of terror as proved
what the weakness was of which he spoke. She clung
with all her failing force to the door which seemed
her only support, and broke out into a shrill cry,
"Walter, Walter, save me!" afraid of she knew not
what, panic seizing her, and the light flickering in her
fainting eyes.

CHAPTER XIV.

WHILE Oona was standing on the verge of these mysteries a trial of a very different kind had fallen to Walter. They had exchanged parts in this beginning of their union. It was his to lead the two elder ladies into those rooms which were to him connected with the most painful moments of his life, but to them conveyed no idea beyond the matter of fact that they were more comfortably furnished and inhabitable than was to be expected in such a ruin. Even to Mrs. Methven, who was interrogating his looks all the time, in an anxious endeavour to know what his feelings were, there seemed nothing extraordinary in the place save this. She seated herself calmly in the chair, which he had seen occupied by so different a tenant, and looking smiling towards him, though always with a question in her eyes, began to express her wonder why, with Auchnasheen so near, it had been thought necessary to retain a dwelling-place among these ruins; but since Walter did from time to time inhabit them, his mother found it pleasant that they were so habitable, so almost comfortable, and answered old Macalister's apologies for the

P 2

want of a fire or any preparations for their coming with smiling assurances that all was very well, that she could not have hoped to find rooms in such careful repair. Mrs. Forrester was a great deal more effusive, and examined everything with a flow of cheerful remark, divided between Lord Erradeen and his old servant, with whom, as with everybody on the loch, she had the acquaintance of a lifetime.

" I must see your wife, Macalister," she said, "and make her my compliment on the way she has kept everything. It is really just a triumph, and I would like to know how she has done it. To keep down the damp even in my little house, where there are always fires going, and every room full, is a constant thought —and how she does it here, where it is so seldom occupied——. The rooms are just wonderfully nice rooms, Lord Erradeen, but I would not say they were a cheerful dwelling—above all, for a young man like you."

"No, they are not a very cheerful dwelling," said Walter with a smile, which to his mother, watching him so closely, told a tale of pain which she did not understand indeed, yet entered into with instinctive sympathy. The place began to breathe out suffering and mystery to her, she could not tell why. It was cold, both in reality and sentiment, the light coming into it from the cold north-east, from the mountains which stood up dark and chill above the low shining of the setting sun. And the cold affected her from his eyes, and made her shiver.

"I think," she said, "we must not stay too long. The sun is getting low, and the cold——"

"But where is Oona?" said Mrs. Forrester. "I would not like to go away till she has had the pleasure too. Oh, yes, it is a pleasure, Lord Erradeen—for you see we cannot look out at our own door, without the sight of your old castle before our eyes, and it is a satisfaction to know what there is within. She must have stayed outside among the ruins that she was always partial to. Perhaps Macalister will go and look for her—or, oh! Lord Erradeen, but I could not ask you to take that trouble."

"My lord," said old Macalister aside, "if it had been any other young lady I wad have been after her before now. Miss Oona is just wonderful for sense and judgment; but when I think upon yon wall——"

"I will go," said Walter. Amid all the associations of this place, the thought of Oona had threaded through every movement of his mind. He thought now that she had stayed behind out of sympathy, now that it was indifference, now—he could not tell what to think. But no alarm for her safety had crossed his thoughts. He made a rapid step towards the door, then paused, with a bewildering sense that he was leaving two innocent women without protection in a place full of dangers which they knew nothing of. Was it possible that his enemy could assail him through these unsuspecting simple visitors? He turned back to them with a strange pang of pity and regret, which he himself did not understand. "Mother," he said, "you will forgive me—it is only for a moment?"

"Walter!" she cried, full of surprise; then waved her hand to him with a smile, bidding him, "Go, go—and bring Miss Forrester." Her attitude, her smile of perfect security and pleasure, went with him like a little picture, as he went down the spiral stairs. Mrs. Forrester was in the scene too, in all her pretty faded colour and animation, begging him—"Dear me, not to take the trouble; for no doubt Oona was just at the door, or among the ruins, or saying a word to Hamish about the boat." A peaceful little picture—no shadow upon it; the light a little cold, but the atmosphere so serene and still. Strange contrast to all that he had seen there—the conflict, the anguish, which seemed to have left their traces upon the very walls.

He hurried down-stairs with this in his mind, and a lingering of all his thoughts upon the wistful smiling of his mother's face—though why at this moment he should dwell upon that was a wonder to himself. Oona was not on the grassy slope before the door, nor talking to Hamish at the landing-place, as her mother suggested. There was no trace of her among the ruins. Then, but not till then, Walter began to feel a tremor of alarm. There came suddenly into his mind the recollection of that catastrophe of which he had been told in Edinburgh by its victim; it sent a shiver through him, but even yet he did not seriously fear; for Oona was no stranger to lose herself upon the

dangerous places of the ruin. He went hurriedly up the
steps to the battlements, where he himself had passed
through so many internal struggles, thinking nothing
less than to find her in one of the embrasures, where
he had sat and looked out upon the loch. He had
been startled as he came out of the shadow of the house,
by a faint cry, which seemed to issue from the distance,
from the other extremity of the water, and which was
indeed the cry for help to which Oona had given utterance when she felt the wall crumbling under her feet,
which the wind had carried far down the loch, and
which came back in a distant echo. Walter began to
remember this cry as he searched in vain for any trace
of her. And when he reached the spot where the
danger began and saw the traces that some other steps
had been there before him, and that a shower of
crumbling mortar and fragments of stone had fallen,
his heart leaped to his throat with sudden horror. This
was calmed by the instant reassurance that had she
fallen he must at once have discovered the catastrophe.
He looked round him bewildered, unable to conceive
what had become of her. Where had she gone? The
boat lay at the landing-place, with Hamish in waiting;
the whole scene full of rest and calm, and everything
silent about and around. "Oona!" he cried, but the
wind caught his voice too, and carried it away to the
village on the other bank, to her own isle away upon the
glistening water, where Oona was not. Where was she?
His throat began to grow parched, his breath to labour

with the hurry of his heart. He stood on the verge of
the precipice of broken masonry, straining his eyes
over the stony pinnacles above, and the sharp irregular-
ities of the ruin. There he saw something suddenly
which made his heart stand still : her glove lying where
she had dropped it in her hurried progress along the
ledge. He did not pause to think how she got there,
which would have seemed at another moment impossible, but with a desperate spring and a sensation as of
death in his heart, followed, where she had passed,
wherever that might be.

Walter neither knew where he was going nor how he
made his way along those jagged heights. He did not
go cautiously as Oona had done, but flew on, taking
no notice of the dangers of the way. The sound of
voices, and of his own name, and Oona's cry for help,
reached his ear as with a leap he gained the stone
balcony of the tower. His feet scarcely touched the
stones as he flew to her who called him, nor did he
think where he was, or feel any wonder at the call, or
at the voices on such a height, or at anything that was
happening. His mind had no room for any observation
or thought save that Oona called him. He flung himself into the dark doorway as if it had been a place he
had known all his life, and caught her as her strength
failed her. She who had thought she could put
herself in his place, and who had been ready to brave
everything for him, turned round with her eyes glazing
and her limbs giving way, with strength enough only

to throw herself upon his breast. Thus Walter found himself once more face to face with his enemy. The last time they had met, Lord Erradeen had been goaded almost to madness. He stood now supporting Oona on his arm, stern, threatening in his turn.

"If you have killed her," he cried; "if you have hurt her as you did before; if you have made her your victim, as you did before!" There was no shrinking in his look now: he spoke out loudly with his head high, his eyes blazing upon the enemy who was no longer his, but *hers*, which had a very different meaning; and though he stood against the door where he had found Oona holding it wide open, this was done unconsciously, with no idea of precaution. The time for that was over now.

And with the sensation of his support, the throb of his heart so near hers, Oona came back to herself. She turned slowly round towards the inhabitant of the tower. "Walter, tell him—that though he can make us miserable he cannot make us consent. Tell him—that now we are two, not one, and that our life is ours, not his. Oh!" she cried, lifting her eyes, addressing herself directly to him, "listen to me!—over me you have no power—and Walter is mine, and I am his. Go—leave us in peace."

"She says true; leave us in peace. In all my life now, I shall do no act that is not half hers, and over her you have no power."

"You expect me then," he said, "to give way to this

bargain of self-interest—a partnership of protection to you and gain to her. And you think that before this I am to give way."

"It is not so," cried Walter, "not so. Oona, answer him. I turned to her for help because I loved her, and she to me for—I know not why—because she loved me. Answer him, Oona! if it should be at this moment for death not for life—"

She turned to him with a look and a smile, and put her arm through his, clasping his hand: then turned again to the other who stood looking on. "If it should be for death," she said.

There was a moment of intense stillness. He before whom these two stood knew human nature well. He knew every way in which to work upon a solitary being, a soul alone, in his power; but he knew that before two, awake, alive, on the watch one for the other, these methods were without power, and though his experiences were so great the situation was new. They were in the first absolute devotion of their union, invulnerable, no germ of distrust, no crevice of possible separation. He might kill, but he could not move them. This mysterious agent was not above the artifices of defeat. To separate them was the only device that remained to him.

"You are aware," he said, "that here if nowhere else you are absolutely in my power. You have come to me. I have not gone to you. If you wish to sacrifice her life you can do so, but what right have you to do it?

How dare you take her from those who love her, and make her your victim? She will be your victim, not mine. There is time yet for her to escape. It is for her to go—Die? why should she die? Are you worth such a sacrifice? Let her go——"

"Hold me fast—do not loose me, Walter," cried Oona wildly in his ear.

And here his last temptation took him, in the guise of love, and rent him in two. To let *her* perish, was that possible? Could he hold her though she was his life, and sacrifice hers? Walter could not pause to think; he tore his hand out of hers, which would not be loosed, and thrust her from him. "Oona," he cried, his voice sinking to a whisper, "go! Oona, go! Not to sacrifice you—no, no, I will not. Anything but that. While there is time, go!"

She stood for a moment between the two, deserted, cast off by him who loved her. It was the supreme crisis of all this story of her heart. For a moment she said nothing, but looked at them, meeting the keen gaze of the tempter, whose eyes seemed to burn her, gazing at Walter who had half-closed his not to see her go. Then with the sudden, swift, passionate action, unpremeditated and impulsive, which is natural to women, she flung herself before him, and seized with her hands the table upon which the light was burning. "You said," she cried, breathless, "that you used small methods as well as great—and this is one, whatever it is." She thrust it from her violently as she spoke. The lamp

fell with a great crash and broke, and the liquid which
had supplied it burst out and ran blazing in great
globules of flames over the floor. The crash, the blaze,
the sudden uproar, was like a wall between the antagonists. The curtains swaying with the wind, the old dry
tapestries, caught in the fire like tinder. Oona, as wild
with fear as she had been with daring, caught at
Walter's hand with the strength of despair, and fled
dragging him after her. The door clanged behind
them as he let it go, then burst open again with the force
of the breeze and let out a great blaze, the red mad
gleam of fire in the sunshine and daylight — un-
natural, devouring. With a sense that death was in
their way before and behind, they went forth clinging
to each other, half-stupefied, half-desperate. Then sense
and hearing and consciousness itself were lost in a roar
as of all the elements let loose—a great dizzy upheaving
as of an earthquake. The whole world darkened round
them ; there was a sudden rush of air and whirl of
giddy sensation—and nothing more.

The two mothers meanwhile talked calmly in the
room below, where Macalister had lighted the fire, and
where, in the cheerful blaze and glow, everything became
more easy and tranquil and calm. Perhaps even the
absence of the young pair, whose high strain of existence at the moment could not but disturb the elder
souls with sympathy, made the quiet waiting, the pleasant talk, more natural. Mrs. Methven had been deeply

touched by her son's all unneeded apology for leaving her. She could have laughed over it, and cried, it was so kind, so tender of Walter, yet unlike him, the late awakening of thought and tenderness to which she had never been accustomed, which penetrated her with a sweet and delightful amusement as well as happiness. She had no reason to apprehend any evil, neither was Mrs. Forrester afraid for Oona. "Oh no, she is well used to going about by herself. There is nobody near but knows my Oona. Her family and all her belongings have been on the loch, I might say, since ever it was a loch ; and if any stranger took it upon him to say an uncivil word, there is neither man nor woman for ten miles round but would stand up for her—if such a thing could be," Mrs. Forrester added with dignity, "which is just impossible and not to be thought of. And as for ruins, she knows them well. But I would like her to see the books, and what a nice room Lord Erradeen has here, for often we have been sorry for him, and wondered what kind of accommodation there was, and what good it could do to drag the poor young man out of his comfortable house, if it was only once in the year——"

"And why should he come here once in the year?" Mrs. Methven asked with a smile.

"That is just the strange story: but I could not take upon myself to say, for I know nothing except the common talk, which is nonsense, no doubt. You will never have been in the north before?" said

Mrs. Forrester, thinking it judicious to change the subject.

"Never before," Mrs. Methven replied, perceiving equally on her side that the secrets of the family were not to be gleaned from a stranger; and she added, "My son himself has not yet seen his other houses, though this is the second time he has come here."

"It is to be hoped," said the other, "that now he will think less of that weary London, which I hear is just an endless traffic of parties and pleasure—and settle down to be a Scots lord. We must make excuses for a young man that naturally likes to be among his own kind, and finds more pleasure in an endless on-going than ladies always understand. Though I will not say but I like society very well myself, and would be proud to see my friends about me, if it were not for the quiet way that Oona and I are living, upon a little bit isle, which makes it always needful to consider the weather, and if there is a moon, and all that; and besides that, I have no gentleman in the house."

"I never had a daughter," said Mrs. Methven; "there can be no companion so sweet."

"You mean Oona? Her and me," said Mrs. Forrester, with Scotch grammar and a smile, "we are but one; and you do not expect me to praise myself? When I say we have no gentleman in the house, it is because we cannot be of the use we would wish to our friends. To offer a cup of tea is just all I have in my power, and

that is nothing to ask a gentleman to; but for all that
it is wonderful how constantly we are seeing our neighbours, especially in the summer time, when the days
are long. But bless me, what is that?" Mrs. Forrester
cried. The end of her words was lost in a tumult and
horror of sound such as Loch Houran had never heard
before.

CHAPTER XV.

THE explosion startled the whole country for miles around.

The old castle was at all times the centre of the land-scape, standing sombre in its ruin amid all the smiling existence of to-day. It flashed in a moment into an importance more wonderful, blazing up to the sky in fire and flame and clouds of smoke like a great battle. The whole neighbourhood, as far as sight could carry, saw this new wonder, and sprang into sudden excite-ment, alarm, and terror. Every soul rushed out of the village on the bank; servants appeared half frantic in front of Auchnasheen, pushing out in skiffs and fishing-cobbles upon the water which seemed to share the sudden passion of alarm, and became but one great reflection, red and terrible, of the flames which seemed to burst in a moment from every point. Some yachts-men, whose little vessel had been lying at anchor, and who had been watching with great curiosity the moving figures on the height of the gallery round the tower, with much laughing discussion among themselves as to the possibility of having seen the ghost—were suddenly brought to seriousness in a moment as the yacht bounded under their feet with the concussion of the air, and the idle sail flapping from the mast grew blood-red in the sudden glare. It was the work of another moment to leap into their boat and speed as fast as the oars could plough through the water, to the rescue, if rescue were needed. Who could be there? they asked each other. Only old Macalister with his wife, who, safe in the lower story, would have full time to escape. But then, what were those figures on the tower? The young men almost laughed again as they said to each other, " The warlock lord!" "Let's hope he's blown himself up and made an end of all that nonsense," said the sceptic of the party. But just then the stalwart boat-load came across a wild skiff dashing through the water, old Symington like a ghost in the stern, and red-haired Duncan, with bare arms and throat, rowing as for life and death.

" My lord is there!" cried the old man with quivering lips, "The leddies are there!"

"And Hamish and Miss Oona!" fell stammering from Duncan, half dumb with horror.

The young yachtsmen never said a word, but looked at each other and flew along over the blood-red water. Oona! It was natural they should think of her first in her sweetness and youth.

The two mothers in their tranquil talk sat still for a moment and looked at each other with pale awe on their faces, when that wild tumult enveloped them,

paralysing every other sense. They thought they were
lost, and instinctively put out their hands to each other.
They were alone—even the old servant had left them
—and there they sat breathless, expecting death. For
a moment the floor and walls so quivered about them
that this alone seemed possible; but nothing followed,
and their faculties returned. They rose with one impulse and made their way together to the door—then,
the awe of death passing, life rising in them, flew down
the stair-case with the lightness of youth, and out to
the air, which already was full of the red flashes of the
rising flames. But once there, a worse thing befell
these two poor women. They had been still in the face
of death, but now, with life saved, came a sense of something more terrible than death. They cried out in one
voice the names of their children. "My boy!"
"Oona!" Old Macalister, speechless, dragging his old
wife after him, came out and joined them, the two old
people looking like owls suddenly scared by the outburst of lurid light.

"Oh, what will be happening?" said the old woman,
her dazed astonishment contrasting strangely with the
excitement and terror of the others.

Mrs. Forrester answered her with wild and feverish
volubility.

"Nothing will have happened," she said. "Oona,
my darling! What would happen? She knows her
way: she would not go a step too far. Oh, Oona,
where are you? why will you not answer me? They

will just be bewildered like ourselves, and she will be
in a sore fright; but that will be for me. Oona! Oona!
She will be frightened—but only for me. Oona! Oh
Hamish, man, can ye not find your young lady? The
fire—I am not afraid of the fire. She will just be wild
with terror—for me. Oona! Oona! Oona!" cried the
poor lady, her voice ending in a shriek.

Mrs. Methven stood by her side, but did not speak.
Her pale face was raised to the flaming tower, which
threw an illumination of red light over everything.
She did not know that it was supposed to be inaccessible. For anything she knew, her boy might be there
perishing within her sight; and she could do nothing.
The anguish of the helpless and hopeless gave her a
sort of terrible calm. She looked at the flames as she
might have looked at executioners who were putting
her son to death. She had no hope.

Into the midst of this distracted group came a sudden
rush of men from the boats, which were arriving every
minute, the young yachtsmen at their head. Mrs.
Forrester flung herself upon these young men, catching
hold of them as they came up.

"My Oona's among the ruins," she said breathlessly.
"Oh, no fear but you'll find her. Oh, find her! find
her! for I'm going out of my senses, I think. I know
that she's safe, oh, quite safe! but I'm silly, silly, and
my nerves are all wrong. Oh, Harry, for the love of
God, and Patrick, Patrick, my fine lad! And not a
brother to look after my bairn!"

"We are all her brothers," cried the youths, struggling past the poor lady, who clung to them and
hindered their progress, her voice coming shrill through
the roar of the flames and the bustle and commotion
below. Amid this tumult her piercing "Oona! Oona!"
came in from time to time, sharp with the derision of
tragedy for anything so ineffectual and vain. Before
many minutes had passed the open space in front of
the house which stood intact and as yet unthreatened,
was crowded with men, none of them, however, knowing
what to do, nor, indeed, what had happened The information that Lord Erradeen and Oona were missing
was handed about among them, repeated with shakings
of the head to every new-comer. Mrs. Methven standing in the midst, whom nobody knew, received all the
comments like so many stabs into her heart. "Was it
them that were seen on the walls just before? Then
nothing could have saved them." "The wall's all
breached to the loch: no cannon could have done it
cleaner. It's there you'll find them." "Find them!
Oh, hon, oh, hon! the bodies of them. Let's hope their
souls are in a better place." The unfortunate mother
heard what everybody said. She stood among strangers,
with nobody who had any compassion upon her, receiving over and over again the assurance of his fate.

The first difficulty here, as in every other case of the
kind, was that no one knew what to do; there were
hurried consultations, advices called out on every hand,
suggestions—many of them impossible—but no author-

itative guide to say what was to be done. Mrs. Methven, turning her miserable looks from one to another,
saw standing by her side a man of commanding appearance, who seemed to take no share in either advice or
action, but stood calmly looking on. He was so different from the rest, that she appealed to him instinctively.

" Oh, sir !" she cried, "you must know what is best
to be done—tell them."

He started a little when she spoke ; his face, when he
turned it towards her, was full of strange expression.
There was sadness in it, and mortification, and wounded
pride. She said after that he was like a man disappointed, defeated, full of dejection and indignation. He
gave her a look of keen wonder, and then said with a
sort of smile—

" Ah, that is true !" Then in a moment his voice
was heard over the crowd. " The thing to be done," he
said, in a voice which was not loud, but which immediately silenced all the discussions and agitations round,
" is to clear away the ruins. The fire will not burn
downward—it has no food that way—it will exhaust
itself. The young lady fell with the wall. If she is to
be found, she will be found there."

The men around all crowded about the spot from
which the voice came.

" Wha's that that's speaking ? "

" I see nobody."

" What were you saying, sir ? "

" Whoever it is, it is the right thing," cried young

Patrick from the yacht. "Harry, keep you the hose going on the house. I'll take the other work; and thank you for the advice, whoever you are."

Mrs. Forrester too had heard this voice, and the command and calm in it gave to her troubled soul a new hope. She pushed her way through the crowd to the spot from whence it came.

"Oh," she cried, "did you see my Oona fall? Did you see my Oona? No, no, it would not be her that fell. You are just deceived. Where is my Oona? Oh, sir, tell them where she is that they may find her, and we'll pray for you on our bended knees, night and morning, every day!"

She threw herself on her knees, as she spoke, on the grass, putting up her quivering, feverish hands. The other mother, with a horror which she felt even in the midst of her misery, saw the man to whom this heart-rending prayer was addressed, without casting even a glance at the suppliant at his feet, or with any appearance of interest in the proceedings he had advised, turn quietly on his heel and walk away. He walked slowly across the open space and disappeared upon the edge of the water with one glance upward to the blazing tower, taking no more notice of the anxious crowd collected there than if they had not existed. Nor did any one notice the strange spectator going away at the height of the catastrophe, when everybody far and near was roused to help. The men running hurriedly to work did not seem to observe him. The two old servants of the house, Symington and Macalister, stood crowding together out of the reach of the stream of water which was being directed upon the house. But Mrs. Methven took no note of them : only it gave her a strange surprise in the midst of her anguish to see that while her Walter's fate still hung in the balance, there was one who could calmly go away.

By this time the sun had set; the evening, so strangely different from any other that ever had fallen on the loch, was beginning to darken on the hills, bringing out with wilder brilliancy the flaming of the great fire, which turned the tower of Kinloch Houran into a lantern, and blazed upwards in a great pennon of crimson and orange against the blue of the skies. For miles down the loch the whole population was out upon the roads gazing at this wonderful sight ; the hillsides were crimsoned by the reflection, as if the heather had bloomed again; the water glowed red under the cool calm of the evening sky. Round about Birkenbraes was a little crowd, the visitors and servants occupying every spot from which this wonder could be seen, and Mr. Williamson himself, with his daughter, standing at the gate to glean what information might be attainable from the passers-by. Katie, full of agitation, unable to bear the common babble inside, had walked on, scarcely knowing what she did, in her indoor dress, shivering with cold and excitement. They had all said to each other that there could be no danger to life in that uninhabited place.

" Toots, no danger at all ! " Mr. Williamson had said, with great satisfaction in the spectacle. " Old Mac-alister and his wife are just like rats in their hole, the fire will never come near them; and the ruin will be none the worse—it will just be more a ruin than ever."

There was something in Katie's mind which revolted against this easy treatment of so extraordinary a catas-trophe. It seemed to her connected, she could not tell how, with the scene which had passed in her own room so short a time before. But for shame she would have walked on to Auchnasheen to make sure that Walter was in no danger. But what would he think of her—what would everybody think ? Katie went on, however, abstracted from herself, her eyes upon the blaze in the distance, her heart full of disturbed thoughts. All at once she heard the firm quick step of some one advanc-ing to meet her. She looked up eagerly ; it might be Walter himself—it might be—— When she saw who it was, she came to a sudden pause. Her limbs refused to carry her, her very breath seemed to stop. She looked up at him and trembled. The question that formed on her lips could not get utterance. He was perfectly calm and courteous, with a smile that be-wildered her and filled her with terror.

" Is there any one in danger ? " he said, answering as if she had spoken. " I think not. There is no one in danger *now*. It is a fine spectacle. We are at liberty to enjoy it without any drawback—now."

" Oh, sir," said Katie, her very lips quivering, " you

speak strangely. Are you sure that there was no one there ?"

"I am sure of nothing," he said with a strange smile.

And then Mr. Williamson, delighted to see a stranger, drew near.

"You need not be so keen with your explanations, Katie. Of course it is the gentleman we met at Kinloch Houran. Alas! poor Kinloch Houran, we will never meet there again. You will just stay to dinner now that we have got you. Come, Katie, where are your manners? you say nothing. Indeed we will consider it a great honour—just ourselves and a few people that are staying in the house; and as for dress, what does that matter? It is a thing that happens every day. Neighbours in the country will look in without preparation; and for my part, I say always, the more the merrier," said the open-hearted millionnaire.

The stranger's face lighted up with a gleam of scornful amusement.

"The kindness is great," he said, "but I am on my way to the other end of the loch."

"You are never walking?" cried Mr. Williamson. "Lord bless us? that was a thing that used to be done in my young days, but nobody thinks of now. Your servant will have gone with your baggage? and you would have a delicacy—I can easily understand—in asking for a carriage in the excitement of the moment; but ye shall not walk past my house where there are conveyances of all kinds that it is just a charity to use.

Now, I'll take no denial; there's the boat. In ten
minutes they'll get up steam. I had ordered it, ready
to send up to Auchnasheen for news. But as a friend
would never be leaving if the family was in trouble, it
is little use to do that now. I will just make a sign to
the boat, and they'll have ye down in no time; it will
be the greatest pleasure—if you are sure you will not
stay to your dinner in the mean time, which is what I
would like best ?"

He stood looking down upon them both from his great
height; his look had been sad and grave when he had
met Katie, a look full of expression which she could not
fathom. There came now a gleam of amusement over
his countenance. He laughed out.

"That would be admirable," he said, offering no
thanks, "I will take your boat," like a prince according,
rather than receiving, a favour.

Mr. Williamson looked at his daughter with a confused air of astonishment and perplexity, but he sent a
messenger off in a boat to warn the steamer, which lay
with its lights glimmering white in the midst of the
red reflections on the loch. The father and daughter
stood there silenced, and with a strange sensation of
alarm, beside this stranger. They exchanged another
frightened look.

" You'll be going—a long journey ?" Mr. Williamson
said, faltering, scarcely knowing what he said.

" I am going—for a long time, at least," the stranger
said.

He seemed to put aside their curiosity as something trifling, unworthy to be answered, and with a wave of his hand to them, took the path towards the beach.

They turned and looked after him, drawing close to each other for mutual comfort. It was twilight, when everything is confusing and uncertain. They lost sight of him, then saw him again, like a tall pillar on the edge of the water. There was a confusion of boats coming and going, in which they could not trace whither he went, or how. Katie and her father stood watching, taking no account of the progress of time, or of the cold wind of the night which came in gusts from the hills. They both drew a long sigh of relief when the steamer was put in motion, and went off down the loch with its lights like glow-worms on the yards and the masts. Nor did they say a word to each other as they turned and went home. When inquiries were made afterwards, nothing but the most confused account could be had of the embarkation. The boatman had seen the stranger, but none among them would say that he had conveyed him to the steamer; and on the steamer the men were equally confused, answering at random, with strange glances at each other. Had they carried that passenger down to the foot of the loch? Not even Katie's keen questioning could elicit a clear reply.

But when the boat had steamed away, carrying into the silence the rustle of its machinery and the twinkling of its lights, there was another great explosion from the tower of Kinloch Houran, a loud report which seemed to roar away into the hollow of the mountains, and came back in a thousand rolling echoes. A great column of flame shot up into the sky, the stones fell like a cannonade, and then all was darkness and silence. The loch fell into sudden gloom; the men who were labouring at the ruins stopped short, and groped about to find each other through the dust and smoke which hung over them like a cloud. The bravest stood still, as if paralysed, and for a moment, through all this strange scene of desolation and terror, there was but one sound audible, the sound of a voice which cried " Oona! Oona !" now shrill, now hoarse with exhaustion and misery, " Oona! Oona !" to earth and heaven.

CHAPTER XVI.

WHEN the curious and the inefficient dropped away, as they did by degrees as night fell, there were left the three youths from the yacht, Hamish, Duncan, and two or three men from the village, enough to do a greater work than that which lay before them; but the darkness and the consternation, and even their very eagerness and anxiety, confused their proceedings. Such lamps as they could get from Macalister were fastened up among the heaps of ruin, and made a series of wild Rembrandt-like pictures in the gloom, but afforded little guidance to their work. The masses of masonry which they laboured to clear away seemed to increase rather than diminish under their picks and spades—new angles of the wall giving way when they seemed to have come nearly to the foundation. And now and then from above a mass of stones penetrated through and through by the fire, and kept in their place only by mere balance, would topple down without warning, dangerously near their heads, risking the very lives of the workers; upon whom discouragement gained as the night wore on, and no result was obtained.

After a while, with a mournful unanimity they stopped
work and consulted in whispers what was to be done.
Not a sound had replied to their cries. They had
stopped a hundred times to listen, one more imagina-
tive than the rest, thinking he heard an answering cry;
but no such response had ever come, how was it
possible, from under the choking, suffocating mass,
which rolled down upon them as they worked, almost
stopping their breath? They gave up altogether in
the middle of the night in dejection and hopelessness.
The moon had risen and shone all round them, appearing through the great chasms in the wall, making a
glory upon the loch, but lending no help here, the
shadow of the lower part of the house lying black over
the new-made ruin. What was the use? They stood
disconsolately consulting over the possibilities. If
Walter and Oona were under those heaps of ruin, it
was impossible that they could be alive, and the men
asked each other, shaking their heads, what chance
there was of any of those fortunate accidents which
sometimes save the victims of such a calamity. The
wall had been already worn by time, there were no
beams, no archways which could have sheltered them—
everything had come down in one mass of ruin. After
many and troubled discussions they prepared reluctantly
to abandon the hopeless work. "Perhaps, in the
morning"—it was all that any one could say. The
young yachtsmen made a last effort, calling out Walter's
name. "If you can speak, for God's sake speak? any

sign and we'll have you out. Erradeen! Erradeen!"
they cried. But the silence was as that of the grave.
A fall of powdery fragments now and then from the
heap, sometimes a great stone solemnly bounding downwards from point to point, the light blown about by
the night air lighting up the dark group, and the
solitary figure of Hamish, apart from them, who was
working with a sort of rage, never pausing, pulling
away the stones with his hands. This was all; not a
moan, not a cry, not a sound of existence under those
shapeless piles of ruin. The only thing that broke
the silence, and which came now with a heartrending
monotony, almost mechanical, was the cry of "Oona!
Oona!" which Oona's mother, scarcely conscious, sent
out into the night.

The men stole softly round the corner of the house
which remained untouched, to get to their boats,
stealing away like culprits, though there was no want
of goodwill in them. But they were not prepared for
the scene that met them there. The little platform
before the door, and the landing-place, were bright
almost as day with the shining of the moon, the water
one sheet of silver, upon which the boats lay black, the
grassy space below all white and clear. In the midst
of this space, seated on a stone, was Mrs. Methven.
She had scarcely stirred all night. Her companion in
sorrow had been taken into the shelter of the house,
but she, unknown and half-forgotten, and strong with
all the vigour of misery, had remained there, avoiding

speech of any one. With all her senses absorbed in
listening, not a stroke had escaped her, scarcely a
word—for a long time she had stood and walked
about, not asking a question, observing, seeing, hearing
all that was done. But as the awful hours went on,
she had dropped down upon this rough seat, little
elevated above the ground, where her figure now
struck the troubled gaze of the young men, as if it
had been that of a sentinel watching to see that they
did not abandon their work. No such thought was in
her mind. She was conscious of every movement they
had made. For a moment she had thought that their
call upon her son meant that they had found some
trace of him—but that was a mere instantaneous thrill,
which her understanding was too clear to continue to
entertain. She had said to herself from the beginning
that there was no hope; she had said from the first
what the men had said to each other reluctantly after
hours of exertion. What was the good? since nothing
could be done. Yet all the while as she said this, she
was nursing within her bosom, concealing it even from
her own consciousness, covering up the smouldering
dying fire in her heart, a hope that would not altogether
die. She would not even go towards the workers
when they called out her son's name to know what it
was; but only waited, waited with a desperate, secret,
half-heathen thought, that perhaps if she did not cry
and importune, but was silent, letting God do what
He would, He might yet relent and bring her back

her boy. Oh be patient! put on at least the guise of patience! and perhaps He would be touched by the silence of her misery—He who had not heard her prayers.

She sat going over a hundred things in her heart. That Walter should have come back to her, called her to him, opened his heart to her, as a preparation for being thus snatched from her for ever! She said to herself that by-and-by she would thank God for this great mercy, and that she had thus found her son again if only for two days: but in the mean time her heart bled all the more for the thought, and bereavement became more impossible, more intolerable, even from that, which afterwards would make it almost sweet. As she kept that terrible vigil and heard the sound of the implements with which—oh, what was it?—not him, his body, the mangled remains of him, were being sought, she seemed to see him, standing before her, leaning upon her, the strong on the weak, pouring his troubles into her bosom—as he had not done since he was a child; and now he was lying crushed beneath those stones. Oh no, no, Oh no, no —it was not possible. God was not like that, holding the cup of blessing to a woman's lips and then snatching it away. And then with an effort she would say to herself what she had said from the first, what she had never wavered in saying, that there was no hope. How could there be any hope? crushed beneath tons of falling stones—oh, crushed out of recognition, out of humanity ! her imagination spared her nothing. When they found him they would tell her it was better, better, she the mother that bore him, that she should not see him again. And all the while the moon shining and God looking on. She was callous to the cry that came continually, mechanically, now stronger, now fainter, from the rooms above. "Oona, Oona!" Sometimes it made her impatient. Why should the woman cry, as if her voice could reach her child under those masses of ruin ? And *she* could not cry who had lost her all ! her only one ! why should the other have that relief and she none—nor any hope ? But all the sounds about her caught her ear with a feverish distinctness. When she heard the steps approaching after the pause of which she had divined the meaning, they seemed to go over her heart, treading it down into the dust. She raised her head and looked at them as they came up, most of the band stealing behind to escape her eye. "I heard you," she said, "call—my son."

"It was only to try; it was to make an effort; it was a last chance."

"A last——" though she was so composed there was a catch in her breath as she repeated this word ; but she added, with the quiet of despair, "You are going away ?"

The young man who was the spokesman stood before her like a culprit with his cap in his hand.

"My brothers and I," he said, "would gladly stay

if it was any use; but there is no light to work by,
and I fear—I fear—that by this time——"

"There is no more hope?" she said. "I have no
hope. I never had any hope."

The young man turned away with a despairing
gesture, and then returned to her humbly, as if she
had been a queen.

"We are all grieved—more grieved than words can
say: and gladly would we stay if we could be of any
use. But what can we do? for we are all convinced—"

"No me," cried Hamish, coming forward in the
moonlight. "No me!" his bleeding hands left marks
on his forehead as he wiped the heavy moisture from
it; his eyes shone wildly beneath his shaggy brows.
"I was against it," he cried, "from the first! I said
what would they be doing here? But convinced, that
I never will be, no till I find—Mem, if ye tell them
they'll bide. Tell them to bide. As sure as God is
in heaven that was all her thought—we will find her
yet."

The other men had slunk away, and were softly
getting into their boats. The three young yachtsmen
alone waited, a group of dark figures about her. She
looked up at them standing together in the moonlight, her face hollowed out as if by the work of
years.

"He is my only one," she said, "my only one.
And you—you—you are all the sons of one mother."

Her voice had a shrill anguish in it, insupportable to

hear: and when she paused there came still more shrilly into the air, with a renewed passion, "Oona! Oona!" the cry that had not ceased for hours. The young man who was called Patrick flung his clenched hand into the air; he gave a cry of pity and pain unendurable.

"Go and lie down for an hour or two," he said to the others, "and come back with the dawn. Don't say a word. I'll stay; it's more than a man can bear."

When the others were gone, this young fellow implored the poor lady to go in, to lie down a little, to try and take some rest. What good could she do? he faltered; and she might want all her strength for to-morrow— using all those familiar pleas with which the miserable are mocked. Something like a smile came over her wan face.

"You are very kind," she said, "oh very kind!" but no more. But when he returned and pressed the same arguments upon her she turned away almost with impatience. "I will watch with my son to-night," she said, putting him away with her hand. And thus the night passed.

Mrs. Forrester had been taken only half-conscious into Walter's room early in the evening. Her cry had become almost mechanical, not to be stopped; but she, it was hoped, was but half aware of what was passing, the unwonted and incredible anguish having exhausted her simple being, unfamiliar with suffering. Mr. Cameron, the minister from the village, had come over

on the first news, and Mysie from the isle to take care
of her mistress. Together they kept watch over the
poor mother, who lay sometimes with her eyes half
closed in a sort of stupor, sometimes springing up
wildly, to go to Oona who was ill, and wanting her, she
cried, distraught. "Oona! Oona!" she continued to
cry through all. Mysie had removed her bonnet, and
her light faded hair was all dishevelled, without the
decent covering of the habitual cap, her pretty colour
gone. Sorrow seems to lie harder on such a gentle
soul. It is cruel. There is nothing in it that is akin
to the mild level of a being so easy and common. It
was torture that prostrated the soul—not the passion of
love and anguish which gave to the other mother the
power of absolute self-control, and strength which could
endure all things. Mr. Cameron himself, struck to the
heart, for Oona was as dear to him as a child of his own,
restrained his longing to be out among the workers in
order to soothe and subdue her; and though she scarcely
understood what he was saying, his presence did soothe
her. It was natural that the minister should be there,
holding her up in this fiery passage, though she could
not tell why.

And thus the night went on. The moonlight faded
outside; the candles paled and took a sickly hue within
as the blue dawn came stealing over the world. At that
chillest, most awful moment of all the circle of time,
Mrs. Forrester had sunk into half-unconsciousness. She
was not asleep, but exhaustion had almost done the

part of sleep, and she lay on the sofa in a stupor, not moving, and for the first time intermitting her terrible cry. The minister stole down-stairs in that moment of repose. He was himself an old man and shaken beyond measure by the incidents of the night. His heart was bleeding for the child of his spirit, the young creature to whom he had been tutor, counsellor, almost father from her childhood. He went out with his heart full, feeling the vigil insupportable in the miserable room above, yet almost less supportable when he came out to the company of the grey hills growing visible, a stern circle of spectators round about, and realised with a still deeper pang the terrible unmitigated fact of the catastrophe. It was with horror that he saw the other mother sitting patient upon the stone outside. He did not know her, and had forgotten that such a person existed as Lord Erradeen's mother. Had she been there all night? "God help us," he said to himself; "how selfish we are, even to the sharers of our calamity." She looked up at him as he passed, but said nothing. And what could he say to her? For the first time he behaved himself like a coward, and fled from duty and kindness; for what could he say to comfort her? and why insult her misery with vain attempts? Young Patrick had pressed shelter and rest upon her, being young and knowing no better. But the minister could not tell Walter's mother to lie down and rest, to think of her own life. What was her life to her? He passed her by with the acute and aching sympathy which bears a share of the suffering it cannot relieve. And his own suffering was sore. Oona, Oona, he cried to himself silently in his heart as her mother had done aloud—his child, his nursling, the flower of his flock. Mysie had told him in the intervals, when her mistress was quiet, in whispers and with tears, of all that had happened lately, and of Oona's face that was like the Sabbath of the Sacrament, so grave yet so smiling as she left the isle. This went to the old minister's heart. He passed the ruin where Hamish was still plucking uselessly, half-stupefied, at the stones, and Patrick, with his back against the unbroken wall, had fallen asleep in utter weariness. Mr. Cameron did not linger there, but sought a place out of sight of man, where he could weep: for he was old, and his heart was too full to do without some natural relief.

He went through the ruined doorway to a place where all was still green and intact, as it had been before the explosion; the walls standing, but trees grown in the deep soil which covered the old stone floor. He leaned his white head against the roughness of the wall, and shed the tears that made his old eyes heavy, and relieved his old heart with prayer. He had prayed much all the night through, but with distracted thoughts, and eyes bent upon the broken-hearted creature by whose side he watched. But now he was alone with the great and closest Friend, He to whom all things can be said, and who understands all. "Give us strength to resign her to Thee," he said, pressing his old cheek against the damp and cold freshness of the stones, which were wet with other dews than those of nature, with the few concentrated tears of age, that mortal dew of suffering. The prayer and the tears relieved his soul. He lifted his head from the wall, and turned to go back again—if, perhaps, now fresh from his Master's presence he might find a word to say to the other woman who all night long, like Rizpah, had sat silent and watched her son.

But as he turned to go away it seemed to the minister that he heard a faint sound. He supposed nothing but that one of the men who had been working had gone to sleep in a corner, and was waking and stirring to the daylight. He looked round, but saw no one. Perhaps, even, there came across the old man's mind some recollection of the tales of mystery connected with this house; but in the presence of death and sorrow, he put these lesser wonders aside. Nevertheless, there was a sound, faint, but yet of something human. The old stone floor was deep under layers of soil upon which every kind of herbage and even trees grew; but in the corner of the wall against which he had been leaning, the gathered soil had been hollowed away by the droppings from above, and a few inches of the original floor was exposed. The old man's heart began to beat with a bewildering possibility: but he dared not allow himself to think of it: he said to himself, but it must be a bird, a beast, something imprisoned in some crevice.

He listened. God! was that a moan? He turned and rushed, with the step of a boy, to where Patrick sat dozing, and Hamish, stupefied, worked on mechanically. He clutched the one out of his sleep, the other from his trance of exhaustion—"Come here! come here! and listen. What is this?" the old minister said.

CHAPTER XVII.

THE two fugitives, holding each other's hands, had fled from the fire without a word to each other. All that needed to be spoken seemed to them both to be over. They hurried on instinctively, but without any hope, expecting every moment when destruction should overtake them. Walter was the last to give up consciousness : but the sickening sense of a great fall, the whirl and resistance of the air rushing madly against him through the void, the sensation mounting up to his brain, the last stronghold of consciousness, and thrill of feeling, as if life were to end there, in a painful rush of blood, were all that were known to him. What happened really was that, holding Oona insensible in his arms, he was carried downwards with the slide and impetus of the part of the ruin on which he was standing, detached by his own weight, rather than thrown violently down by the action of the explosion. The force of the fall, however, was so great, and the mass falling with them so heavy, that some of the stones, already very unsteady, of the pavement below gave way, and carried them underground to one of the subterranean cellars, half filled up with soil, which ran under the whole area

of the old castle. How long they lay there unable to
move, and for some part of the time at least entirely
without consciousness, Walter could never tell. When
he recovered his senses he was in absolute darkness and
in considerable pain. Oona had fallen across him and
the shock had thus been broken. It was a moan from
her which woke him to life again. But she made no
reply to his first distracted question, and only gave
evidence of life by a faint little cry from time to time—
too faint to be called a cry—a breath of suffering, no
more. The suffocating terrible sensation of the darkness, a roar of something over them like thunder, the
oppression of breathing, which was caused by the want
of atmosphere, all combined to bewilder his faculties
and take away both strength and will to do anything
more than lie there quietly and gasp out the last breath.
Walter was roused by feeling in Oona an unconscious
struggle for breath. She raised first one hand, then
another, as if to take away something which was stifling
her, and he began to perceive in the vagueness of his
awakening consciousness that her life depended upon
his exertions. Then, his eyes becoming more accustomed to the darkness, he caught a faint ray of light,
so attenuated as to be no more than a thread in the
solid gloom. To drag himself towards this, and with
himself the still more precious burden, thus in utter
helplessness confided to him, was a more terrible work
than Walter in all his life had ever attempted before.
There was not room to stand upright, and his limbs

were so shaken and aching that he could scarcely raise
himself upon them; and one of his arms was useless,
and, when he tried to raise it, gave him the most
exquisite pain. It seemed hours before he could
succeed in dragging her to the little opening, a mere
crevice between the stones, through which the thread
of light had come. When he had cleared the vegetation
from it, a piercing cold breath came in and revived
him. He raised Oona in his arms to the air, but the
weight of her unconsciousness was terrible to him in
his weakened condition, and though she began to
breathe more easily, she was not sufficiently recovered
to give him any help.

Thus she lay, and he crouched beside her, trying to
think, for he could not tell how long. He heard sounds
above him indeed, but the roar of the falling stones
drowned the human noises, and his brain was too much
clouded to think of the search which must be going on
overhead for his companion and himself. The worst of
all was this dazed condition of his brain, so that it was
a long time before he could put one thing to another
and get any command of his thoughts. In all likelihood
consciousness did not fully return until the time when
the men above in despair relinquished their work, for
some feeble sense of cries and human voices penetrated
the darkness, but so muffled and far off that in the
dimness of his faculties he did not in any way connect
them with himself, nor think of attempting any reply.
Perhaps it was, though he was not aware that he heard

it, the echo of his own name that finally brought him to the full possession of himself—and then all his dull faculties centred, not in the idea of any help at hand, but in that of fighting a way somehow to a possible outlet. How was he to do it? The pain of his arm was so great that at times he had nearly fainted with mere bodily suffering, and his mind fluctuated from moment to moment—or was it not rather from hour to hour?—with perplexity and vain endeavour. He was conscious, however, though he had not given any meaning to the sounds he heard, of the strange silence which followed upon the stopping of the work. Something now and then like the movements of a bird (was it Hamish working wildly above, half-mad, half-stupefied, unable to be still?) kept a little courage in him, but the silence and darkness were terrible, binding his very soul.

It was then that he had the consolation of knowing that his companion had come to herself. Suddenly a hand groping found his, and caught it; it was his wounded arm, and the pain went like a knife to his heart, a pang which was terrible, but sweet.

"Where are we?" Oona said, trying to raise herself—oh, anguish!—by that broken arm.

He could not answer her for the moment, he was so overcome by the pain—and he was holding her up with the other arm.

"Do not hold my hand," he said at last; "take hold of my coat. Thank God that you can speak!"

"Your arm is hurt, Walter?"

"Broken, I think; but never mind, that is nothing. Nothing matters so long as you have your senses. Oona, if we die together, it will be all right?"

"Yes," she said, raising her face in the darkness to be nearer his. He kissed her solemnly, and for the moment felt no more pain.

"As well this way as another. Nothing can reach us here—only silence and sleep."

She began to raise herself slowly, until her head struck against the low roof. She gave a faint cry— then finding herself on her knees, put her arm round him, and they leant against each other. "God is as near in the dark as in the day," she said. "Lord, deliver us—Lord, deliver us!" Then, after a pause, "What happened? You saved my life."

"Is it saved?" he asked. "I don't know what has happened, except that we are together."

Oona gave a sudden shudder and clung to him. "I remember now, the flames and the fire: and it was I that broke the lamp. What did it mean, the lamp? I thought it was something devilish—something to harm you." She shivered more and more, clinging to him. "Do you think it is He—that has shut us up in this dungeon, to die?"

Walter made no reply; it was no wonder to him that she should speak wildly. He too was tempted to believe that accident had no part in what had befallen them, that they had now encountered the deadly vengeance of

their enemy. He tried to soothe her, holding her close
to his breast. "I think we are in some of the vaults
below—perhaps for our salvation." As her courage
failed there was double reason that he should maintain
a good heart. "There must be some outlet. Will you
stay here and wait till I try if I can find a way?"

"Oh no, no," cried Oona, clinging to him, "let us
stay together. I will creep after you. I will not hinder
you." She broke off with a cry, echoing, but far more
keenly, the little moan that came from him unawares
as he struck his arm against the wall. She felt it far
more sharply than he did, and in the darkness he felt
her soft hands binding round his neck something warm
and soft like their own touch in which she had wound
the wounded arm to support it. It was the long white
"cloud" which had been about her throat, and it
warmed him body and soul; but he said nothing by
way of gratitude. They were beyond all expressions of
feeling, partly because they had reached the limit at
which reality is too overpowering for sentiment, and
partly because there was no longer any separation of
mine and thine between them, and they were but
one soul.

But to tell the miseries of their search after a way of
escape would demand more space than their historian
can afford. They groped along the wall, thinking now
that they saw a glimmer in one direction, now in
another, and constantly brought up with a new shock
against the opaque resistance round them, a new corner,

or perhaps only that from which they started; under
their feet unequal heaps of damp soil upon which they
stumbled, and broken stones over which Oona, with
childlike sobs of which she was unconscious, caught her
dress, falling more than once as they laboured along.
In this way they moved round and round their prison,
a long pilgrimage. At length, when they were almost .
in despair, saying nothing to each other, only keeping
close that the touch of each to each might be a moral
support, they found themselves in what seemed a
narrow passage, walls on each side, and something like
an arrowslit over their heads, the light from which
showed them where they were, and was as an angel of
consolation to the two wounded and suffering creatures,
stumbling along with new hope. But when they had
reached the end of this narrow passage, Walter, going
first, fell for a distance of two or three feet into the
lower level of another underground chamber like that
which he had left, jarring his already strained and
racked frame, and only by an immense effort hindered
Oona from falling after him. The force of the shock,
and instant recovery by which he kept her back and
helped her to descend with precaution, brought heavy
drops of exhaustion and pain to his forehead. And
when they discovered that they were nothing the better
for their struggles, and that the place which they had
reached at such a cost, though lighter, was without any
outlet whatever except that by which they had come,
their discouragement was so great that Walter had hard

ado not to join in the tears which Oona, altogether prostrated by the disappointment, shed on his shoulder.

"We must not 'give in," he tried to say. "Here there is a little light at least. Oona, my darling, do not break down, or I shall break down too."

"No, no," she said submissively through her sobs, leaning all her weight upon him. He led her as well as he was able to a heap of earth in the corner, over which in the roof was a little opening to the light, barred with an iron stanchion, and quite out of reach. Here he placed her tenderly, sitting down by her, glad of the rest, though it was so uninviting. The light came in pale and showed the strait inclosure of their little prison. They were neither of them able to resume their search, but sat close together leaning against each other, throbbing with pain, and sick with weariness and disappointment. It gave Walter a kind of forlorn pride in his misery to feel that while Oona had failed altogether, he was able to sustain and uphold her. They did not speak in their weakness, but after a while dozed and slept, in that supreme necessity of flesh and blood which overcomes even despair, and makes no account of danger. They slept as men will sleep at death's door, in the midst of enemies : and in the depths of their suffering and misery found refreshment. But in that light sleep little moans unawares came with their breathing, for both were bruised and shaken, and Walter's broken arm was on fire with fever and pain. It was those breathings of unconscious suffering that

8

caught the ear of the minister as he made his prayer. His step had not disturbed them, but when he came back accompanied by the others, the light was suddenly darkened and the stillness broken by some one who flung himself upon his knees with a heavy shock of sound and a voice pealing in through the opening— "Miss Oona, if ye are there, speak ! or, oh for the love of the Almighty, whoever is there, speak and tell me where's my leddy ? " It was Hamish, half mad with hope and suspense and distracted affection, who thus plunged between them and the light.

They both woke with the sound, but faintly divining what it was, alarmed at first rather than comforted by the darkness into which they were plunged. There was a pause before either felt capable of reply, that additional deprivation being of more immediate terror to them, than there was consolation in the half-heard voice. In this pause, Hamish, maddened by the disappointment of his hopes, scrambled to his feet reckless and miserable, and shook his clenched fist in the face of the minister who was behind him.

"How dare ye," he cried, "play upon a man, that is half wild, with your imaginations ! there's naebody there ! " and with something between a growl and an oath, he flung away, with a heavy step that sounded like thunder to the prisoners. But next moment the rage of poor Hamish all melted away into the exceeding and intense sweetness of that relief which is higher ecstasy than any actual enjoyment given to men, the very sweetness of heaven itself—for as he turned away the sound of a voice, low and weak, but yet a voice, came out of the bowels of the earth; a murmur of two voices that seemed to consult with each other, and then a cry of "Oona is safe. Oona is here. Come and help us, for the love of God."

"The Lord bless you!" cried the old minister, falling on his knees. "Oona, speak to me, if you are there. Oona, speak to me! I want to hear your own voice."

There was again a pause of terrible suspense. Hamish threw himself down, too, behind the minister, tears running over his rough cheeks, while the young man, who was overawed by the sight, and affected too, in a lesser degree, stood with his face half hidden against the wall.

"I am here," Oona said feebly, "all safe—not hurt even. We are both safe; but oh, make haste, make haste, and take us out of this place."

"God bless you, my bairn. God bless you, my dearest bairn!" cried Mr. Cameron: but his words were drowned in a roar of laughter and weeping from the faithful soul behind him—"Ay, that will we, Miss Oona—that will we, Miss Oona!" Hamish shouted and laughed and sobbed till the walls rang, then clamorous with his heavy feet rushed out of sight without another word, they knew not where.

"I'll follow him," said young Patrick; "he will know some way."

The minister was left alone at the opening through

which hope had come. He was crying like a child, and ready to laugh too like Hamish.

"My bonny dear," he said; "my bonny dear——" and could not command his voice.

"Mr. Cameron—my mother. She must be breaking her heart."

"And mine," Walter said with a groan. He thought even then of the bitterness of her woe, and of all the miserable recollections that must have risen in her mind: please God not to come again.

"I am an old fool," said Mr. Cameron, outside : "I cannot stand out against the joy; but I am going. I'm going, my dear. Say again you are not hurt, Oona. Say it's you, my darling, my best bairn !"

"And me that had not the courage to say a word to yon poor woman," he said to himself as he hurried away. The light was still grey in the skies, no sign of the sun as yet, but not only the hills distinct around, but the dark woods, and the islands on the water, and even the sleeping roofs so still among their trees on the shores of the loch, had come into sight. The remaining portion of the house which had stood so many assaults, and the shapeless mass of the destroyed tower, stood up darkly against the growing light : and almost like a part of it, like a statue that had come down from its pedestal was the figure of Mrs. Methven, which he saw standing between him and the shore, her face turned towards him. She had heard the hurrying steps and the shout of Hamish, and knew that something had happened. She had risen against her will, against the resolution she had formed, unable to control herself, and stood with one hand under her cloak, holding her heart, to repress, if possible, the terrible throbbing in it. The face she turned towards the minister overawed him in the simplicity of his joy. It was grey, like the morning, or rather ashen white, the colour of death. Even now she would not, perhaps could not, ask anything ; but only stood and questioned him with her eyes, grown to twice their usual size, in the great hollows which this night had opened out.

The minister knew that he should speak carefully, and make easy to her the revolution from despair to joy ; but he could not. They were both beyond all secondary impulses. He put the fact into the plainest words.

" Thank God ! your son is safe," he cried.

" What did you say ? "

" Oh, my poor lady, God be with you. I dared not speak to you before. Your son is safe. Do you know what I mean ? He is as safe as you or me."

She kept looking at him, unable to take it into her mind ; that is to say, her mind had flashed upon it, seized it at the first word, yet—with a dumb horror holding hope away from her, lest deeper despair might follow—would not allow her to believe.

" What—did you say ? You are trying to make me think ——" And then she broke off, and cried out " Walter ! " as if she saw him—as a mother might cry who saw her son suddenly, unlooked for, come into the house when all believed him dead—and fell on her knees,—then from that attitude sank down upon herself, and dropped prostrate on the ground.

Mr. Cameron was alarmed beyond measure. He knew nothing of faints, and he thought the shock had killed her. But what could he do? It was against his nature to leave a stranger helpless. He took off his coat and covered her, and then hurried to the door and called up Macalister's wife, who was dozing in a chair.

"I think I have killed her," he said, "with my news."

"Then ye have found him?" the three old people said together, the woman clasping her hands with a wild "Oh hon — oh hon!" while Symington came forward, trembling, and pale as death.

"I had hoped," he said, with quivering lips, "like the apostles with One that was greater, that it was he that was to have delivered—— Oh, but we are vain creatures! and now it's a' to begin again."

"Is that all ye think of your poor young master? He is living, and will do well. Go and take up the poor lady. She is dead, or fainted, but it is with joy."

And then he went up-stairs. Many an intimation of sorrow and trouble the minister had carried. But good news had not been a weight upon him hitherto. He went to the other poor mother with trouble in his heart. If the one who had been so brave was killed

by it, how encounter her whose soft nature had fallen
prostrate at once ? He met Mysie at the door, who
told him her mistress had slept, but showed signs of
waking.

"Oh, sir, if ye could give her something that would
make her sleep again! I could find it in my heart to
give her, what would save my poor lady from ever
waking more," cried the faithful servant; "for oh,
what will she do—oh, what will we all do without
Miss Oona ? "

"Mysie," cried the minister, "how am I to break it
to her ? I have just killed the poor lady down-stairs
with joy; and what am I to say to your mistress ?
Miss Oona is safe and well—she's safe and well."

"Oh, Mr. Cameron," cried Mysie, with a sob, " I
ken what you are meaning. She's well, the Lord
bless her, because she has won to heaven."

Mrs. Forrester had woke during this brief talk, and
raised herself upon the sofa. She broke in upon them
in a tone so like her ordinary voice, so cheerful and
calm, that they both turned round upon her with a
kind of consternation.

"What is that you are saying—safe and well—oh,
safe and well. Thank God for it; but I never had a
moment's doubt. And where has she been all this
weary night; and why did she leave me in this
trouble ? What are ye crying for, Mysie, like a daft
woman ? You may be sure, my darling has been
doing good, and not harm."

" That is true, my dear lady—that is true, my dear
friend," cried the minister. " God bless her ! She
has done us all good, all the days of her sweet life."

" And you are crying too," said Oona's mother, almost
with indignation. " What were you feared for ? Do
you think I could not trust God, that has always been
merciful to me and mine ? or was it Oona ye could
not trust ? " she said with smiling scorn. " And is
she coming soon ? For it seems to me we have been
here a weary time."

" As soon—as she can get out of the—place where
she is. The openings are blocked up by the ruin."

" I had no doubt," said Mrs. Forrester, " it was something of that kind."

Then she rose up from the sofa, very weak and
tottering, but smiling still, her pale and faded face
looking ten years older, her hair all ruffled, falling out
of its usual neat arrangement. She put up her hands
to her head with a little cry.

" Bless me," she said, " she will think I have gone
out of my senses, and you too, Mysie, to take my
bonnet off and expose me, with no cap. I must put
all this right again before my Oona comes."

Mr. Cameron left her engaged in these operations,
with the deepest astonishment. Was it a faith above
the reach of souls less simple ? or was it the easy rebound of a shallow nature ? He watched her for a
moment as she put up her thin braids of light hair, and
tied her ribbons, talking all the time of Oona.

"She never was a night out of her bed in all her life before; and my only fear is she may have gotten a chill, and no means here of making her comfortable. Mysie, you will go down-stairs, and try at least to get the kettle to boil, and a cup of tea for her. Did the minister say when she would be here?"

"No, mem," said Mysie's faltering voice; "naething but that she was safe and well; and the Lord forgive me—I thought—I thought——"

"Never mind what you thought," said Mrs. Forrester briskly, "but run down-stairs and see if you can make my darling a good cup of tea."

By the time she had tied her bonnet strings and made herself presentable, the full light of the morning was shining upon the roused world. The air blew chill in her face as she came down the staircase (strangely weak and tottering, which was "just extraordinary" she said to herself), and emerged upon the little platform outside. Several boats already lay on the beach, and there was the sound of the voices and footsteps of men breaking the stillness. Mrs. Forrester came out with those little graces which were part of herself, giving a smile to old Symington, and nodding kindly to the young men from the yacht who were just coming ashore. "This is early hours," she said to them with her smile, and went forward to the little group before the door, surrounding Mrs. Methven, who still lay where Mr. Cameron had left her, incapable of movement. "Dear me," said Mrs. Forrester, "here have I been taking up a comfortable room, and them that have a better right left out of doors. They have given us a terrible night, my child and yours, but let us hope there has been a good reason for it, and that they will be none the worse. They are just coming, the minister tells me. If ye will take the help of my arm, we might step that way and meet them. They will be glad to see we are not just killed with anxiety, which is what my Oona will fear."

CHAPTER XVIII.

THE news that Lord Erradeen, and it was supposed several others—some went so far as to say a party of visitors, others his mother, newly arrived as all the world was aware, and to whom he was showing the old castle, with a young lady who was her companion—had perished in the fire, streamed down the loch nobody knew how, and was known and believed to the end of the country before the evening was over. It came to the party at Birkenbraes as they were sitting down to dinner, some time after everybody had come in from gazing at the extraordinary spectacle of the fire, got up, Mr. Williamson assured his guests, entirely for their amusement. The good man, however, had been much sobered out of that jocose mood by his encounter with the strange visitor whom he had first seen at Kinloch Houran, but had begun to draw a little advantage from that too, and was telling the lady next to him with some pride of Lord Erradeen's relation, a very distinguished person indeed. " I'm thinking in the diplomatic service, or one of the high offices that keep a man abroad all his life. (I would rather for my part live in a cottage at home, but that is neither here nor there.) So as he was leaving and naturally could not trouble the family about carriages just at such a moment, I offered him the boat: and you could see them getting up steam. I find it very useful to have a steam-boat always ready, just waiting at the service of my friends." The lady had replied as in duty bound, and as was expected of her, that it was a magnificent way of serving your friends, which the millionnaire on his side received with a laugh and a wave of his hand, declaring that it was nothing, just nothing, a bagatelle in the way of cost, but a convenience, he would not deny it was a convenience; when that discreet butler who had ushered Lord Erradeen into Katie's private sitting-room, leaned over his master's shoulder with a solemn face, and a "Beg your pardon, sir. They say, sir, that Lord Erradeen has perished in the fire."

"Lord bless us!" said Mr. Williamson, "what is that you say?"

"It is only a rumour, sir, but I hear Kinloch Houran is all in a commotion, and it is believed everywhere. The young lord was seen with some ladies going there in a boat this afternoon, and they say that he has perished in the flames."

Sanderson was fond of fine language, and his countenance was composed to the occasion.

"Lord bless us!" cried Mr. Williamson again. "Send off a man and horse without a moment's delay to find out the truth. Quick, man, and put down the sherry, I'll help myself! Poor lad, poor lad, young Erradeen! He was about this house like one of our own, and no later than yesterday— Katie, do you hear?" he cried, half rising and leaning over the forest of flowers and ferns that covered the table, "Katie! do you hear this terrible news? but it cannot be true!"

Katie had been told at the same moment, and the shock was so great that everything swam in her eyes, as she looked up blanched and terror-stricken in mechanical obedience to her father's cry. "That man will have killed him," she said to herself: and then there came over her mind a horror which was flattering too, which filled her with dismay and pain, yet with a strange sensation of importance. Was it she who was to blame for this catastrophe, was she the cause——

"It seems to be certain," said some one at the table, "that Erradeen was there. He was seen on the battlements with a lady, just before the explosion."

"His mother!" said Katie, scarcely knowing why it was that she put forth this explanation.

"A young lady. There is some extraordinary story among the people that she—had something to do with the fire."

"That will be nonsense," said Mr. Williamson. "What would a lady have to do with the fire? Old stone walls like yon are not like rotten wood. I cannot understand for my part——"

"And there could be no young lady," said Katie.
"Mrs. Methven was alone."

"Well, well!" said her father. "I am sorry—sorry
for Lord Erradeen; he was just as fine a young fellow
——— . But we will do him no good, poor lad, by letting
our dinner get cold. And perhaps the man will bring
us better news—there is always exaggeration in the
first report. I am afraid you will find that soup not
eatable, Lady Mary. Just send it away; there is some
fine trout coming."

He was sincerely sorry; but, after all, to lose the dinner
would have spared nothing to poor young Erradeen.

Katie said little during the long meal. Her end of
the table, usually so gay, was dull. Now and then she
would break in with a little spasmodic excitement, and
set her companions talking: then relapse with a strange
mingling of grief and horror, and that melancholy elation
which fills the brain of one who suddenly feels himself
involved in great affairs and lifted to heroic heights.
If it was for her—if it was she who was the cause of
this calamity——— She had dreamed often of finding
herself with a high heroic part to fulfil in the world,
though it seemed little likely that she would ever
realise her dream; but now, Katie said to herself, if
this was so, never more should another take the place
which she had refused to him. If he had died for her,
she would live—for him. She would find out every
plan he had ever formed for good and fulfil it. She
would be the providence of the poor tenants whom he

had meant to befriend. She imagined herself in this poetical position always under a veil of sadness, yet not enough to make her unhappy—known in the county as the benefactor of everybody, described with whispers aside as "the lady that was to have married poor young Lord Erradeen." Katie was profoundly sorry for poor Walter—for the first few minutes her grief was keen; but very soon this crowd of imaginations rushed in, transporting her into a new world. If this were so! Already everybody at table had begun to remark her changed looks, and to whisper that they had been sure there was "something between" Katie and the poor young lord. When the ladies went to the drawing-room they surrounded her with tender cares.

"If you would like to go to your room, my dear, never mind us."

"Oh, never mind us," cried the gentle guests, "we can all understand——"

But Katie was prudent even at this crisis of fate. She reflected that the report might not be true, and that it was premature at least to accept the position. She smiled upon the ladies who surrounded her, and put her handkerchief to her eyes.

"Of course," she said, "I can't help feeling it—every one will feel it on the loch—and we had seen so much of him! But perhaps, as papa says, when the messenger comes back, we may have better news."

The messenger did not come back till late, when the party were about to separate. He had found the

greatest difficulty in getting information, for all that
was known at Auchnasheen was that the young lord
and his mother had gone in the boat from the isle with
the ladies, to see the old castle. With the ladies!
Katie could not restrain a little cry. She knew what
was coming. And he had been seen, the man went on,
with Miss Oona on the walls—and that was all that was
known. This stroke went to Katie's heart. "Oona!"
she cried, with something of sharpness and bitterness in
the cry; though in the wail that rose from all around
who knew the isle, this tone that broke the harmony
of grief was lost. But her little fabric of imaginary
heroism fell into the dust: and for the moment the
shock of a genuine, if alloyed, sentiment thrown back
upon herself, and the secret mortification with which
she became conscious of the absurdity of her own self-
complacence, kept Katie from feeling the natural pity
called forth by such a catastrophe, and the deeper pang
which by-and-by awakened her heart to the thought of
Oona—Oona no rival, but the friend of her youth, Oona
the only companion of her mother, the young and
hopeful creature whom everybody loved. To think
that she should have indulged a little miserable rivalry
—on account of a man for whom she did not care the
hundredth part so much as she cared for Oona, before
realising this real grief and calamity! Katie's honest
little soul was bowed down with shame. She, too,
watched that night with many a prayer and tear, gazing
from her many-windowed chamber towards the feathery

crest of the isle which lay between her and Kinloch
Houran. Oh, the desolation that would be there and
Oona gone! Oh, the blank upon the loch, and in all
the meetings of the cheerful neighbours! Another
man on horseback was sent off by break of day for
news, and not only from Birkenbraes, but from every
house for miles round the messengers hurried. There
had been no such excitement in the district for gener-
ations.

The news reached the Lodge—Sir Thomas Herbert's
shooting-box—early in the morning when the family
met at breakfast. The previous night had been
occupied with an excitement of their own. Major
Antrobus, Sir Thomas's friend, brother in sport and
arms, had been from the moment of his arrival a
disappointment to Sir Thomas. The first evening
Julia had caught him in her toils. She had sung and
laughed and talked his heart, so much as remained to
him, away. He was the man of all others who, his
friends were convinced, was not a marrying man. He
had a good estate, a house full of every bachelor comfort,
and was useful to those in whom he was interested as
only a bachelor can be. Nor was it only to men that
he was invaluable as a friend. He had a box at Ascot;
he had ways of making the Derby delightful to a party
of ladies; he was of infinite use at Goodwood; he knew
everybody whom it was well to know. Lady Herbert
was almost as inconsolable as her husband at the idea of
losing him. And that such a man should be brought

by Sir Thomas himself into harm's way, and delivered
over to the enemy by the very hands of his friends, was
more than flesh and blood could bear.   The Herberts
saw their mistake before he had been at the Lodge two
days.   But what could they do ?   They could not send
him away—nor could they send Julia away.   Had they
done so, that young lady had already made herself
friends enough to have secured two or three invitations
in a foolishly hospitable country, where everybody's
first idea was to ask you to stay with them !   Sir
Thomas acted with the noble generosity characteristic
of middle-aged men of the world in such circumstances.
He told his friend, as they smoked their cigars in the
evening, a great many stories about Julia, and all she
had been "up to" in her chequered career.   He described how Lady Herbert had brought her down here,
because of some supposed possibility about Lord
Erradeen.   "But young fellows like that are not to be
so easily taken in," Sir Thomas said, and vaunted his
own insight in perceiving from the first that there was
nothing in it.   The major listened, and sucked his
cigar, and said nothing ; but next day on the way
home, when the fire at Kinloch Houran was reddening
the skies, took his host aside, and said—

"I say, all that may be true, you know. I don't know
anything about that. Girls, you know, poor things !
they've devilish hard lines, when they've got no tin. If
she's tried it on, you know, once or twice before, that's
nothing to me. That's all their mother's fault, don't

you know. She's the jolliest girl I ever met, and no end of fun. With her in the house, you know, a fellow would never be dull, and I can tell you it's precious dull at Antrobus on off days, when all you fellows are away. I say! I've asked her—to be mine, you know, and all that; and she's — going to have me, Tom!"

"Going to have you! Oh, I'll be bound she is! and everything you've got belonging to you!" in the keenness of his annoyance, cried Sir Thomas.

The major, who was somewhat red in the face, and whose figure was not elegant (but what trifles were these, Julia truly said, in comparison with a true heart!), hemmed a little, and coughed, and set his chin into his shirt collar. He stood like a man to his choice, and would have no more said.

"Of course she is—if she's going to have me, you know. Fixtures go with the property," said Major Antrobus, with a hasty laugh. "And, I say, by-gones are by-gones, you know—but no more of them in the future if we're going to be friends."

The men had a quarrel, however, before Sir Thomas gave in—which was stopped fortunately before it went too far by his wife, who met them all smiles with both hands extended.

"What are you talking loud about, you two?" she said. "Major, I'm delighted. Of course I've seen it all along. She'll make you an excellent wife, and I wish you all the happiness in the world."

"Thank you: he don't think so," the major said with a growl.

But after this Sir Thomas perceived that to quarrel with a man for marrying your cousin whom he has met in your house is one of the foolishest of proceedings. He relieved his feelings afterwards by falling upon the partner of his life.

"What humbugs you women are! What lies you tell! You said she would make him an excellent wife."

"And so she will," said Lady Herbert, "a capital wife! He will be twice as happy, but alas! no good at all henceforward," she ended with a sigh.

The excitement of this incident was not over, when to the breakfast-table next morning, where Julia appeared triumphant, having overcome all opposition, the news arrived, not softened by any doubt as if the result was still uncertain, but with that pleasure in enhancing the importance of dolorous intelligence which is common to all who have the first telling of a catastrophe. There was a momentary hush of horror when the tale was told, and then Julia, her expression changed in a moment, her eyes swimming in tears, rose up in great excitement from her lover's side.

"Oh, Walter!" she cried, greatly moved. "Oh that I should be so happy, and he——" And then she paused, and her tears burst forth. "And his mother— his mother!"

She sat down again and wept, while the rest of the

party looked on, her major somewhat gloomy, her cousin (after a momentary tribute of silence to death) with a dawning of triumph in his eye.

"You always thought a great deal of young Erradeen, Ju—at least since he has been Lord Erradeen."

"I always was fond of him," she cried. "Poor Walter! poor Walter! Oh, you can weigh my words if you like at such a time, but I won't weigh them. If Henry likes to be offended I can't help it. He has no reason. Oh, Walter, Walter! I was always fond of him. I have known him since I was *that* high—and his mother, I have always hated her. I have known her since I was *that* high. If you think such things go for nothing it is because you have no hearts. Harry, if you love me as you say, get your dog-cart ready this moment and take me to that poor woman—that poor, poor woman! His mother—and she has only him in all the world. Harry, take me or not but I will go——"

"You said you hated her, Julia," cried Lady Herbert.

"And so I did: and what does that matter? Shall I keep away from her for that—when I am the only one that has known him all his life—that knew him from a child? Harry——"

"I have ordered the dog-cart, my dear; and you are a good woman, Julia. I thought so, but with all your dear friends and people hang me if I knew."

Julia gave him her hand: she was crying without any disguise.

"Perhaps I haven't been very good," she said, "but I never was hard-hearted, and when I think upon that poor woman among strangers——"

"By Jove, but this is something new," cried Sir Thomas; "the girl that liked young men best without their mothers, Antrobus, hey?"

"Oh hush, Tom," cried his wife; "and dear Julia, be consistent a little—that you're sorry for your old—friend (don't laugh, Tom; say her old flame if you like, but remember that he's dead, poor fellow), that we can understand. Major Antrobus knows all that story. But this fuss about the mother whom you never could bear. Oh that is a little too much! You can't expect us to take in that!"

Julia turned upon her relations with what at bottom was a generous indignation. "If you don't know," she said, "how it feels to hear of another person's misfortune, when you yourself are happier than you deserve—and if you don't understand that I would go on my knees to poor Mrs. Methven to take one scrap of her burden off her! oh all the more because I never liked her—— But what is the use of talking, for if you don't understand, nothing I could say would make you understand. And it does not matter to me now," cried Julia, less noble feelings breaking in, "now I have got one who is going to stand by me, who knows what I mean, and will put no bad motive—"

The real agitation and regret in her face gave force
to the triumph with which she turned to her major,
and taking his arm swept out of the room. He, too,
had all the sense of dignity which comes from fine
feeling misunderstood, and felt himself elevated in the
scale of humanity by his superior powers of understanding. Lady Herbert, who remained behind, was saved
by the humour of the situation from exploding, as Sir
Thomas did. To think that the delicacy of the major's
perceptions should be the special foundation of his
bride's satisfaction was, as she declared with tears of
angry laughter, "too good!"

But the second and better news arrived before Julia
could set out on her charitable mission. Perhaps it
was better that it should end so: for though the first
outburst of feeling had been perfectly genuine and
sincere, the impulse might have been alloyed by less
perfect wishes before she had reached Kinloch Houran.
And it is doubtful in any case whether her ministra-
tions, however kind, would have been acceptable to
Walter's mother. As it was, when she led her major
back, Julia was too clever not to find a medium of
reconciliation with her cousins, who by that time had
come to perceive how ludicrous any quarrel open to
the world would be. And so peace was established,
and Julia Herbert's difficulties came in the happiest
way to an end.

CHAPTER XIX.

THE miseries of the night's imprisonment were soon forgotten. Oona, elastic in youthful health, recovered in a few days, she said in a few hours, from its effects, and the keen reality of the after events dimmed in her mind the mystery of that extraordinary moment which appeared now like a dream, too wonderful to be true, too inexplicable and beyond experience to come into natural life at all. They spoke of it to each other with bated breath, but not till some time after their rescue, when the still higher excitement of their near approach to death—a thing which reveals the value and charm of life as nothing else does—had somewhat subsided in their minds. But their recollections were confused, they could not tell how ; and as Walter had never been sure after they were over, whether the terrible conflicts which he had gone through were not conflicts between the better and worse parts of his own nature, without any external influence, so they asked each other now whether the mysterious chamber, the burning lamp, the strange accessories of a concealed and mysterious life, were dreams of disordered fancy, or something real and

actual. They could not explain these things to each
other, neither could they understand what it was that
made the throwing down of the light of such vital
importance. Was it common fire, acting after the
ordinary laws of nature and finding ready fuel in the
dry wood and antique furniture? or was it something
more mystic, more momentous? They gave little explanation to questioners, not so much because they were
unwilling, as because they were unable; and when they
discussed it between themselves became more and more
confused as the days went on. It became like a phan-
tasmagoria, sometimes suddenly appearing in all the
vivid lines of reality, sometimes fading into a pale
apparition which memory could scarcely retain.

To the world in general the fact of a great fire, a
thing unfortunately not very rare in the records of
ancient houses, became after a while a very simple piece
of history; and the wonderful escape of Lord Erradeen
and Miss Forrester, and their subsequent betrothal and
marriage, a pretty piece of natural romance. The
tower, now preserving nothing more than a certain
squareness in its mass of ruins, showed traces of two
rooms that might have been, but everything was
destroyed except the stones, and any remains that
might have withstood the action of the fire were buried
deep under the fallen walls; nor could any trace be
found of concealed passages or any way of descent
into the house from that unsuspected hiding-place.
One thing was certain, however, that the being who

had exercised so strange an influence on a year of his life never appeared to Walter more. There were moments in which he felt, with a pang of alarm, that concentration of his thoughts upon himself, that subtle direction and intensification of his mind, as if it had suddenly been driven into a dialogue with some one invisible, which had been the worst of all the sufferings he had to bear; but these, after the first terror, proved to be within the power of his own efforts to resist and shake off, and never came to any agonising crisis like that which he had formerly passed through. His marriage, which took place as soon as circumstances would permit, ended even these last contentions of the spirit. And if in the midst of his happiness he was sometimes tortured by the thought that the change of his life from the evil way to the good one had all the results of the most refined selfishness, as his adversary had suggested, and that he was amply proving the ways of righteousness to be those of pleasantness, and godliness to be great gain, that thought was too ethereal for common use, and did not stand the contact of reality. Mr. Cameron, to whom he submitted it in some moment of confidence, smiled with the patience of old age upon this overstrained self-torment.

"It is true enough," the minister said, "that the right way is a way of pleasantness, and that all the paths of wisdom are peace. But life has not said out its last word, and ye will have to tread them one time or other with bleeding feet, or all is done—if the Lord has not given you a lot apart from that of other men. And human nature," the old man said, not without a little recollection of some sermon, at which he smiled as he spoke, "is so perverse, that when trouble comes, you that are afraid of your happiness will be the first to cry out and upbraid the good Lord that does not make it everlasting. Wait, my young man, wait—till perhaps you have a boy at your side that will vex your heart as children only can vex those that love them—wait till death steps into your house, as step he must——"

"Stop!" cried Walter, with a wild sudden pang of that terror of which the Italian poet speaks, which makes all the earth a desert—

> "Senza quella
> Nova, sola, infinita,
> Felicità che il suo pensier figura."

He never complained again of being too happy, or forgot that one time or other the path of life must be trod with bleeding feet.

"But I'll not deny," said the minister, "that to the like of you, my young lord, with so much in your power, there is no happier way of amusing yourself than just in being of use and service to your poor fellow-creatures that want so much and have so little. Man!" cried Mr. Cameron, "I would have given my head to be able to do at your age the half or quarter of what you can do with a scratch of your pen!—and you must mind that you are bound to do it," he added with a smile.

But before this serene course of life began which

Walter found too happy, there was an interval of
anxiety and pain. Mrs. Methven did not escape, like
the rest, from the consequences of the night's vigil. She
got up indeed from her faint, and received with speechless thanksgiving her son back from the dead, as she
thought, but had herself to be carried to his room in the
old castle, and there struggled for weeks in the grips of
fever, brought on, it was said, by the night's exposure.
But this she would not herself allow. She had felt
it, she said, before she left her home, but concealed it,
not to be hindered from obeying her son's summons.
If this was true, or invented upon the spur of the
moment to prove that in no possible way was Walter
to blame, it is impossible to say. But the fever ran
very high, and so affected her heart, worn and tired by
many assaults, that there was a time when everything
was hushed and silenced in the old castle in expectation
of death. By-and-by, however, that terror gave place to
all the innocent joys of convalescence—soft flitting of
women up and down, presents of precious flowers
and fruits lighting up the gloom, afternoon meetings
when everything that could please her was brought
to the recovering mother, and all the loch came with
inquiries, with good wishes, and kind offerings. Mrs.
Forrester, who was an excellent nurse, and never
lost heart, but smiled, and was sure, in the deepest
depth, that all would "come right," as she said, took the
control of the sick-room, and recovered there the bloom
which she had partially lost when Oona was in danger.

And Oona stole into the heart of Walter's mother, who
had not for long years possessed him sufficiently to
make it bitter to her that he should now put a wife
before her. Some women never learn this philosophy;
and perhaps Mrs. Methven might have resisted it, had
not Oona, her first acquaintance on the loch, her tenderest
nurse, won her heart. To have the grim old house in
which the secret of the Methvens' fate had been laid
up, and in which, even to indifferent lookers-on, there
had always been an atmosphere of mystery and terror,
thus occupied with the most innocent and cheerful com-
monplaces, the little cares and simple pleasures of a long
but hopeful recovery, was confusing and soothing beyond
measure to all around. The old servants, who had borne
for many years the presence of a secret which was not
theirs, felt in this general commotion a relief which words
could not express. "No," old Symington said, " it's not
ghosts nor any such rubbitch. I never, for my part, here
or elsewhere, saw onything worse than myself; but, Miss
Oona, whatever it was that you did on the tap of that
tower—and how you got there the Lord above knows,
for there never was footing for a bird that ever I saw—
it has just been blessed. ' Ding down the nests and the
craws will flee away.' What am I meaning? Well,
that is just what I canna tell. It's a' confusion. I
know nothing. Many a fricht and many an anxious
hour have I had here : but I am bound to say I never
saw anything worse than mysel'."

" All yon is just clavers," said old Macalister, waving

his hand. "If ye come to that there is naething in this life that will bide explaining. But I will not deny that there is a kind of a different feel in the air which is maybe owing to this fine weather, just wonderful for the season ; or maybe to the fact of so many leddies about, which is a new thing here—no that I hold so much with women," he added, lest Oona should be proud, "they are a great fyke and trouble, and will meddle with everything ; but they're fine for a change, and a kind of soothing for a little whilie at a time, after all we've gone through."

Before the gentle *régime* of the sick-room was quite over, an unusual and unexpected visitor arrived one morning at Loch Houran. It was the day after that on which Mrs. Methven had been transferred to Auchnasheen, and a great festival among her attendants. She had been brought down to the drawing-room very pale and shadowy, but with a relaxation of all the sterner lines which had once been in her face, in invalid dress arranged after Mrs. Forrester's taste rather than her own, and lending a still further softness to her appearance, not to be associated with her usual rigid garb of black and white. And her looks and tones were the most soft of all, as, the centre of everybody's thoughts, she was led to the sofa near the fire and surrounded by that half-worship which is the right of a convalescent where love is. To this pleasant home-scene there entered suddenly, ushered in with great solemnity by Symington, the serious and somewhat stern " man of business " who had come

to Sloebury not much more than a year before with the
news of that wonderful inheritance so unexpected and
unthought of, which had seemed to Mrs. Methven, as
well as to her son, the beginning of a new life. Mr.
Milnathort made kind but formal inquiries after Mrs.
Methven's health, and offered his congratulations no less
formally upon her recovery.

"I need not say to you that all that has happened
has been an interest to us that are connected with the
family beyond anything that I can express. I have
taken the liberty," he added, turning to Walter, "to
bring one to see you, Lord Erradeen, who has perhaps
the best right of any one living to give ye joy. I told
her that you would no doubt come to her, for she has
not left her chamber, as you know, for many a year;
but nothing would serve her but to come herself, frail as
she is——"

"Your sister!" Walter cried.

"Just my sister. I have taken the liberty," Mr. Mil
nathort repeated, "to have her carried into the library,
where you will find her. She has borne the journey
better than I could have hoped, but it is an experiment
that makes me very anxious. You will spare her any—
emotion, any shock, that you can help?"

The serious face of the lawyer was more serious than
ever: his long upper lip trembled a little. He turned
round to the others with anxious self-restraint.

"She is very frail," he said, "a delicate bit creature
all her life—and since her accident—"

He spoke of this, as his manner was, as if it had happened a week ago.

Walter hurried away to the library, in which he found Miss Milnathort carefully arranged upon a sofa, wrapped up in white furs instead of her usual garments, a close white hood surrounding the delicate brightness of her face.   She held out her hands to him at first without a word ; and when she could speak, said, with a tremble in her voice :

"I have come to see the end of it.   I have come to see—her and you."

"I should have come to you," cried Walter, "I did not forget—but for my mother's illness——"

"Yes?" she said with a grateful look.   "You thought upon me?   Oh, but my heart has been with her and you ! Oh, the terrible time it was ! the first news in the papers, the fear that you were buried there under the ruins, you —and she ; and then to wait a night and a day."

"I should have sent you word at once—I might have known ; but I did not think of the papers."

"No, how should you ? you were too busy with your own life.   Oh, the thoughts of that night.   I just lay and watched for you from the darkening to the dawning. No, scarcely what you could call praying—just waiting upon the Lord.   I bade Him mind upon Walter and me —that had lost the battle.   And I thought I saw you, you and your Oona.   Was not I wise when I said it was a well-omened name ? "   She paused a little, weeping and smiling.   "I could not tell you all the thoughts that

went through my mind. I thought if it was even so, there
might have been a worse fate. To break the spell and
defeat the enemy even at the cost of your two bonnie
lives—I thought it would not be an ill fate, the two of
you together. Did I not say it? Two that made up
one, the perfect man. That is God's ordinance, my dear?
that is His ordinance. Two—not just for pleasure, or for
each other, but for Him and everything that is good.
You believed me when I said that. Oh, you believed
me! and so it was not in vain that I was—killed yon
time long ago——" Her voice was broken with sobs.
She leant upon Walter's shoulder who had knelt down
beside her, and wept there like a child—taking comfort
like a child. "Generally," she began after a moment,
" there is little account made, little, little account, of
them that have gone before, that have been beaten,
Walter. I can call you nothing but Walter to-day.
And Oona, though she has won the battle, she is just
me, but better. We lost. We had the same heart;
but the time had not come for the victory. And now
you, my young lord, you, young Erradeen, like him, you
have won, Oona and you. We were beaten; but yet I
have a share in it. How can you tell, a young man
like you, how those that have been defeated, lift their
hearts and give God thanks?" She made a pause and
said, after a moment, "I must see Oona, too." But when
he was about to rise and leave her in order to bring Oona,
she stopped him once more. "You must tell me first,"

she said, speaking very low, "what is become of *him?*
Did he let himself be borne away to the clouds in yon
flames?   I know, I know, it's all done ; but did you see
him?   Did he speak a word at the end ?"

"Miss Milnathort," said Walter, holding her hands,
"there is nothing but confusion in my mind. Was
it all a dream and a delusion from beginning to
end ?"

She laughed a strange little laugh of emotion.

" Look at me then ," she said, "for what have I
suffered these thirty years ? And you—was it all for
nothing that you were so soon beaten and ready to
fall? . Have you not seen him ? Did he go without
a word ?"

Walter looked back upon all the anguish through
which he had passed, and it seemed to him but a dream.
One great event, and then weeks of calm had inter-
vened since the day when driven to the side of the loch
in madness and misery, he had found Oona and taken
refuge in her boat, and thrown himself on her mercy ;
and since the night when once more driven distracted
by diabolical suggestions, he had stepped out into the
darkness, meaning to lose himself somehow in the gloom
and be no more heard of—yet was saved again by the
little light in her window, the watch-light that love kept
burning. These recollections and many more swept
through his mind, and the pain and misery more remote
upon which this old woman's childlike countenance had

shone. He could not take hold of them as they rose before him in the darkness, cast far away into a shadowy background by the brightness and reality of the present. A strange giddiness came over his brain. He could not tell which was real, the anguish that was over, or the peace that had come, or whether life itself—flying in clouds behind him, before him hid under the wide-spreading sunshine—was anything but a dream. He recovered himself with an effort, grasping hold of the latest recollection to satisfy his questioner.

"This I know," he cried, "that when we were flying from the tower, with flames and destruction behind us, the only words I heard from her were a prayer for pardon —'forgive him,' that was all I heard. And then the rush of the air in our faces, and roar that was like the end of all things. We neither heard nor saw more."

"Pardon!" said Miss Milnathort, drying her eyes with a trembling hand, "that is what I have said too, many a weary hour in the watches of the night. What pleasure can a spirit like yon find in the torture of his own flesh and blood? The Lord forgive him if there is yet a place of repentance! But well I know what you mean that it is just like a vision when one awaketh. That is what all our troubles will be when the end comes: just a dream! and good brought out of evil and pardon given to many, many a one that men are just willing to give over and curse instead of blessing. Now

go and bring your Oona, my bonnie lad ! I am thinking
she is just me, and you are Walter, and we have all won
the day together," said the invalid clasping her thin
hands, and with eyes that shone through their tears,
" all won together ! though we were beaten twenty
years ago."